BALLINA AND BEYOND

BALLINA AND BEYOND

AUBREY MALONE

First published Nov 2020

ISBN 978-1-913144-18-0

PENNILESS PRESS PUBLICATIONS
Website :www. pennilesspress. co. uk/books

CONTENTS

Poetry Book

Being the youngest of a family
I never got to know
what it was like
to go away from home.
I never had the experience
of travelling to Dublin
knowing I could come back.
When I made the 1969 trip there
it was for good.
There were holidays
in Sandymount
and Roscommon
but I didn't count these.

Not having been away
I didn't know how badly
I'd take it
when I had to leave forever.
There was no prelude,
nothing to soften the blow.
I was cossetted
by my young age.

I always told myself
I'd write a book about Norfolk
some day.
I was over sixty
when that happened.
I put a photo of the house
on the cover.

It was a community centre now.
The people there
said they'd like to see it
when it came out.

I put a copy in an envelope
for them.
It was strange
sending it to Norfolk.
It was my first time
writing home
except it wasn't home now.

Sixty seven years
after I was born
in that house
my words returned to it
through the postal system.
It was like looking
in a mirror of shadows
like waving at a festival
that wasn't there.
I resented the arrival
of the book
through a letterbox
that had once been ours,
resented it falling on a floor
I'd walked on
for sixteen years.

Other feet walked on it now.
Another hand
would pick up my book
and put it on the hall table.
It would be viewed
by a committee member
who would decide
either to keep it
or throw it out.

Graduate

Stranded on the edges of nothingness,
the future arrowing in,
your father urging 'Now, now'
as the application forms pile up
for jobs that would kill you
even sooner than poverty.

On the streets the drunks sidle by
as obstreperous as yourself.
They're in love with the next fix,
the next gamble,
the next love.

'Lower your standards,' the manuals say
'and improve your performance'.
But who wants performances now?
The search is better,
even for a chimera
At the end of a smoking summer
there are false dawns.

You look out at the disapproving sun
at the hills that are on fire.
A crazy lethargy
overtakes you.
Slaughter the pig of plenty,
you tell yourself,
before it slaughters you.
Stack up resentments
against the expectations of time.
Become the family skeleton.

You are now an official nobody,
your badge of honour a crucifix
screaming vitriol
as it smokes inside the corridors
of your mind.
You wear testaments
to decade-long lies
as your enemies climb the ladder
to their better selves.

Gambling

It was a summer of endless sunshine, tourists checking their tans like scones you'd put in the oven, the eternity of flesh almost nauseating along the strand.

She worked in the casino beside the boardwalk, flicking the cards nightly at the blackjack table as I gobbled her up with my eyes.

I pretended I was just there to play. She was always dressed in a frilly costume. It made her look like a cross between a cowgirl and a lapdancer.

One night she asked me why I continued to come back when I kept losing.

'That's what all compulsive gamblers do,' I said. I didn't want to tell her I was infatuated with her. I was afraid she'd become nervous of me, that she'd pack me off to one of the other tables.

As the summer went on I got my courage up. One night I asked her if she'd like to come for a walk with me when her shift ended. Miraculously she said yes.

We walked across the bridge that was down the road from the casino. The boardwalk led onto the beach. Gulls cawed around us. some people were feeding them chips from plastic containers.

I told her I'd been afraid to ask her out before.

'I knew you liked me,' she said, 'Anyone could tell a mile away.'

'Why didn't you register it?' I said.

'You don't know anything about women,' she said, 'I wanted to make you try harder to win me over.'

Our first few evenings together were forced. I talked too much. I always did that when I was nervous with people. When I got to know her better she opened up about herself. Hearing about her life made me less awed by her. She became a person rather than a goddess in sequins who dispensed cards to the hordes of tourists who were trying to beat the house.

She told me her ambition in life was never to be tied down.

'Up to now,' she said, 'My life has been one long party.'

My own one was boring by comparison. I'd left Ballina for Dublin after my father retired. A few months beforehand I'd finished First

Arts. I was in America for the summer with some friends. We'd intended to travel to San Francisco but when we got to Atlantic City we fell in love with it. We decided to spend the summer there instead.

I disengaged myself from the people I'd gone there with. The more time we spent together the more relaxed I became with her. I spent a lot of time in her chalet. During the day we sat watching the waves thrashing in on the shore for hours on end. We had nobody to impress but one another and nothing to live up to. Days enwreathed themselves around us as time stood still. I had no energy for anything but I didn't mind. It was an allowable lethargy. We swam and slept. The lifeguard did press-ups in his hut. Nobody drowned. In fact nobody did anything.

I was almost afraid of my happiness with her. I thought nothing this perfect could last. One night we went gambling together and nearly cleaned the place out. Then our luck deserted us. Like all gamblers we lost eventually.

Some nights we didn't bother going out, sitting around the chalet as if we knew each other all our lives. I was nervous if any of my friends rang. She seemed not to want them to be in my life. She was amused by my stories of growing up in Ireland, about mothers who cooled their sons' porridge, about sons who stayed at home till they were thirty. Her own life had been lived on the road. She was rootless. And ruthless.

She ran away from home when she was sixteen and never went back. 'Parents suck,' she said. The way she said it made me shiver at the thought of ever falling out with her.

My friends from the university warned me away from her.

'You're getting in over your head,' they said. I laughed away their comments.

'She's only a fling,' I said. If I told the truth about her to anyone I felt it would all end between us. I was that superstitious.

One day I asked her if she was happy with me.

She seemed thrown by the question. When I asked her if she ever wanted to get married she laughed at me. She didn't think in terms like that. Her life was lived for the moment.

On other days I saw her looking at children playing in the park. If she saw me she stopped. It was as if I'd caught her out in something. She seemed afraid of any feelings she had. It was a kind of pride against being old-fashioned.

Maybe it was inevitable that we'd move in together. When we did I felt uneasy with myself. It was my first time living with a woman and maybe her twenty-first with a man. I never knew for sure. I was too shy to ask her.

The morning after my first night with her the sun came up with more ice than heat in it. I looked out at the cerulean blue of the sky and felt I was in heaven,

'Well,' I said, 'That wasn't so bad, was it?'

'You'll do for the moment,' she replied.

As the summer died we settled into a mellowness together. Seeing her for dates had been a trauma to me, an artificial arrangement. Each evening had had a beginning and an end. Now that I was with her constantly it changed the goalposts.

There was a swimming pool outside the chalet. Most days I sat beside it. It was kidney-shaped. You couldn't swim for long in it without hitting the edge. I preferred watching her.

My friends got ready to go back to Dublin. One of them rang me to ask if I was going back with them. I was tempted to cut her out of my life before I got to the stage where I'd have no choice in the matter.

'She's dangerous,' he said to me. 'She'll drag you in farther than you want to go.' I told him that was a chance I had to take.

'You have to strike while the iron is hot in life,' I said, the cliché that hides a deeper fear of isolation.

'The iron is red-hot,' he said, 'It'll burn you.'

A couple of hours later I went with him to the train station. He was cool with me on the journey. I made no arrangement to see him back in Dublin.

'Do you want me to say anything to your parents?' he said as he headed for the plane.

'Tell them I'm still a virgin,' I said, 'That's the only thing they'll be worried about.'

'What about your future?' he said.

'What about it?' I said.

I felt guilty. It was as if I was looking for something out of life beyond what I deserved, as if I was being untrue to my deeper nature. But there was no going back now. Maybe I enjoyed the danger of it. I told him she was just another woman but deep down I knew I was cemented to her. A parting between us could never be clean.

In the absence of my friends she grew closer to me. Suddenly I wasn't just a transient to her anymore. It wasn't just a holiday romance.

She was quieter now. I started to see a new side to her, a side that was more like me. I wondered if she might have been intimidated by my friends, if her bravado hadn't been a pose. How I loved that bravado. I missed it when it wasn't there.

The closer she got to me the more unsure I became about my feelings for her. Despite myself I began to hanker after the road not taken.

August burned into September. I knew I had no chance of getting back to the university on time. I felt like a footnote to the summer, somebody who'd outstayed his welcome on a cheap package deal. The tourists were starting to disappear and with them my own assumed relevance in this seasonal city.

When the carnival closed the casino lost business. The coldness of autumn set in. I started to see new people, the bread and butter of the city's existence, people who came out of the woodwork once all the festivities were over, the dull Monday souls that are all of us at base. Emotionally I felt naked in their presence. The illusion was over now, the neon-lit suntrap no more adventurous than my own home town. Maybe, I thought, all places were the same if you spent long enough in them.

When my visa expired I got nervous. I became an illegal immigrant now. I knew each day could be my last if the authorities discovered me. In a strange way that relaxed me. I had no deadline to fear anymore. Being illegal for a day was the same as being illegal for a lifetime.

14

I was glad my friends had gone home. I wanted to cut myself off from my Irishness. I even began to speak in an American accent. After a few weeks I got a job selling enchiladas. Every morning I stood at a counter pedalling my wares to Puerto Rican visitors on exchange programmes, fat slackers who'd outstayed their welcome at the casino. In the evenings I sat in the silence of the boardwalk, imprisoned in a vacuum of confusion and desire. What was I doing here? Who did I think I was?

'You wanted to go home with your friends, didn't you?' she said to me one night. I tried to deny it but there was no conviction in my voice. She saw through me.

My parents phoned me but I didn't pick up. Afterwards letters started arriving from them. They asked me what was happening about my degree, what was going to happen to all the money they'd invested in their darling son to help him make good. I soul-searched about my so-called umbilical connection to Mother Ireland.

'Maybe I'm corrupting you,' she said to me one night as we lay on the beach. 'Maybe you'd be better off back in the island of saints and scholars.'

I felt my blood rising inside me as she spoke, maybe because I believed she was right. I pulled her towards me in an embrace that had as much anger in it as need, pinioning her arms under me on the sand. As she struggled to get free I saw an expression on her face I'd never seen before. It was one of excitement. Did she like me dominating her? Was it the thing that had been missing in our relationship up to this?

She started to spoil me. I should have been pleased by that but I wasn't. I felt a claustrophobia beginning to grow in me, even an independence of her. She'd given birth to a new identity in me but it had the wrong effect. It seemed to preclude the need of her.

'What's happening to you?' she said. I said I wished I knew.

'You're not the same,' she said.

I told her I needed some space, the old cliché. I moved out of the chalet into a run-down room in a motel a few hundred yards down the road. I was using the last of my money to be away from a woman I'd fantasised about all too recently.

She started to look up her old friends again, to immerse herself in a clique that was as alien to me as a foreign species. One night she asked me to join them. Was she trying to make me jealous? If she was it didn't work. They were people she knew from the casino, nothing people with nothing lives. They drank into the small hours telling stories about gamblers they knew who'd risked their fortunes on the roll of a dice. She flirted casually with them, whether to annoy me or not I didn't know.

'If that's what you want you can have it,' I said to her at the end of the night. She laughed dismissively.

I couldn't survive without her. The loneliness got too much. I felt tied to her like to a disease. I didn't know if she'd take me back but she did. We did the same things together as we'd done at the beginning of the summer but it was different now. A hardness had come into both of us. Maybe we'd both showed too much of our hands. The mystery was gone.

'Would you have preferred it if we never became a couple?' I asked her one night when she was being unusually crabby with me. She burst out laughing at the suggestion.

'Isn't that the way it works?' she said, 'Perennial love of the chase? Duh?'

She started to live a separate life from me. I sold my enchiladas and came home to the empty rooms. She went out drinking most nights. Even when she stayed home she didn't talk much to me. In the mornings she slept off her hangovers.

I watched her blowing her money in the casino. She almost seemed to enjoy it when she lost. I tried to drag her away once or twice but she resisted. Our arguments often came to blows.

One night when I came home she was standing in the kitchen with her overcoat on. She had a case beside her.

'What are you doing?' I said. I had to ask her even though I knew the answer. I'd seen it a hundred times in her eyes in the previous weeks.

'What does it look like?'

I poured myself a drink. Her words were inevitable but that didn't make them any easier to hear. I felt an ache in my head that might have been part relief.

'I thought it would be easier for both of us if I moved out.'

'That's ridiculous.'

'Don't drag it out. You know it's for the best.'

'Is there any way I can change your mind?' I wasn't sure if I wanted to.

'I'm doing you a favour. Don't pretend you didn't notice how bad things were. The way we were going either one of us could have ended up in the looney bin.'

'I never saw it like that.'

'How could you? You always loved the lie.'

I had another drink. Its bitterness comforted me. I was glad for her strength. I had so little of it myself.

'Where will you go?' I said. She told me once that she'd left particles of her brain in every place she'd visited. Her adolescence had been one long odyssey across Europe. She'd probably return to that identity now. Maybe she never left it.

'Somewhere. Anywhere. What does it matter? I might go to Dublin and see all the leprechauns.' That was a joke we had between us. I was from the land of leprechauns and she from a place where mad bohemians roamed.

'What about this leprechaun left behind?'

'You'll survive. Your kind always do.' No matter where she went she'd never lose her cruelty.

'Are you not sad at all?'

She gave a sardonic laugh.

'It's not the first time something ended for me. I doubt it'll be the last. We had some fun together. What else is there to say?'

I looked out at the crashers hugging the shore. The wind blew a sandstorm across the boardwalk. I felt frozen like a statue. We were finished but neither of us could walk away. It was like a machine that carried on whirring after you switched it off.

'What about yourself?' she said, 'What will you do?' Maybe she imagined me running home to my mother's apron-strings.

'I don't know.'

'You can stay here if you like. The rent is paid.'

'Do you think that will solve everything?'

'I'm not trying to solve things. Go home tomorrow if you like.'

I wondered where we went wrong. Or was ending going wrong? Maybe the relationships that went on forever were the ones that went wrong.

'So that's it,' I said.

It was like a game of blackjack that ended. You folded your tent and went out into the night without your chips.

'Look me up in a few decades,' she said. Her face looked more relaxed now that the set-piece was over.

'That soon?' I said.

She smiled.

'It's not the end of the world.'

'For a while it will be.'

In her absence all my old insecurities came back. My friends were gone too. I had no shoulder to cry on. Were they right about her? Had I been punching over my weight? I didn't know and I didn't care. What mattered now was just getting through the days, pretending she'd never existed so that I could piece some kind of a new life together for myself, either in Atlantic City or Ireland. I didn't let myself hope she'd come back. If she did I could never be sure she'd stay.

I thought about going back to Dublin but decided against it. Didn't people say never to make decisions in a crisis?

I signed on for a business course but I couldn't do it. I had to drop out when they asked me for my Social Security number. I tried tending bar afterwards but that didn't work either. I couldn't be sociable with the customers. Drinking at home was easier.

Most nights I drank myself sober. What good was it to me when she wasn't there to share it? I needed her to alchemise my ordinariness into her high gaiety.

'You have me on too much of a pedestal,' she said to me once. Was it true? Maybe I needed a goddess in my life. It didn't matter if it was an illusory one or not. I didn't want the genie put back in the bottle.

I wandered around the chalet trying to figure out my next move. How long was the rent paid for? She didn't say. Maybe I'd just let it run out and then vamoose.

The more I thought about things the less choices I seemed to have. I needed a job to get my mind off her but I didn't have my J1 anymore. My options were limited. Maybe I'd get lucky at blackjack and clean the casino out.

I remembered the night we'd got on a toll together there. For a few hours we were rich. We contemplated a life of luxury in Las Vegas. By midnight we had only 3 dollars and 47 cents left between us. We bought a milk shake on the way home with two straws, gurgling it into our mouths until the last drop was gone. That was probably the best part of the night.

I went on the buildings for a while. 'Construction' they called it. I didn't know one end of a scaffolding from another but that didn't seem to matter. They were only paying me slave wages. The foreman didn't mind.

I became a gofer, enduring his easy banter about Paddy from the bogs. One day I jumped from a wall wearing only a pair of tennis shoes. I landed on a rusty nail. He said he was worried about gangrene. Maybe the danger of me suing him was more on his mind. He drove me to the hospital to get a tetanus shot. Afterwards an orderly put something on my foot that looked like treacle. He scrubbed it so hard I felt he was going to take the skin off. 'Don't wear sneakers the next time,' the foreman told me on the way back to the chalet. I decided there wouldn't be a next time. I was, as the Americans put it, 'out of there.'

I found myself searching for her without realising it. I went to places she might have been, places we went to together. The echo of her absence was like a record played at the wrong speed. Now and again I ran into her friends. When they asked me what happened I said we just drifted apart. It was close enough to the truth.

'Sorry, buddy,' one of her co-workers from the casino said, 'You guys really looked like an item.'

'I have someone else now,' I said but I could see he didn't believe me. Trying to pretend I didn't care as much as I did never worked for me. My face always told another story.

I didn't see her for a few months. Then she re-appeared without warning. I spotted her in an arcade. She was in her gladrags, picking up bric-a-brac at a counter. I wasn't sure if she saw me. If she did she didn't pretend. There was a man with her, one of her casino friends. She looked drunk.

In a bar one night a man told me she was on heroin. Someone else said she'd gone to Europe. Such stories I listened to with a vague curiosity. I was amused that it wasn't only Dublin that had its valleys of squinting windows. They were here as well.

The next time I saw her was on the boardwalk. She was doing what appeared to be a striptease for some surfers. They were whooping in delight. I tried to work up an emotion as I watched her, some sense of shame or even disgust, but nothing came. Afterwards I saw her a few times falling out of bars. There was usually someone to tend to her and drive her home, wherever that was. I picked up the phone to ring her a hundred times a day but something always held me back, some innate cowardice.

One night I got a call to say she'd taken an overdose. I was hardly surprised. She'd been on this precipice for many months now. When I visited her in hospital she had tubes coming out of various parts of her. She looked like a Mummy. She was strangely jaunty.

'Why did you do it?' I asked her.

'It beats the monotony,' she said.

Suicide, I thought, the ultimate fix.

'How do you feel?' I asked her.

'Like a million bucks,' she said. 'Where's the party?'

'Did you know what you were doing?' I asked her.

'People like me never mean business the first time,' she said, 'It was a call for help. Didn't you know that?'

'So who were you calling?' I was playing her own game now.

'If it was you, would you have answered?' She was teasing me now.

'Don't do this to yourself,' I said.

20

'You sound like my mother. The two of you would make a good match.'

'Could I see you when you get out of here?'

'That's noble of you but no thanks. Pity is an emotion I can do without at the moment.'

'It isn't pity. I need you.' The words were out before I formed them. I wondered what ridiculous part of me they'd come from.

'You were always a good actor,' she chided.

'You're looking for an excuse to do damage to yourself.'

'I was damaged from birth. Nothing can change that.'

'Don't dramatise yourself.'

She fiddled with one of the tubes coming out of her.

'How many women have you had since me?' she said, 'Ten? Fifteen? I'd say a nice conservative one would suit you.'

The words sputtered out of her as she fought for breath.

'Don't talk. You need to relax.'

After a few minutes a doctor came in to sedate her. I wanted to talk to him about her but she put up her hand to stop me.

'Please go,' she said, 'I'm not able for people.'

The last time I saw her she was in the company of the man who spun the roulette wheel in the casino. She was wearing a dress I'd bought her some months before. At the time it fitted her perfectly. Now she was swimming in it. If it wasn't for that I wouldn't have known how much weight she'd lost. When I looked closer at her face I saw the paleness, the lack of expression.

She looked happy to see me. When she hugged me I felt her bones against me.

'Well, Mr Philosopher,' she said to me, 'Have you found the meaning of life yet?'

I tried to force a smile. Her humour seemed oddly pathetic now. She started to introduce me to her friend but I walked away. He had a beaver-like grin on his face that suggested he was already looking forward to where the two of them would end up that night. I felt like grabbing him and beating him into the ground.

A friend of hers rang me last week to say that she'd been taken into hospital after another overdose. When I asked him how she was it was a long time before he answered.

'She died,' he said.

I heard the words and didn't hear them.

'What?' I said.

'She died,' he said again. This time it registered. It was a shock but I probably expected it.

'Can I see her?' I said.

I could sense him waiting for me to say something else but I didn't. What else could I have said? I didn't want to hear the circumstances.

The silence extended. I wanted him to be off the line, to be able to break down without him hearing me.

'How did you get my number?' I said. There was coldness in my voice. He must have thought I was a hard bastard. Maybe I was.

'They found it on a piece of paper she had. It was by her bed.'

Was this her final valentine to me? Her final call for help?

'Thanks for telling me,' I said.

I sat for a while in the room. The gulls were wailing outside as if for her. Would she have anyone else to mourn her? Were all her contacts flotsam and jetsam like me?

I walked down by the casino. I remembered the way she was at her table, flicking the deck like a card sharp. I'd been in awe of her on those nights. What did it matter now how good she was at what she did? What did anything matter?

I started to think about her funeral, about the practical things that come into your mind when someone dies, the things you don't like to say to anyone in case they think you aren't sad enough.

I thought about her parents. They'd seen little enough of her in recent years. Now they'd only see the people who knew her. They'd walk through the church looking at her coffin. They would have expected to walk through it on her wedding day. The funeral would be a substitute for the reception she denied them.

The following day I took up the newspaper to read the report of her demise. 'Death by misadventure,' was written in big letters across the page. It was a phrase that said everything and nothing. The article was slotted into a column usually reserved for the racing results. The headlines that day were devoted to news about a governmental decision to reduce the interest rates on mortgages for newlyweds. She would have been amused.

I walked down to the causeway. Sailboats creaked in the wind. The boardwalk was deserted. Gulls screeched furiously above it, swirling round in the sky like so many buzzards. I listened to the lost chant of a busker somewhere in the night. The waves lashed up against the rocks. A piece of driftwood made a splash as it was thrown up by the departing waves.

It would have been easy to forget but I withstood forgetting. Instead I indulged the memory of her, the memory of her petulance and her wild laughter, those eyes that had the moods of the sea in them. I was locked in self-pity. There was no way to avoid it. Maybe it was therapy. In brooding there seemed to be more fidelity to the moment than the lie we called oblivion.

I didn't go to the funeral. It would have been too complicated trying to explain to everyone what my relationship with her was. I might have broken down. That would have made things worse for her parents.

I got the plane back to Dublin the following day. The weather was fine. That made me feel even worse than I might otherwise have done. It was as if it was mocking me.

'You brought the sun with you,' my mother said.

She welcomed her wandering son back to the fold. The way she embraced me reminded me of the apostle who put his hand into the wound of Jesus to make sure it was really him. Behind her my father winked at me knowingly. It was if we shared some dark and terrible secret.

Later in the night he brought me out on the town. I could see he was expecting to be regaled with the kind of risqué anecdotes that were the psychic baggage of any Irish neophyte making his first incursion into the New World. I gave him as many as would have satisfied his own deprived longings.

The more I entertained him the emptier I felt inside. I felt responsible for some obscure breach of confidence.

The following day I met my friends from the university for a drink. They'd heard about her death. I didn't ask how. Everyone always seemed to know everything about my life. Maybe they knew it even before I did.

One of them asked me how things ended with her.

'It fizzled out,' I said. It was the same thing I'd said to her co-worker from the casino. I doubt he believed it either.

The mention of her name caused me to tense up. When I got back to my room later in the night a vision of her stamped itself on to me like an old scar. I pulled the curtains open and looked up at the sky. In my mind's eye I saw her whirling around out there somewhere, a liberated spirit of some alien paradise. I wondered what she'd have been thinking of me all those light years away, what she'd have been thinking of all of us. I imagined her smiling down at us from her privileged vantage point, smiling down at all the leprechauns myopically picking their way around our quaint little land mass in the sea.

Golden Evening

Autumn fringed the day.
The ship glided across the ocean.
You were sailing away from me.
I waved to you
but you didn't see me.
How could you?
You'd left me long before.

Clouds streaked the horizon.
The waves gave no inkling
of passion or unease.
They did what they always do.

Mountains sloped lazily
towards the sea.
A couple danced on the beach,
reminding me of you, of us.
I watched lights
fluttering on the bay
as the night came on.
Your ship became small
and then nothing.

The way the sun went down
made me think
of the end of the world.
Two lovers embracing on the dunes
made me think
of a different kind of end.
I walked through scuffed sand
to a lighthouse.
The searchlights pierced the dark.
Lost ships clamoured.
My soul sank like the sun.

I called you
but you didn't answer.
The moon followed me home.
My road looked different.
My home looked different.
Trees on the avenue hovered
like benevolent ghosts.
I worried the wound.
I was in love with memories,
in love with what we were
and could be again.

You didn't agree.
You wanted to re-invent yourself
on the streets of London.
You'd grown away from me
and everything I knew.
You wanted to embrace
differentness
an alien culture.
You taunted me
with the person
you were going to be
on foreign soil.

I clutched a brooch
you gave me
on a Tuesday in Swinford
in the summer of our love.

The Grace of God

Flames from the campfires lick the night. He's getting ready to spend his last night at the grotto. Around him a group of students strum their guitars, the harmonies echoing plaintively down the valley in the soft heat. Pilgrims pass by him in little clusters. He joins them once or twice, vaguely chanting the litanies. He passes by the rosary stalls, the amusement arcades, the infinity of toffee apples that gleam in the dusk like pumpkins. Every now and then a cripple hobbles along with a look of intensity in his eyes. Maybe an epiphany awaits behind the next hill. Planes drone by overhead. A man in a turban crouches in fear. It's as if a war has begun for him, or the memory of a war.

The night grows deeper. The prayers go on, sporadic at first and then in unison, resounding through the grottos. Across the river a group of young men are drinking from beer cans.

'Did you hear the one about the actress and the bishop?' a redheaded boy enquires. When he gets to the punchline there's laughter. It's exaggerated in that way it often is with drink.

When the noise dies down they talk about what will happen later tonight at the discotheque. They talk about the women they've been chasing for the last few days, about the excitement of seducing devout young mademoiselles from conservative homes.

Behind them in a tent a different kind of conversation is going on. A delicate-boned nun discusses the prophecies of an ancient saint with her friends. She says there may only be one more Pope before the end of the world. She read that somewhere.

'It will be a black one,' she says.

'As long as it's not another Pole,' a round-faced man sitting opposite her whispers. She stares sternly at him.

'I'm a Pope Paul man myself,' he says. ''John the 23rd opened the windows to let the cobwebs out but he brought in a tornado instead of a breath of fresh air. He threw the baby out with the bathwater.'

He deals cards for a game of whist. Across the table from him the nun says, 'I can't stop thinking about that armless woman we saw today. It got me thinking about the stupid we complain about in our lives.'

A jolly-eyed man with a bald patch smiles at her.

'We all have our crosses to bear, Sister,' he says, 'be they physical or otherwise. Sometimes I think the handicapped people are happier than any of us. They look that way to me, anyway. And of course it will all be made up to them on the last day.'

'Whom the Lord loveth, he chastiseth,' the round-faced man says, 'Though if that's actually the way it is I think I'd prefer to be despised.'

The orderly walks down by the stream. It gullies gently beneath him like water swivelling down a plug-hole. The pilgrims are at the top of the hill. They're bent in adoration. As he looks at them, something about the starkness of the situation moves him. He listens to the rustle of their garments as they shift from knee to knee.

Across from him a woman is holding her baby so tightly she seems to be on the point of suffocating it. There are men in uniforms selling holy water. Emaciated figures on stretchers give slight waves as he passes. Many of them have their eyes closed. It's as if they're reaching some kind of revelation the outside world has no right to intrude upon.

When he gets to the office he signs himself in. He feels a hand on his shoulder. When he looks around he sees it's Peter Gallagher, the group leader.

'Well,' he says, beaming over at him, 'Not much longer to go now. How do you feel?'

'Tired,' he says. He hopes the remark will dissuade Gallagher from pursuing the conversation but it has the opposite effect.

'The first time I came here I was shattered. It was a week after I got home before I was myself again. It's the psychological drain rather than the physical one that gets to you eventually.' Something in his tone of voice annoys him. It's been annoying him all week. He can't put his finger on the reason.

'So what's the story for tonight?'

'I'm afraid you're on the graveyard shift with Hanratty again. Do you think you'll be able for her?'

'I think so.'

It doesn't matter to him who he has now as long as the night passes. He's been operating on his reserve energy for the past few days. It's just a matter of bodies to push, afflictions to ignore. Or at least pretend to.

'She seems to have taken quite a fancy to you. She asked for you especially tonight. Don't say I told you.'

'I don't know how you call throwing crutches at someone taking a fancy to them.'

'She did that?'

'Last night.'

'I wouldn't worry about it. With the rest of us it's tables and chairs.'

He walks to the annex where all the paraplegics are sitting. They're lined up regimentally in their wheelchairs like before a race. Some of them are mentally disturbed as well. They eye him strangely as he appears, not recognising him even though he's been pushing them all week.

'Since it's the last night,' Gallagher says, 'Maybe we'll give them ringside seats at the altar.'

'Good idea.'

When he gets over to Mrs. Hanratty she grunts at him.

'I'll be having nightmares about you yet,' she says.

Why does she ask for him when she takes such delight in abusing him? Or is that the reason?

He wheels her out into the air. She cringes as the wind comes up.

'Do you want to give me pneumonia as well as everything else?' she shrieks. 'Get me another blanket for God's sake.'

He drapes one around her shoulders. The wheels grate on the cobblestones as he wheels her down the pathway.

'You're late,' she says, 'No doubt you were detained chatting up some senorita.'

Her comments will go on like this until midnight. He's grown immune to them by now. Maybe a part of him enjoys them. He finds her preferable to the others in the group, the long-suffering types who say little but convey it all in their expressions. Their stoicism annoys him. There's something mock-saintly about it. At least she' honest about herself. She has her wit to get her through.

'Don't let me fall whatever you do,' she says as they get to a hill, 'That'd fix me nicely now, wouldn't it?'

'Maybe it'd cure you,' he says.

They reach the patch of ground where the sermon is to be held He looks around him at the sea of bodies on the grass. He has a sensation of the past, of what life might have been like thousands of years ago in these fields. Across from him there's a tree that has branches filled with relics, so many offerings to appease the Gods. If you pray at it often enough, they say, a cure is certain.

The moon appears from behind a cloud. Everyone is bathed in its mellowness. A guitar is plucked somewhere lower down in the valley. The voice accompanying it is like the keening at a wake.

A priest emerges from the shadows. He begins to speak in a gruff voice.

'There are no shortcuts to the Almighty,' he says, 'If you're someone who's sceptical of our Lord's mercy I ask you to do one thing for me. Pray to him. Not just for a physical cure but a spiritual one too. We're all sick, my dear brethren, sick in our hearts and in our minds. We're sick with hatred and vengeance, sick in our relationships with our fellow man and with ourselves, many of us sick beyond cure. What I would ask you all to do if you haven't been blessed with the miracle cure of the young Bernadette is to pray for the grace to accept your suffering.'

He finishes speaking. A man on crutches on the other side of the hill starts to scream, 'I can walk! I can walk!' He drops his crutches and takes a step forward. He shouts, 'I see her! She's here!' A moment later he falls down on the ground again. He searches vainly for his crutches.

A couple of stewards rush over to him. He swings a crutch at them. They hoist him up. They stand back from him, nervous suddenly as he gets ready to take another step forward without the crutches. He falls again. This time he lets them help him up, throwing himself into their arms. They lift him into an ambulance.

The torchlight procession begins. Pilgrims move up the hill with their candles in their hands. He gazes at them from the hilltop. Flames flicker like fairy lights on some gigantic Christmas tree. Mrs Hanratty has been disturbed by the man with the crutches.

'Bloody eejit,' she says, 'Gave me the fright of my life with his antics he did. Another Lazarus.'

'What did you think of the sermon?' he asks her.

'Accept your suffering how are ye. He's a fine one to talk all right, buzzing around the Riviera in his BMW.'

'How did you come to be disabled?' he says, sensing she might be in the mood to talk about herself.

'It happened when I was married. There you go now. I bet you didn't think any man would be bothered with a hussy like me. Well I had one once all right. Before I got like this.'

'Did you have an accident?'

'I was in a dinghy with him. The bloody thing capsized on us. He was able to swim to the shore. I had to hang on to the edge of it while he went for help. I nearly froze to death waiting for the rescue squad. Sometimes I think I should have died. Lost the circulation of my legs I did.'

'Did you have an operation on them?'

'Multiply that by twenty. I've spent more of my life in hospitals than out of them. Not that they did me any good. You'd need money to get a proper job done on the likes of me. Money is one thing I never had.'

'Do you ever think you could be cured by a miracle?'

'Ha! After fourteen years traipsing along to this dump? I'd be better off if I never heard of the place.'

'Why do you keep coming then?'

'I wish I knew. Sure what's the alternative? Maybe one of these days the man upstairs will get fed up of my groaning and wave his wand.'

'Is your husband with you?'

'Sure who'd want to live with someone like me? He skedaddled shortly after it happened. That's men for you.'

'Does he send you money?'

'A few bob now and then when I threaten to take him to court. Not enough to wet your whistle with. God love his innocence if he thinks a body could get by on the buttons he gives me.'

'Would you like him back?'

'Not in a month of Sundays. Amn't I bad enough on my own? If there were two of us in it there'd be murder.'

She continues prattling as he wheels her. When they get to the village the awnings are coming down over the street-stalls. In the distance the grotto looks lethargic in the twilight. The locals gaze at him as he passes. It's as if no foreigner has a right to be here. Or no healthy foreigner.

They reach the centre of the village. He watches the scalpers selling off the last of their wares. A man at a stall stands with a bunch of crucifixes in his hands. He places them in people's hands as they pass. It's as if he's giving them away for nothing but if they take them he walks along beside them asking for a 'small donation, *s'il vous plait.*'

The last pilgrims disperse to the taverns. On the balconies he sees children waving. In the distance the neon lights of the discotheque gleam.

Her mood is subdued. When they get to the *pension* he wonders if the night hasn't been an anti-climax for her.

He puts her on the stairlift and presses the button. When they get to her room he starts to help her out of her chair.

She shrugs him off.

'I'm not quite ga-ga yet,' she snarls.

She throws herself onto the bed. Her face shows pain but she says nothing. He pulls the clothes over her.

'Well,' she says as she straightens a pillow behind her head, 'What are you waiting for – a tip?'

'I thought you might want something to eat or drink.'

'If you could fix me up with a new pair of legs that would be nice. I hear there's an all-night shop around the corner.'

'I'll look in on you in the morning before I go,' he says. She shrugs as if it doesn't matter one way or the other. Before he goes out the door he thinks he sees a tear in her eye.

As he walks down the stairs he finds himself wondering why he came here at all. A part of him shares her cynicism. Maybe he's trying to fight it.

He thinks of his youth, of how religion had been fed into him with his mother's milk during his adolescence. It culminated in his decision at seventeen to become a priest. He remembered the day. He was about to do his Leaving Cert. He'd been five years preparing for it. Now suddenly it didn't matter. All that mattered was his vocation. It was three years before the bubble burst, his zeal for proselytising compromised into the laicised vocation of the social worker.

He wonders if he could someday return to the seminary now. He's often thought of it. Would he have the discipline? The belief? Sometimes he thinks reflection is his greatest enemy.

He walks through the village again. The moon leers above him, the last grudging light in a plaintive sky. In the woods the students are still sitting around their campfires. The wind blows into their faces as they sing. Their voices rise and fall like a group of birds at dawn. Now and then someone stands up to get fuel to fan the dying embers of the fire.

He arrives at the base tent. The other volunteers are bubbling over with end-of-season buoyancy. Is this an act or their real selves? They steer conversations away from anything that might hint at the disenchantment he suspects they all secretly feel.

Over cappuccinos doled out by the nuns they congratulate one another on the fine ecumenical job they've done since they got there. It was a sacrifice for them. They could have been sunning themselves in the Canaries with a bunch of other couch potatoes anxious to improve their tan lines.

He stands in the doorway. Chairs are being stacked away, food-plates being scraped.

When he looks around he sees her standing in front of him. The woman who's kept him sane the past two weeks, whose good humour has acted as an antidote to his brooding. His lifeline.

'I believe you were saddled with Mrs Hanratty again. How was she?'

33

'The same as ever. She gets a bad press but I have a soft spot for her.'

'Me too.'

'Have you any plans for the rest of the evening? I thought we might go for a walk.'

'I better go in to Peter first. He's doing his farewell thingie tonight. If I'm not there he'll blow a head gasket.'

'I'm sure it'll be second only to Robert Emmet's speech from the docks.'

'Will you join me?'

'I'm afraid not.'

She knew he didn't get on with him.

'Come on. You can suffer him for one last night.'

'It would do my head in. If it hasn't been done in already.'

'Okay Mr Angry. Put my name on a bottle of vino and I'll see you later.'

'Give Peter my love,' he says going out. She sticks her tongue out at him.

He walks to the inn with a sense of expectancy. He feels he's earned the right to some indulgence now, particularly tonight, the most difficult night so far. He orders a glass of wine.

He feels a pang of guilt as he thinks of the other volunteers. They'd be clearing out the tents now, maybe treating themselves to a cup of tea afterwards. He wonders what Peter will say when he notices his absence. He'll think it was deliberate, that he wouldn't allow him wrap up the fortnight in his little pink ribbons. Maybe he should have suffered him after all. There was little to be gained by this eleventh hour defection.

Over another glass of wine he thinks about the seminary years, the years he gave his all to what was then a viable goal, the illusion dissolving only when his mother died. Maybe she was the one responsible for his vocation. And for the dying of it. .

'*Alors*,' says the barman as he orders a third glass of wine, 'I think you go back to Ireland tomorrow, yes?'

When he doesn't respond he says it again in French.

'*Vous rentrez demain, ne'est ce pas?*'

He's sobered by the comment, not having realised the man knew who he was.

'That's right,' he mutters, '*Oui. Ca va.*'

Tomorrow, he thinks, the day when it all comes together for you, all the deep philosophical resonance, all the inconsequential hype.

Tomorrow he'll trudge down these sickly streets again. He'll trade anodynes with fellow Good Samaritans. He'll tend to little old ladies who bathe themselves in the miraculous waters, pining afterwards about the built-in obsolescence of dreams.

There'll be a pilgrimage to the grottoes again, a re-reading of reverential ruminations, the obsequious kissing of the bishop's ring. There'll be the adoring of statues, the therapeutic scent of incense, a reflection on the woman with hands growing out of her shoulders. She'll make her last visit down to the baths that don't have any disinfectants in them because miracles are beyond questions of hygiene. And of course there'll be a visit to the hospital wards. Abandoned crutches hang on their walls like billiard cues, so many testaments to the Almighty's gentle touch.

As he downs the wine he thinks of his life back in Ballina, the things he left behind to come here, things he may or may not return to once his interlude is over. And he thinks of all the comforts he takes for granted, comforts he'll sample again as soon as the plane touches down in Collinstown and he slots himself back into his old grooves.

As he prepares to leave the bar she walks in. She looks resplendent to him.

'Wakey wakey,' she says, snapping her fingers in front of him.

'Sorry,' he says, 'I was in another world.'

'Did I miss anything?'

'Not really. Would you like a drink?'

'Does the Pope pray?'

'I'll get it for you.'

'No, let me. I'll order a pitcher for us. We'll get nicely snockered. It's time for a different kind of spirit than the one we've been savouring for the last two weeks.'

She goes up to the counter. When she comes back she snuggles up beside him. He asks if Peter Gallagher missed him.

'Like a hole in the head,' she says, 'He was too busy listening to everyone else licking his arse. Me included.'

'Hypocrite. You probably told him he was wonderful.'

'Hypocrisy makes him bearable. You should try it.'

'I doubt it would work for me.'

'I don't know why you get so riled about him.'

'It's that God complex of his.'

'He's not the only volunteer with one of those.'

'I wish I had your way for dealing with him.'

'It's not something I even think about.'

She pours a glass of wine for him. As he drinks it he feels all the tension of the fortnight evaporating.

'You're like a tonic to me,' he tells her, 'You make me feel ten years old.'

'You *are* ten years old,' she says, 'That's what I like about you. The day you grow up will be the day I'll jilt you.'

'Thanks.'

After they finish their drinks they go across the courtyard to a fountain. Jets of water squirt around them in the soft heat.

'Make a wish,' she says, throwing a coin in.

The ripples of the water extend outward in little circles.

'I wouldn't know what to wish for.'

'What about Peter Gallagher developing humility? Or Mrs Hanratty becoming mannerly? Or everyone we've seen in the past fortnight becoming miraculously cured of their maladies overnight?'

'Come here to me,' he says.

He holds her in his arms.

'We'll make our own miracles,' he says as they sink into the night's embrace.

Contemporary Ireland

Contemporary Ireland is wonderful
despite certain problems -
horrific car crashes
drive-by shootings
spousal abuse
galloping obesity
overcrowded hospitals
alcoholism
teenage suicides
breakdown of the law
one parent families
no parent families
latchkey kids
drug deaths
cartels
contract killings
a crumbling economy
lying lawyers
car crash TV
lousy weather
an obsession with sex
corrupt politicians
terrorist threats
a lack of religion
a lack of courtesy
among all men.

Let that be as it may.
Let's not forget
we also have world famous singers
fantastic writers
red-hot celebs.
We've also won medals
at the Olympics

even if some of them
were taken back afterwards.
We started the whole
Riverdance thing too
and the holy grail of 'the craic'.
Shouldn't that count for something?

Pearse and Connolly
wouldn't dance at the crossroads
if they came back
but neither would they be
under the thumb
of John Charles McQuaid.

More importantly
we don't allow
smoking in pubs any more,
only people
getting shot in the head.

The Unforgiving Minute

I try to surface from under the bedclothes. It's the same as yesterday and the day before, this effort to meet the world. I do my forty hours and get my pay cheque, fabricating brittle gaiety along with the rest of the wage slaves. Meanwhile the fat continues to grow on my soul.

One of these days, I fear, someone will see me for what I am. when they do, everything will come unstuck. That might be for the best. Maybe people would like me more if I stopped acting. Maybe I'd start getting my old hunger for life back again.

It's a couple of seconds before I realise I've got the mother and father of all hangovers. My head feels as if a juggernaut has capsized on it. Too much wine last night, of course, so what could I expect? The wrath of grapes. Must get some Alka-Seltzer. The cure-all. System must be half full of the stuff by this stage.

Daylight dawns. Skyful of clouds. Behind them the sun reclines. I contemplate another day of slavery in my computerised cage. I wish I was that helium ball - clockless, jobless, bossless. Rising at its discretion.

My first impulse is to swoon backwards. I want to savour once more the multiple delights of marital slumberland. Sadly, the impertinent chirp of a treeful of sparrows enjoying squatters' rights on my favourite birch tree puts paid to that ambition. Not with Shelley's profuse strains of unpremeditated art, I might add, nor Keats' light-winged Driadic chant. No, more the local tone deaf choir.

I know now why T.S. Eliot said romanticism was impossible for the modern world. There are no ornithological singing classes any more, just a monopoly of atonal feathered creatures making my hangover even worse. They say there's providence in the fall of a sparrow. Who can knock one down for me?

My lady wife awakes, her belly big with its nine-month load. The soon-to-be-born infant kicks nightly against her. He brings a different kind of nausea to her by day. Perhaps this is to prepare us for the delights he will no doubt bring to our lives for the next half century or so. Already an aggro merchant.

'I wonder which of us he'll look like?' she says.

'His mother,' I hope,' I answer.

Palaver her before the day starts. One of the main duties of a father-to-be. Besides begetting the bloody things.

'How are you feeling?

'Not too bad.'

'Did you have a good night?'

'Reasonable.'

'Any pain?'

'The usual. Anyway, less of your questions. Get that ass in high gear. It's twenty past.'

She digs me unceremoniously in the ribs, remembering no doubt that this is the day bosses give out little brown envelopes with rectangular pieces of paper in them that rustle and crease, causing mirthful grins to appear on the faces of butchers, bakers and candlestick-makers when produced in wads.

'To hell with it. I think I'll stay home today.'

'What's the problem?'

'I have a headache.'

'Hmm. Sounds serious. Do you think it'll need surgery?'

Cruelty, thy name is woman. I once used to have conversations with my mother that went like this. Petty histrionics on the eve of a new school term. She didn't fall for them either. Has time wreaked no changes at all?

'Come on, bucko, out.'

Soul-searching decision to heave obsolescent bones of 41 summers and what seems like 141 winters onto the carpet. The floorboards creak under me like in a Dracula movie. I do my morning sit-ups. Midway through a stretch I hear some apocryphal sounds emanating from my nether regions. They summon up charming thoughts of me shuffling off the mortal coil even before I get to the breakfast table.

My corporate ulcer also joins in the fun. This overused, underpaid carcass is decaying prematurely as another few hundred chromosomes bite the dust.

By some inexplicable miracle I reach the bathroom without mishap, bestowing gratitude on my creator for such tender mercies. So far so good but what I espy in the mirror gives me pause.

Skin shrivelled up like a dried pea, head approaching the Kojak stations. And a stomach nearly as large as her own. Come to think of it, isn't it a pity men can't deliver babies? Plop, out it goes. Job done. Tummy down to nothing in an instant to make yet more room for Arthur Guinness's fine brew once again.

Ablutions complete, I lurch down to the kitchen. After a few minutes my progeny appear. They wipe the sleep from their eyes as they dig their grubby little claws into the Rice Krispies.

'Daddy,' says Shauna, the younger one, 'Lennie won't let me sit at the window. I bagsed that last night, remember?'

In the background the morning news informs me of carnage on our streets. Elsewhere a drug war looms. Never mind that. I have to confront a more urgent civil war building up closer to home.

'Let her sit at the window, Lennie, and I'll give you an extra dollop of Angel's Delight at dinner time. How about that?'

Frantically biting his thumb. Lennie gives an Oscar-winning pout.

'Okay, but only if you drive me to school.'

And so it goes on, the petty briberies of our days that keeps them ticking over. He'll go far in life, methinks. Farther than his father anyway. Not that that would be saying much.

I start to shave. Shauna follows me to the mirror.

'Daddy, why do you have to shave?'

'You better ask Charles Darwin about that.'

'Who?'

'Charles Darwin.'

'Where does he live?'

'Nowhere. He's dead now.'

'You're stupid.'

Out of the mouths of babes...

41

'Granted.'

'So answer the question.'

'What question?'

'Why do you have to shave?'

'Because hair grows on my face.'

'But you shaved yesterday.'

'I know, but I ate yesterday too and I'm going to eat again today. At least if your mother gets up in time and manages to cook my breakfast.'

'She told me it's you that should be making her breakfast.'

'She did? Why?'

'Because she's getting a baby.'

I realise I'm losing the conversation. I have nothing to add to that.

'Daddy,' she says.

'What?'

'I don't want to go to school today.'

'I know, but you have to.'

'Why?'

'Because.'

'That's not an answer.'

'Okay, for the same reason I have to go to work.'

'Why do you have to go to work?'

'To keep you in Maltesers, my little chickadee. To tickle the mahogany with those seminal spondulicks that give you your cornflakes and your chipped potatoes and your Buttons and your ice cream and your dolls and DVDs and Nintendo games and -'

'We could manage. Mammy has lots of coins in a jam-jar upstairs.'

So that's who's been rifling the small change from my pockets every night.

'And when they run out?

'She could get a job.'

'God bless your innocence. Mammies don't work, you should know that. They just sit around on their bottoms all day waiting for Daddies to come home.'

42

'She says she works harder than you.'

'Does she?'

This is the type of brainwashing that goes on when I'm out earning a crust?

'Can I ask you a question, Daddy?'

Why do children always ask if they can ask a question when they're going to ask the question anyway?

'Go ahead.'

'Are you happy with Mammy?'

'Of course I am, my darling. Need you ask? Does it not radiate from my every pore?'

She looks at me as if I'm from outer space.

'Daddy?'

'Yes?'

'Why do you use stupid words when you're answering my questions?'

'I wish I knew.'

She works her face into a frown.

'Daddy?'

'Yes?'

'How did Mammy's belly get big?'

Oh damn, not this one again. The crazy thing is, I know she knows. She just likes making her father feel embarrassed. God be with the days when children were a few years out of the cradle before they knew the facts of life.

'From a stork, Shauna, that's where.'

'Mammy told me that's only a fairy story.'

'Then go ask Mammy why she got so fat.'

She sees she's not going to get anywhere on this one so she adopts a different tack.

'When are you going to take me and Lennie out for the day?'

'Soon, chicken, very soon. I'm too busy at work at the moment.'

'You're no fun. You never take us out anywhere.'

Here we go again.

'Now you're being ridiculous. Didn't we go to Killarney last summer?'

'Last summer? Tracey Crofton's father takes her to the park every day.'

'Tracey Crofton's father is on the dole.'

'What does that mean?

'It means he doesn't have to go to work.'

Her eyes light up.

'Why don't you get on that?'

If I had a penny for every time I've thought about it.

'I can't.'

'You can't do nothing?'

'Nothing, my dear girl, is the hardest thing in the entire world to do. Unless, of course, you're a politician.'

'What's that?'

'Somebody who makes a living by telling us lies.'

'So you're not going on the dole.'

'Unfortunately not. Anyway, you can't make a living on it.'

'Tracey Crofton's father is making a living on it.'

'That's because he does nixers as well.'

'What's a nixer?'

'It's sort of like a job.'

'But I thought you said he did nothing.'

It's time to stop the conversation.

'Just eat your Rice Krispies, Shauna.'

'I will if you let me off school.'

My Better Half arrives down to breakfast. She showers Shauna and Lennie with kisses and gives me a smack on the head. This is either a subtle gesture of affection or an indication that I should be making tracks for the Dart.

'Shauna isn't well,' I say.

'Again?'

She puts on her sick face.

'We'll let you stay home today,' she says, 'but that's it.'

She blows me a kiss. Mission accomplished.

'What about breakfast?' I ask.

'What did your last servant die of?'

'Indolence.'

She makes her way to the toaster. A few minutes later I'm presented with two slices of toast. They taste like leather left out in the rain. And a cup of tea that looks like a mouse died in it. My wife is slowly poisoning me and I'm blithely going along with it. An accessory after the fact. Or during it.

I say nothing because I don't want to be on tonight's news as a victim of domestic violence, especially when she's sitting dangerously close to the steak knife she cut the toast with. It is at least viaticum for my journey to work. I wash it down with a cup of coffee after throwing the tea down the sink.

'That stuff is bad for you,' she tells me.

A few moments later I'm ready to face the world. As I make my way towards the door she roars at me. It's the kind of roar one should reserve for national emergencies.

'Are you not bringing Lennie to school?'

She brings him out.

We clamber into my house on wheels. It's fifteen years old and still unpaid for, like everything else in my life. If the bills get any worse I'll probably have to start selling off the tyres with the bricks of the house so we can continue to eat.

The engine gasps and dies, gasps and dies. It finally spits into life at the tenth or eleventh turn.

I motor through Fairview, waving good morning to half-remembered faces. It's a bit harder trying to kick-start my brain to life as the streets race by. When I get to Lennie's school he makes me park around the corner in case some of his classmates see the excuse for a human being he has for a father.

I wave goodbye to him but he ignores me. He's already in his other world, the one I can't be a part of. He'll never believe me when I tell him I was young once.

I drive to my place of work, parking in the same spot as I've done for the past 16 years. I'm starting to wake up. At my age it takes this long.

Lock car, trudge up driveway, press code, enter building, wave to secretary. At this stage I could do it from memory.

When I arrive at the office I shuffle through the sea of papers that await my attention. I read glorified pap from intellectually-challenged executives that I have to brown-nose to ensure my future in this antediluvian boneyard.

Tom Healy comes in. Tom is my boss. He's as fresh-faced as always, rubbing his hands in glee at the prospect of another day's work. Or what passes for it.

'There you are,' he says, 'The main man. Going to give it hell today, are we?'

'Don't I always?'

'But of course. You know someday I want to see you running this plant.'

I'm sure you do, I think, when you're brown bread.

'I wouldn't exactly have considered myself a candidate for that role.'

'On the contrary. Your main problem is your lack of confidence. I've always thought of you as the most under-rated man in the factory.'

'Really?' I say. Is that why you passed me over at the last promotion?

'Well I won't delay you. Did you say good morning to Miss Jackson yet?'

I didn't. In fact I rarely do. Years ago we both came to the conclusion that, despite (or because of?) spending so many years in such close proximity to one another, we have less in common than a lumberjack and a ballet dancer.

'Good morning, Ms Jackson,' I intone.

She likes to be addressed as Ms. It's short for miserable.

'Good morning,' she replies.

A cackle of typewriter keys begins. I face the teeming avalanche of print that awaits my attention. As I ready myself for the day's tortuous labours there's a knock on the door.

Joe Daly enters. Joe has been in the office as long as myself. We share a mutual disdain for everything it represents. Like myself he's a prisoner here, probably until they cart him away.

'Have you a minute for a chat?' he asks. Most of Joe's chats last several hours. Some of them have come dangerously close to lasting as long as the work day.

'Get lost, Daly,' I tell him, 'I 'm busy. I'll see you in the canteen at eleven. Have you no work to do?'

'Fuck that for a game of marbles. I did ten minutes when I came in. That'll do me for the day unless Healy is on the warpath. Is it my fault if I can do a day's work in the time it takes the rest of you gobdaws to wipe your collective arses?'

Ms Jackson isn't too impressed by this less than noble form of expression. She exits stage left.

'I wouldn't say too much in front of Her Ladyship,' I whisper to Joe when she's out of earshot, 'Everything she hears gets back to you-know-who.'

'Let it. I'm too old for him to sack me now. He knows I'd have him in the Labour Court in jig-time.'

'Good thinking Robin.'

'How did you get over the weekend?'

'Nothing too exciting. I climbed Niagara Falls in a barrel on Friday then went round the Cape of Good Hope on Saturday. Yesterday I went scuba diving to wind down.'

'I was thinking more of the club scene.'

'I'm cash and carried. Has that little detail escaped your mind?'

'I suppose that means you spent the weekend in front of the goggle box. Or cleaning up kiddie's puke.'

'Near enough. What about you? Did you meet the woman of your dreams?'

'Almost. I spent a few hours chatting one up on Friday but that was as far as it went.'

'You probably came on too strong. You always do.'

'I wanted whiskey and sofa and she was more the gin-and-platonic type.'

'It's about time you realised you were past it. There's no fool like an old fool.'

'Better to have loved and lost, my friend. I refuse to bow out as long as there's life in the old dog.'

Ms Jackson reappears, murdering Joe with her eyes. He gets the message and leaves, winking at me on the way out.

After he's gone I get to wondering wonder if Ms Jackson is into whiskey and sofa or gin and platonic. I conclude neither. In fact I don't think she's into anything.

'So how are you today, Ms Jackson,' I enquire.

'As well as can be expected. Terrible weather we're having, isn't it?'

'Now you've said it. Do you think it'll get worse before it gets better?'

'You never know in this godforsaken country, do you?'

'That you don't, Ms Jackson, that you don't.'

'How is Aoife? She must be due any day now.'

'Last Friday actually. The little fellow doesn't want to come out. Can't say I blame him considering the state of the world.'

'Oh don't say that now. I hope there's no medical problem.'

'I don't think so. The gynaecologist said everything was hunky dory.'

'I'm delighted to hear that.'

She looks at me with an expression that says the conversation is now over. This gives me much relief. She puts on her specs and starts typing.

I try to do the same but can't. Any kind of conversation kills my concentration. Already I know today will be one of those days where I get nothing done.

So what. As Joe says, I'm too old to sack. Poverty averted once more. At least for the foreseeable.

In a week or less I'll have another mouth to feed. When will I learn? Loving beyond my means. Shauna put the kibosh on Gran Canaria a few years ago. Lennie killed off a Datsun I had my eye on. Sacrifices, sacrifices. Looks like Killarney again next year on the restricted budget. Another week in a maggoty B&B eating stale fries as the kids go ape in the local playground. Not exactly what I expected fourteen years ago when we tied the knot in the Burlington. What's next? Keep reproducing until they render me sterile? Or the bank manager repossesses the house? I can't go on I must go on, or whatever it was that miserable git Beckett said. Maybe one day I'll get the guts to tell Healy to put his job where the monkey put the nuts. Sometime before I'm 97 maybe.

My eyes glaze over mildewed pages, debit credit debit credit, debit credit. Figures for incoming goods and outgoing goods. Profits, losses. Increases, decreases.

I would prefer to be drilling machinery. Would prefer to have my eyes pulled out slowly by Tom.

'Blue collar more than white?' Joe asks me. His world is that simple. Mine is locked between the two of them. I tell him the worst day of my life was when I was kicked upstairs.

'That's where all the dead wood is,' I say.

He thinks I'm only saying it because I'm not up there. He'd like to be.

The hours, somehow, pass. I skite off for a cup of coffee with Joe in mid-afternoon and somehow get through the day. The secret is not to think, not to think and not to feel. When I do that I find that suddenly, without warning, it's 5.30.

I clock out as I clocked in, mindlessly, brainlessly, soullessly. Ms Jackson bids me adieu. I make my way to the metal coffin that got me here. Turn ignition, wave goodbye to Stalag 17. Thank Christ I won't see it for another 16 hours.

Driving, like working, is easier if you don't know you're doing it. My car could nowfind its own way home now without me driving it, without me even using satnav.

I stop off at the off-licence to buy a six-pack and a hip flask of vodka. I'm planning on spending another night in. If I go to the pub I know I'll end up on the shorts. If I do that I'll dig into the ESB money again and Aoife will go through me for a shortcut.

Instead I'll sit with her watching the late night movie. We'll be polite and civilised with one another. We'll talk about the bump for a while and then she'll phone her mother and natter with her for a while and then she'll come back to the room and tell me her news and another night will pass. She'll go up to bed before me and I'll have a few vodka chasers to kill my mind. When I go up to join her she'll be snoring gently and I'll sleep my drunken sleep beside her.

Tomorrow I've promised to tidy the garage. On Wednesday I'll bring Shauna to the local playground. She'll come with me if she's up to it. We'll watch the children playing before coming home for the soaps and the game shows. Thursday is shopping day. We'll join the other millions to stock up on provisions as if we're building nuclear shelters. Then Friday, Crunchie day. Little treats on the way home, a few extra bevvies at night. Saturday means a lie-in to reward myself for my week's labours.

Her mother is with her when I reach the house. She always seems to pick Monday to visit. It's as if she knows it's the one night I like to be left alone.

She gives me a gruff hello when I enter but nothing else. She always makes me feel I've committed some crime anytime I see her. I feel like apologising for being alive. Or for marrying her daughter. I know I've failed in her estimation as a son-in-law. Too irresponsible, too much Jack the Lad. Once upon a time that might have mattered to me. No more. Maybe I even get some sadistic satisfaction out of her disapproval of me.

One thing she's been unsuccessful at, which seems to pain her deeply, is turning her daughter against me.

'There you are,' I say, 'How goes it?'

'Not too bad.' She gives me the hatchet face.

'And how is my lady love?' I kiss my other half. Or as I call her since she got pregnant, my other three-quarters.

'Okay. We're just exchanging gossip about the battle of the bulge. She was telling me how it was with me.'

'It won't be long now.'

'Not long at all.'

'Are you ready for him?' Hatchet Face asks.

'I hope so. I should be an old hand at this stage.'

'There's always something new to learn. Don't take it for granted.'

'Have no fear of that.'

'How are you keeping yourself?'

'So-so. I suppose you walked over.' She lives just up the road, worse luck.

'I always do, as you know. Isn't the weather ferocious?'

'That it is. You'd want to be well muffled up. Aoife told me you had the 'flu.'

'I did. Couldn't shake it off for some reason.'

'You better watch yourself. They say if you get it a second time it's a curse.'

We stand awkwardly, wondering what to say next. Then mercifully she stands up.

'Well I'll be off. I wouldn't want to give any of you my dose.'

'That's very considerate of you.'

Aoife isn't too pleased. She looks at me with aggressive eyes that say, 'Press her to stay longer.' I can't do that. We despise one another. Why pretend different?

'Would you like a cup of tea?'

'No thanks. I have to go.'

She puts on her overcoat.

'I'll be in touch, ' Aoife says, 'The doctor says any day now. Don't be too far from the phone.'

'How could I be?'

'You're going to be my rock on this.'

'I'll try anyway.'

I want to say, 'So will I' but the words won't come out.

She gives me another look. It's a sickly smile that says, 'How did you manage to persuade my precious daughter to marry you?'

I've never yet had a run-in with this woman. Maybe we'd be better off if we did. There's a tension there that only an argument could break. They say Irish girls never fully leave their mothers. Could this one drive Aoife away from me one day? Or me away from Aoife?

She goes out.

'You were rude to her,' Aoife says.

It's a familiar taunt, one I'm tired defending myself about.

'I asked her if she wanted to have a cup of tea,' I say, 'What else could I do?'

'It was obvious you didn't want her to. A blind person could see that.'

'She had a mouth on her. If she wanted it all she had to do was ask.'

'It's not the tea, it's the attitude.'

'She puts me on edge. You know that. She's your mother, not mine.'

'So that gives you a licence to be rude to her.'

'I wasn't rude. That's your imagination. I treat her the same way I treat everyone else.'

'That's not true and you know it.'

'Okay, so I was rude to her. I apologise. What do you want me to do about it? Run after her and beg her to come back?'

'She doesn't come round much. You could have made an effort.'

'I've had a rough day. I'm tired.'

'There's always something, isn't there? A rough day, a hangover, stress about money. It's always about you. I'm about to bring another human being onto the planet and you're tired.'

'Okay, I'm a horrible person. Anything else?'

'Now you're being childish.'

'I don't get on with your mother. Is that a crime?'

'She's never done anything against you. What have you got against her?'

'Nothing. I just know she hates me.'

'She never said anything like that to me.'

'She doesn't need to.'

'We're going around in circles as usual. Maybe we'll just let it rest for now.'

'Good idea.'

Aoife, I think, you're turning into a bitch. If you keep this up I'll swing for you. Or for your mother. Or both of you. Your old lady has got at you again. Every time she calls you're gone from me for the rest of that day. Will it always be like this?

She puts a meal in front of me that I don't want. I can't tell her that because it would set her off on another rampage. Instead I pick at it like a bird. When she leaves the room I deposit it in the bin.

She comes back after a minute. She suspects something.

'Have you finished your meal already?' she says

'I wasn't hungry. I ate what I could.'

'And thrown the rest away?'

'Yes.'

'It's a pity you didn't tell me. I could have saved some for Lennie's lunchbox.'

'Sorry.'

'I suppose it would kill you to compliment me on my cooking sometime.'

'You're a wonderful cook. I've often told you that. I'm just not hungry tonight. My stomach is at me.'

She begins to laugh.

'You poor thing. you must have all the problems of the world on your shoulders.'

It's the last straw.

'If you don't stop I'll put my head in the oven.'

My remark seems to get through to her.

'I know I'm spoiling for a fight,' she says. 'Don't mind me. What do they call it – pre-natal tension?'

She grimaces.

'What's wrong?'

'Nothing.'

'Is it kicking again?'

'A bit.'

'I'm sorry for you. I know it doesn't look like that sometimes.'

'This is the last one - okay?'

'Amen to that. Next week it's the snip for me.'

'If you don't sign yourself in for it, I will.' She gives me a half-smile. Maybe there's hope for us yet.

'So your day was rough?'

'Aren't they all? But it passed. That's all I ask any more.'

'Get out of that job. It's killing you.'

'There's a small problem called money if I do. We'd be in the poor house.'

'Can you afford to die? Would that be preferable?'

'In some ways yes.'

She grimaces again. Suddenly I don't know what to say. I turn
on the television in a kind of trance. There's a James Bond film
showing. Daniel Craig is having a karate fight with someone who
looks like a *Playboy* bunny. What's interesting is that she's beating
him.

'I'd prefer you to sweep the streets than to be in a job you don't
like,' she says.

'So would I. If you can get me a job sweeping the streets, I'll do
it.'

'Now you're being melodramatic again.'

'Half the country is out of work. Wake up and smell the coffee.'

I want to be nice to her but something is stopping me. Maybe
it's the residue of pain I've been building up these last few months.
Something I want to take out on the world, her included.

I crack open a beer. All my problems seem to disappear as I
swallow it. I become Daniel Craig, become James Bond. I'm ten
years old as the bullets fly.

She goes upstairs. After a few minutes I hear her reading a
bedtime story to Shauna.

It's something I should be doing but I can't. I'm an absent
parents these days. For a while Shauna seemed to draw us together.
At the moment she's more like a wedge between us, a weapon we use
to alienate us from one another.

Her mother is another one. Maybe mothers-in-law always were.
There's a thousand years of negative publicity riding on that one. I
wonder if cavemen from the Palaeozoic era went around pummelling
their mothers-in-law with clubs. They probably did. I'd love to have
been a caveman.

It would have been nice to live in that time for other reasons as
well. No navel-gazing or shrink visitations or Spock or Freud or
books on Mothercare or Parenting with a capital P or pseudo-
intellectual posing or psychoanalytic bullshit or trial marriages or
trial separations or pre-nuptial agreements or dead end jobs. Just two
people in a cave doing what people do. Maybe the ambitious ones
moved to bigger caves when they got a promotion. At least if the
pterodactyls didn't object.

Aoife tells me I should try harder with her. I tell her I do, repeatedly, but it never works. Maybe her problem is that she has too much time to think since her husband passed away. Nothing to do and all day to do it. On the phone to Aoife twenty times a day as a substitute. Her new cause.

She says they don't talk about me but I doubt it. I can imagine the way the conversations might go. 'Is he on the bottle again? Doing his bit around the house? Still moaning about the job, no doubt.'

Where it starts to get problematic is when she starts comparing me to her father. 'There's no man in Ireland that can live up to him,' she said to me once. What a wonderful attitude with which to start marriage. Maybe the miracle is that we survived this long.

It's past midnight. I sit watching static on the television, Daniel Craig has defeated the *Playboy* bunny and stopped a nuclear holocaust. Well done Daniel.

Her voice calls down to me.

'Is the film over? Will you be up soon?'

'I'm on the way.'

'Bring me a Panadol, will you? And a glass of water.'

Tomorrow I'll try to take more of an interest in her pregnancy. She's the easiest woman in the world to get on with and the hardest. For half the year we seem to be on a perpetual honeymoon and for the other half on a collision course with disaster. Is there any middle ground? If there was, maybe the world would have no need for marriage counsellors.

In a couple of days there'll be a new person in the house. We'll be back to the horror of night feeds, throwing up on the carpet and various accidents in the bathroom. Afterwards the arguments will begin. Whose turn is it to stay in? Whose turn to change the nappy? Whose turn to try and be sane?

Will it be a bundle of joy or one of misery? Will I be allowed father it or will I be shoved into the background as she showers it with the affection that was once directed at me.

Fools can ask more questions than wise men can answer, as she's fond of telling me. I decide to put these particular ones on the back boiler. As for now I should be grateful for the fact that I've got through another week without killing anybody - or myself.

Look at the positives, she says. Be grateful for what you have. Health not too bad, sort of. Still in a job, sort of. And still in a marriage, sort of. So stop being so glum.

Life, after all, does have something to offer. And as the lady says, you never know.

Redeemed

Peripheral
she floated through my days one time,
a monolith to me,
a doom.
Abducting me with alcohol
she swooned into my path
but later she annulled me,
carved a gypsy wrath.
In spring I saw her bonded,
husband-led,
her trolley in the marketplace,
her kindergarten love.
Conversing
she assured me all was well,
the pregnancy
a false alarm
the continental trip a cert,
When bidding her goodbye,
I washed away my dreams,
the man I might have been,
delinquent, part serene.
'You spared me different deaths,'
I told her surreptitiously
by waking prematurely,
making deals.

Uncle Edwin

The atmosphere at UCD was electric that year. In the cafeteria the conversations ranged from Watergate to Kent State, the horrors perpetrated by Lieutenant Calley in Mi Lai. We were all full of how we were going to change the world. A more pressing concern was getting a cup of coffee that didn't taste as if the waitress hadn't spat in it.

'Where are you off to for the summer?' a pimply-faced first year asked me.

'To Uncle Edwin, ' I said.

'Oh.'

I didn't go into any more details. Didn't everyone have an Uncle Edwin stashed away somewhere in America? He was going to fill in my last summer for me, the one between doing the B.A. and entering that horrible place called The World.

I'd spent three years examining my bellybutton. Now it was wake-up time. What would I do for a living? My father wanted me to join him in his car business. My mother had her mind on more exalted things. Teaching, maybe. forming the minds of a generation. Or reading The News out in RTE. I'd have preferred to be in Vietnam than that.

Edwin had been asking me over since I was knee-high to a grasshopper. I was about that height the last time he'd seen me. Since then it was just phone calls and letters. Now I felt the time was ripe. Maybe he'd clean my head out for me. I might even stay over there with him and try to become as rich as he was.

I got the train down to Ballina to say goodbye to my parents.

'Have you not enough of the world seen?' my mother said to me when she met me at the station. It was hard to explain to her that I had to keep moving or my brain would shrivel into jelly. That was what youth was about. She'd have been happier for me to hang around Ballina for the summer, making the occasional trip to Costa del Enniscrone for kicks.

She scrutinised me like a police officer as I stuffed the last of my Bob Dylan cassettes into my travelling case. Last summer it was

58

Croatia, the year before that Greece. She hadn't been outside Ireland herself. She envied me my status as one of the 'Follow the Sun' generation - even though I hated the sun. I needed to get away for the sake of it.

'You know me and my itchy feet,' I said. 'Anyway I'll be home long enough. It's probably going to be my last chance to spread my wings.'

'I'll phone you when your exam results come through.'

A masochistic part of me wanted to fail it. It would give me an extra few months of dossing while I did the repeats. I didn't have a conscience about wasting my father's money.

'Tell Edwin we'd love to see him over here,' she said. There was sadness in her voice when she spoke. I wondered why my father didn't mention him. He was his brother after all.

She examined the final contents of my case herself. I wasn't old enough at twenty to negotiate such convoluted manoeuvres on my own. Sometimes I wondered why she didn't do my shaving for me or accompany me to the toilet. She went close sometimes.

She stuffed a bunch of lettercards into the case. They were addressed to herself. This was to make sure I didn't drift off the radar. It was just as well she didn't have Skype. She'd have had me on it 24/7.

'Don't forget to keep warm,' she said, 'We don't want you coming down with anything.'

'It's America. They fry eggs on the sidewalks over there.'

'Sidewalks. Fair play to you. You're getting in on the language already. Whatever happened to footpaths?'

She put so many jumpers into the case I had to sit on it to get the zip closed. Even after that she insisted on squeezing a last pair of socks in at the side.

'I'm not Ernest Hemingway going into the jungle,' I told her, 'There are shops over there. Or should I say stores.'

'Hemingway even had to wear socks,' she snapped, 'jungle or no jungle.'

The next morning I got up at the crack of dawn to get the train to Dublin.

'Don't be out late at night,' my father said, 'and keep your money in your socks. It's a good trick if you get mugged. Nobody ever thinks of looking there.'

'It's just as well,' I said, 'the way mine smell. They're enough to turn any robber off.'

The last thing my mother gave me was a bunch of sausages for Edwin. 'He eats them till they come out his ears,' she said. 'Even with all his money he can't get them over there.'

'Give him a few boxes of matches as well,' my father said, 'I believe he lights his cigars with $100 bills. They might prove a more economic substitute.'

I made a beeline out the door. I was never a fan of goodbyes.

'Make sure you eat healthy,' my mother shouted as I ran towards the train station.

'Of course,' I said, inwardly fantasising about a non-stop diet of Big Macs.

I wanted to sleep on the train but I couldn't. The year's study had burned me out. Being over-tired made it harder to sleep than being under-tired.

When we got to Dublin I felt sick.. I hailed a taxi at the station.

'Airport,' I said when one stopped. I threw myself across the seat. I fell asleep now just when I didn't want to. It seemed only a minute later when the driver said, 'We're here.'

It was black with people. I had to queue for ages at the check-in. It seemed hours later before I finally reached the embarkation area.

As I got on the plane I wondered how many thousands of others like me had ridden the big bird to the U.S. of A. In the last century it would have been the coffin ships of the Great Famine. We were the privileged generation, the one that went out for fun rather than necessity. We had our J1 visas in our pockets along with our Traveller's Cheques, hungry for laughter.

I wondered how Edwin would receive me. It was so long since I saw him. I wouldn't even have remembered what he looked like if my mother hadn't given me a photograph of him. He sent it to her just after he left Ireland. It was when he went to join the Navy. He looked sad in it. It was as if he didn't want to be there. No one knew why he let Ireland so suddenly after seeming to be so happy there.

He made his fortune in real estate. My father professed to be proud of him for that but I always felt there was resentment buried beneath his praise.

Like many brothers I knew, they seemed to have been rivals in childhood. Or was the rivalry just on my father's side? Was he jealous of the fact that Edwin made so much money?

'Make sure you relieve him of a few of his dollars when you see him,' he'd said to me the night before I left Ballina, 'They came easy enough to him.'

That couldn't have been true. My mother told me he started out as a dishwasher in the Sheraton Hotel. Afterwards he became an elevator operator. He earned enough from it to put himself through college. He was probably lucky to get into 'Realty,' as he called it. It was during a property boom. But there was nothing lucky about the way he worked himself to the bone afterwards.

I spent most of the plane journey wondering how he'd receive me. People sometimes made offers for you to visit them without meaning it. If you took them up they got a seizure. Would that be the way with Edwin? I knew precious little about him except that he was rich.

Everyone on the plane seemed to be under thirty. I spoke to people going to San Francisco to work on the buildings. Others were off to the mid-west to theme parks. A few were lazyboneses like myself visiting relations to just goof off. I envied the ones who were going to work their socks off to earn those precious dollars. It always seemed easier to do that in another country. The Irish had done it in England and in the States. Why were we loth to break sweat in our own country?

As the plane touched down I sampled for the first time the wonder of The Land of Opportunity. I walked through the airport feeling I'd been plummeted into some kind of intergalactic netherworld. The constellation of neon made my heart race. I looked around me at the teeming crowds. I didn't properly believe I was here yet.

I felt I knew more about America than I did about Ireland. I'd grown up listening to its music. I watched its sports stars and

politicians. I absorbed its irrepressible energy. I knew what time it
got up in the morning, how many pills it swallowed before breakfast,
how many diseases it accumulated before it went to bed at night.
Even before I saw the country I both loved and hated it. I'd learned to
immortalise the plastic gods it splurged across cinema screens at me
for two decades.

That was all very well. For now there was the small business of
trying to get where I was going.

I took my case from the conveyor belt and walked towards the
exit. All around me tannoys were barking out instructions. There was
a sniffer dog at the counter. He expressed such an interest in my
luggage that the Customs lady decided to have a peek. When she
opened it she saw the item that interested the dog.

'Sausages,' she bellowed in a deep Texan drone, 'Sausages from
Ireland.' It could have been worse, I thought. It could have been
cocaine.

'They're for my uncle,' I explained. Surely she was aware Edwin
liked sausages. Surely the President had transmitted a message to her
from the White House about his love of bacon.

'We usually impound stuff like that,' she said, 'but I could hardly
deny your uncle his bacon.' She gave me a smile. 'I love the Irish,'
she said, 'I have a cousin in Gollway.'

I thanked her and marched on. No sooner was I out of the Customs
area than a burly black man came up behind me. He snatched my
case. I was about to scream for the cops when I saw he had a badge
on him. It had 'Airport' written on it. Underneath it was another one
that said 'No Tipping.' I was reminded of the 'Don't Feed the
Animals' signs in the zoo in the Phoenix Park. Would racism ever get
that bad in Ireland?

When I got outside I saw my first sidewalk. The night felt humid.
Hot air wafted itself up at me from a vent under the ground. I thought
of that Marilyn Monroe movie where she's doing her best to keep the
air from blowing up her dress (but not really). A flurry of yellow cabs
sped by me, reminding me of any number of Hollywood films.
Especially the ones where the hero gets into a cab and says to the
driver, 'Follow that car!'

I was just about to hail one of them when I saw Edwin. He was waving frantically at me from a Corvette. At first sight he seemed to be more American than the Americans. He looked like one of those tourists who came to see 'Kelly's Book' in TCD and drank pints of Guinness with shamrock designs on the top of the cream as they sang 'I'll Take You Home Again, Kathleen' in some rip-off pub over Irish coffees.

He was dressed in a three-piece suit with a silk handkerchief sticking out of the top pocket. His tie was like something out of Damon Runyon. It was all the colours of the rainbow. All he was missing was a 'Have a Nice Day' badge on his lapel.

His face was double the size of what it was in the photograph I had of him. So was his stomach. It wasn't too hard to figure out why. Twenty years of easy living.

'Wo!' he said getting out of his car, 'If it isn't yourself that's in it.' His accent was thicker than the soup we used to get at my cousin's house in Foxford. I wasn't sure if he was mimicking the stage-Irishry or if it was really him. He gave me a bonecrusher of a handshake. I got a hug afterwards. A big one. I thought he was going to come out the other side of me.

'How did you recognise me after all these years?' I asked him. He guffawed.

'Are you jokin' me? I smelled the bogdirt from across the street. That sensation never leaves you no matter how long you're out of the old country.'

'The last time I saw you I was in nappies,' I said.

'Diapers,' he corrected.

'Whatever you call them, it wasn't today or yesterday.'

'And that's for sure. So how the bejesus are ya anyhow? Marian told me you'd grown up into a fine strappin' lad. Well she wasn't tellin' a word of a lie.' Marian was my mother.

'It's probably all the spuds,' I said, deciding to go along with his blarney. This caused him to let out another guffaw.

He put my case into the boot of the car and zoomed out of the airport. He kept talking to me all the way down the Interstate but I couldn't hear a word he said. The Rolling Stones were blaring out over his stereo.

I had the sausages in my hands. I'd kept them separate from everything else because of the Customs lady. When I showed them to him he almost ran us off the road in his excitement.

'Jeez,' he said, 'Irish sausages! Now I can die happy. I bet herself was responsible for these. I told her if she sent you over to me without them I'd pack you back to her on the next 747.'

We continued to speed down the motorway at the rate of knots. As he zig-zagged between lanes without looking into his mirror I contemplated the prospect of being the shortest-living tourist in American history. As we screeched to a halt at the toll booth he said, 'Don't happen too have sixty cents on you, do you?' Before I had time to search my ragged Levis we were off again in overdrive down the four-laner. The sun beamed down on us mercilessly as Mick Jagger complained about not being able to get any satisfaction.

'Have you got rid of those pigs in the kitchen yet?' he asked me when we got out of the thick of the traffic. It was a question I'd almost expected since I first clapped eyes on him, the question all expatriate uncles probably felt they had to ask. It was as if the old cliché would put me at my ease.

'We're so affluent now,' I said, 'We've moved them to the living-room.' He giggled like a schoolboy.

'So you're here to get the dope on me,' he said, 'To find out why the old rake never married.'

'I'm here to enjoy myself,' I told him, 'and to recover from the insanity of three years studying for a piece of paper I can wave in the fasces of people who'll probably have their minds made up not to employ me.'

'Take your time before you start working. You'll be a wage slave long enough. In the meantime it's up to me to show you just about as many bright lights as I can. And maybe a few red ones as well.'

I doubted that. My father said to me once, 'If Ed tries to pull any of that raunchy stuff on you, don't believe a word of it. He's an altar boy at heart.'

The needle of the speedometer hit 80. My heart continued to palpitate. When we came to a red light he screeched to a halt. He took the opportunity to show off the technological delights of his vehicle: a drinks cabinet in the glove compartment that opened out at the flick of a switch, a television in the back seat.

'You've really got it all,' I said to him. 'Who owned this car before you – the president of General Motors?'

'Not too bad for an oul fella, is it?' he said.

I thought of how my mother described him to me once, 'The nicest capitalist I ever met.'

So far the comment seemed apt. The thought made me postpone all those speeches about the unequal division of wealth in the world that I'd spent the past three years delivering to anyone who cared to listen in the Belfield bar. The socialist ideal could wait until the summer was over before I unleashed it on him.

'Did you know it was St. Brendan who discovered America,?' he said then, 'not Christopher Columbus? He just didn't want to boast about it.'

'Is that what you tell your customers?' I said, 'when you're trying to sweeten them up?'

'Of course. Most of my houses have pictures of Saint Patrick in the windows.'

He pummelled me with questions all the way to the apartment. How was college? Was his brother behaving himself? What did I plan to do with my life? I answered him with the cliches that are all you can manage in situations like that. I wondered if there was anything behind his bluff exterior. Was there any way through to the real Edwin or was that too big an ambition for me to have over a few weeks?

When we got to his apartment he took out a device that opened the gates to an underground car park. A huge beam crossed his face. He might have been a child that had just been given a new toy.

He hit his device again after we parked. The trunk popped open for me to get my bag. We got the elevator up to the 11th floor of the building. That was where his apartment was.

I'd never been in an apartment before. When he opened the door it was like walking into heaven. It was the biggest room I'd ever seen in my life, an open plan kitchen-cum-living-room that could have accommodated a family of thirteen back in Dublin. It looked out over the vast expanse of Manhattan.

'This is where you'll be sleeping,' he said, leading me down a corridor to a bedroom, 'Joleen and myself are in the one next to you in case you need anything.'

'Joleen?'

'Did I not mention her to you in the car? She's my partner.'

'Your partner?'

'We've been together nearly a year now.' I'd never heard a thing about her.

'Really?'

'She's an actress.'

I was stunned. Somehow I never had Edwin down as someone who'd have a partner. He was my bachelor uncle, wasn't he? And as my father put it, an altar boy. I'd never heard of him even going out with a girl in Ireland, never mind living with one. I assumed it would be the same over here.

'I'll introduce you to her in the morning. She's at a shoot in Philadelphia tonight.'

The way he said 'shoot' didn't sound like him. It was as if he made up the word.

'I hope you don't mind her being here. I didn't like to mention her when I invited you over. I thought it might put you off. I know how Marian thinks about things like that.'

'So this is a serious relationship then?'

'You betcha. I'm gonna marry her when her divorce comes through.'

Things were getting more complicated by the second.

'So she was married before?'

'That's right. She was in a bad marriage but that's all over now. She might even get it annulled. If she does I can come clean to the Irish contingent. That way I could marry her in the church. Then we'd all be hunky-dory, right?'

He poured himself a glass of Jack Daniels.

'Like a can of Bud?' he said. I nodded. He lit a cigar. Not with a $100 bill as my father had led me to expect but rather a match.

'What's Joleen like?' I said.

'An 18-carat beauty. Wait till you see her. The day they made her they threw the mould away.'

He downed a few glasses of 'Jack,' as he called it, while I dug into my Budweiser. It went straight to my head. He kept topping both of us up.

The more he drank the more he talked. He told me about his plans for having approximately 30 children with Joleen and living happily ever after in a ranch in Montana that he planned to buy when he retired.

The last thing I remember is falling onto a bed in a heap with my clothes still on. When I woke up the next morning my head felt like there were a million rats crawling around inside it.

Edwin was standing in front of me with a tray in his hand. He was wearting a pair of multi-coloured pyjamas about three sizes too big for him.

'I thought any nephew of mine would be able to hold his drink,' he said as he handed me a glass of something called Aunt Jemima, 'I had to put you to bed like a five-year-old.'

I couldn't eat the breakfast he'd cooked for me despite the inclusion of the famous sausages. As I crawled out to the living-room a strange apparition greeted me. Joleen was sitting there. She was a peroxide blonde with very big breasts. She looked like the cat that got the cream.

She was six feet tall if she was an inch. Her dress was so tight I thought she must have been sewn into it. She was beautiful to be sure but it seemed to me to be the kind of beauty that came out of a bottle.

'Hi,' she said. She stood up to embrace me but held herself back as she did so. The kiss she aimed for my cheek missed its target. It was one of those Californian ones I'd seen on television.

'You must be Joleen.'

'Got it in one.'

'I wasn't expecting you to be here this early.'

'Me either. I jumped on a red eye from Philly. Sorry I missed you last night. You guys must have been shooting the breeze into the wee hours judging from all the cans on the table. Pity I missed it.'

'We had a lot to catch up on.'

'I bet you had.'

'Edwin tells me you're an actress.'

'For my sins.'

'Do you like it?'

'It's dog-eat-dog out there but, hey, it's a job.'

'So you work in TV?'

'Used to. I'm getting out of it now. I was on a sitcom on Channel 8 last year. Dullsville. Edwin thinks I can break into movies. And as you know, Edwin's instincts are always right.'

It was hard not to suspect she was with him for his money. I told myself to stop thinking like that, to stop making spot judgments of people.

'That would be great,' I said.

'Awesome.'

She fastened her big eyes on me. I felt she was X-raying my soul.

'So how long are you over for?'

'Just a few weeks.'

'Ed tells me you're a bit of a brainbox.'

'I wouldn't say that. Educated idiot would probably be a more apt description.'

'But you got your degree, right?'

'Hopefully. The results won't be out until I get back.'

'I bet you got straight As in everything.'

'Don't be too sure. I just read a few books and memorised what was in them.'

'Stop playing yourself down. That's so Irish! You've got to get over that national inferiority complex. People will take advantage of it.'

Edwin appeared.

'She's right,' he said. I tried not to look at his pyjamas.

He gave her a kiss on the cheek. She made a face at him as she wiped it away.

'Ugh,' she said, 'What's that on your breath?'

'Too much Jack. Sorry. I'll spray something on it.'

'You do that.'

'So what have you two been gabbin' about? How do you like my delightful nephew?'

'Adore the accent. What a pity we can't bottle it.'

'Two weeks in Ireland and you'd be wishing it could be outlawed,' I said.

She looked into a saucepan.

'Ed cooked some sausages for you,' she said.

'He brought me in some already. I couldn't eat them.'

'Why not?'

'I'm hungover. He'll have to have them himself.'

'I don't know if that's a good idea. He has high cholesterol.'

'What about yourself – would you like some?'

'I don't think so. I'd get like an elephant. I only have to look at food and I put on weight.'

I doubted that. She looked almost anorexic.

'My figure is my fortune,' she said, 'Every calorie is magnified by a hundred with a camera lens.'

Edwin started to dig into them. She gave him a dirty look.

'If you have any more of them you'll explode, she said, 'and so will I – with anger.'

'I have a few decades of deprivation to make up for,' he explained.

She got up from the table.

'I give up,' she said.

'Come on. It's a special day.'

'Screw that. I'm going to the studio.'

She put on her coat.

'Already?' he said.

'Some of us gotta work. If I'm late again they'll can me. Anyway I wouldn't like to be in the way with you two. I'm sure you have a lot of things planned.'

'I was hoping to show him the delights of 42nd Street,' Edwin said.

'Don't corrupt him,' she said.

'It's too late,' I said, 'I've been corrupted already.'

'I doubt that, Irish boy. Anyways, I have to split. You guys have a great day. See y'all at teatime.'

She gave Edwin another air kiss.

'Don't worry if you're late home,' she said, 'I'll probably be at the studio late tonight.'

'That's fine, honey.'

He gave her a kiss on the cheek. She blew me one and floated out the door.

'Well,' said Edwin, sporting a large grin, 'What do you think of her?'

'She's a knock-out,' I said.

'I know. Every day I wake up I thank God for her.'

I didn't want to talk about her too much. I knew if I did I might say something negative about her.

We didn't go to 42nd Street. Instead he drove me to a Mexican restaurant. I ate things I'd never heard of before (and couldn't pronounce). He talked about the phenomenal cost of the houses he was selling, probably imagining I'd be impressed. What impressed me more was how he'd managed to be so successful without selling out his Irishness.

'They go for the mother machree stuff so I just keep giving it to them,' he explained.

'What about Joleen? Do you give it to her too?'

'When she lets me. Most of the time she sees through me. I feel out of her league.'

I wanted to say he was worth ten of her but I didn't. He always put a low value on himself. Because he did that, I thought she did too.

'Tell me about Marian,' he said, 'Is there any chance she'd ever grace me with a visit?'

'It's hard enough to get her on a bus to Foxford, never mind a plane to America. She's one of those mothers whose idea of variety is a trip from the kitchen to the living-room.'

'She hasn't changed much then. It's such a pity. She's a sweet lady. I'd really love to see her again.'

He showed me a photograph he had of her. It was from way back. I found it strange seeing her with black hair.

'That's amazing,' I said, 'You've kept it all this time.'

'It's my most treasured possession,' he said. I thought there was a catch in his voice as he spoke but he quickly dropped the subject. Afterwards he talked mostly about Joleen. There didn't seem to be many other women in his life before her. Maybe he was too busy making money. And yet he didn't seem to care about money. It was as if some great insecurity inside him was wiped out by being rich. Maybe that was the only function his wealth performed.

After we got home from the restaurant neither of us knew what to do. The apartment yawned with Joleen's absence.

'I'd like to take you out somewhere,' he said, but I could see he was tired.

'Why don't we just sit in,' I suggested, 'As well as being hungover I'm a bit jetlagged.'

'Jeez,' he said, 'Wait till you're my age. Don't get old before your time.'

I unpacked my luggage. He kept talking ninety to the dozen, following me in and out of rooms as if he was in my house instead of me being in his. It was the kind of talk you expected from someone who hadn't seen anyone in a long time.

I was relieved when he suggested watching a ballgame on the television. I'd never seen one. He talked most of the way through it. There were more stops than in a rugby game. It meant nothing to me despite his best efforts to explain the rules.

His mind seemed to be elsewhere after the game ended. The room suddenly became very quiet. Was he thinking about Joleen? He kept looking at his watch.

'Why isn't she calling me?' he said.

'Did she say she would?'

'Not specifically.'

'Maybe she thinks you're still caught up with me.'

'That's probably it.'

I went to bed early. The adrenalin of the previous night was replaced with a kind of flatness.

I fell into a deep sleep. When I got up the next morning I found him sitting alone in the kitchen. There was a lost look in his eyes.

'Well,' he said as I went in, 'You finally decided to get up. You were snoring so much I didn't think you were going to surface until evening.'

'Where's Joleen?'

'Gone to work, believe it or not. She told me to give you a hug for her.'

'What time did she get in?'

'Late. I was out for the count. I didn't speak to her until this morning. It was only for a few minutes. She had to be at the studio at cockcrow.'

As I fixed myself breakfast he talked about a film he'd been watching on the television after I went to bed. He tried to be cheery but he didn't make a very good job of it.

'What's on the agenda for today?' I said.

'I have a heavy schedule. Maybe you'd like to hang around here for a few hours. I'll bring you somewhere after lunch.'

'That's putting too many demands on you. Why don't I tour for a few days on my own? We can meet up later in the week.'

'But you've only got here.'

'I have a ticket for a bus tour,' I said. It wasn't true. The words came out without my planning to say them. Maybe I sensed a tension between himself and Joleen that I felt I was contributing to. I needed to escape from it.

'I was planning to take the rest of the week off to show you the sights.'

'We can do that next week instead. I feel like a spare part here at the moment.'

'Nonsense. Why do I get the impression this is something to do with Joleen?'

'It's not. I never planned to be here all the time.'

'She's nuts about you. You know that, don't you? I've been telling her about you for months. She couldn't wait to meet you. She'll be shattered if you're gone when she gets in.'

'I love being here but I can't go back to Dublin without having seen some things of my own. If I got away for a few days I'd have more stuff to talk about with you.'

'What are you on about? We already have millions of things to talk about. But if you want to go I won't stand in your way.'

'I appreciate that. Sorry for messing you around. This way you can get your work sorted out. We'll all be more organised by the weekend.'

'Whatever works for you. I'll drive you to the bus.'

I got some of my things together. We were both quiet on the way to the station. He wanted to come in with me but I didn't let him. I didn't want him to know I didn't have a pre-paid ticket.

'Go west, young man!' he chirped as he waved goodbye to me, 'See you in a few days.' Before he left he thrust a wad of notes into my hand. He gave me some bumpf about places I might be interested in seeing that he'd torn from tourist magazines.

I spent the next few days going round Staten Island and the Bronx. It was mindless. I was doing the things tourists do to kill time. I tried my best to keep my mind off the situation between himself and Joleen. It was difficult to do that. I wasn't sure why it was affecting me so much. Maybe I was only imagining there was something wrong between them. I hardly knew either of them.

For a lot of the time I was bored to tears. I went around museums taking photographs. In previous summers I'd worked. Work always made me feel more energised.

At the end of the week I went back to the apartment. Edwin welcomed me with the same enthusiasm as he'd had at the airport. Or did he? Maybe this time it was more forced.

Joleen seemed forced too but then she always had been. Edwin asked me if I enjoyed myself touring around. I told him I wasn't good at goofing off.

'Have you thought about what you'd like to do when you get back to Dublin?' he asked me. Suddenly he was beginning to sound like my father.

'No,' I said, 'Anything that's been suggested to me so far seems only slightly preferable to being roasted alive while having my eyes gouged out by burning coals.'

'You paint a beautiful picture of the job market.'

'That's how it looks to me at the moment.'

'You could work for me for a while,' he suggested. 'Why don't you come into the office with me for a few days and see how you get on? I could make it worth your while financially. You wouldn't be on any books.'

'How do you mean?'

'Not having a work visa wouldn't be an issue.'

I didn't go for it. Maybe I'd have got too fond of it. My future lay back in Ireland. I didn't want anything to get in the way of that.

The next few days were even more fraught than the ones before I went travelling. I felt in their way when I was around the apartment. I tried to stay out as much as I could.

Most of my time I spent wandering around New York. I sat in coffee-houses watching the panoply of life unfold around me. It was so difficult to my confined life in Dublin and my even more confined one in Ballina.

People did what they liked. That impressed me. I saw anything and everything - Indian chiefs, circus clowns, a man in a tuxedo on a skateboard, a policeman on a horse. You never knew what was going to come down the street.

I could hardly see the sky because of the height of the buildings. Cars sped recklessly through the boulevards. I watched members of the Hari Krishna beating on tom-toms. Weird music spilled out of bars. At a fountain a semi-clad waitress did a flamenco dance for her boyfriend under a multi-coloured dome of light. A man with an ankle-length coat wore a billboard around his neck bearing the message: 'Jesus is Coming Soon.'

After a while the abnormal became normal. It even became boring. I found myself longing for my old life back. It was time to go back to the two of them.

The original plan was to stay with them for a few weeks and then go travelling. I hadn't the appetite for that now. I decided to cut the trip short even if it cost me money changing the date of the ticket.

I didn't know what was wrong with me. Maybe I was tired after all my years of study. Or was it simply the fact that the Real World was looming up?

Edwin said he was delighted to see me back. Joleen acted like her usual self. She was so laidback she was horizontal. I felt like asking her how she worked up the energy to breathe.

She spent most of her time admiring herself in the mirror. Every day she appeared in a different get-up. Edwin looked at her like someone watching a model on a catwalk. They never seemed to have much to say to each other. Edwin concealed that fact by talking too much. Shy people always did that.

I spent most of my time sitting around the apartment. It was too tempting to wallow in all the luxury. I was afraid to go shopping tor fear I'd blow my small budget on junk. My money disappeared as money always disappears in big cities, especially when you have nothing to do except spend it. I'd like to have treated Edwin to a few nights on the town but he insisted on paying for everything any time we went out. He brought me to a show on Broadway one evening and to a film another night. It was an adventure one that bored us all out of our minds. We just kept munching candy to take our minds off that fact. We went to a party another night but we left early. We had enough of New York intellectuals within the hour.

'These are the sort of people I have to indulge in meetings so I can sell brownstones to them,' Edwin said to me in the taxi on the way home, 'The secret is to go to the john every fifteen minutes and throw up.' It was the first time the mask of the ditsy expatriate slipped. The truth was coming out. Maybe he was like the rest of us at the back of it all, putting a bright face on a dull life to ease the pain.

Joleen was out a lot. That made me wonder what she was up to. Was she seeing another man on the side?

One night I heard her on the phone to someone. It sounded like a boyfriend from the way she was speaking. I was supposed to be out. She almost jumped out of her chair when she saw me walking into the room. It was the first time I saw her coolness disappear. She made an excuse before hanging up with a hurried goodbye.

I asked her who it was. She fell over herself trying to explain that he was only a casual acquaintance but the more she tried to talk herself out of it the more I became convinced she was involved with him.

'Please don't hurt Edwin,' I said. If she was going to leave him I hoped she'd do it sooner rather than later for both of their sakes.

I didn't tell him about the phone call. She was edgy with me after it. There was even more tension between us than there had been before. In a way that was better than the false politeness of the first few days.

A few days later the airport rang to say they were able to change my ticket. I could see they were both relieved.

'I hope Joleen didn't cramp your style, ' Edwin said to me the night before I went home.

'She's a beautiful girl,' I said, deflecting the issue, 'I hope you two will make a go of it.'

'If we don't, I think I'll resign myself to bachelordom.'

'I hope you wouldn't be marrying her just for the sake of it.'

'I didn't mean it that way,' he said but I felt he did.

He was in low spirits the following morning. Joleen was already gone to the studio by the time I got up. She'd put a love heart on a piece of paper for me with some Xs around it. There was also a note: 'Come back to us next summer. We won't take no for an answer.'

'That's your 'Undying Troth' pledge,' Edwin said as he showed it to me over breakfast. I pretended to be touched but I felt if I never saw the girl again it would be too soon.

On the way to the airport he was quiet. Did he know I disliked her or was there something else worrying him? I couldn't see them lasting long together but I knew he didn't want to spend the rest of his life alone either. From the way he talked about his work I didn't feel it was giving him enough of a buzz any more. What was the alternative? He was hardly a candidate for retirement. He had no hobbies worth talking about.

'Instead of me coming to you,' I said as we got to the airport, 'Maybe you'll come over and visit us sometime. I'd like to try and spoil you the way you spoiled me.'

'You've got a deal,' he said, giving me his trademark wink, but I doubted he meant it. He looked old suddenly. I couldn't understand why he wouldn't want to come to Ireland even if only to see my mother. He obviously thought highly of her but he hadn't brought up her name after that first day.

'Tell them all I sent my love,' he said as we got out of the car. I said I would. He gave me the inevitable bonecrusher hug.

'Get into that car,' I said, 'I hate goodbyes.' He gave me a wave before driving off. It wasn't the usual Edwin wave. I wouldn't have been surprised if he was crying to himself behind the wheel.

My mind was all over the place on the flight back to Dublin. Was there something he was hiding from me? For all his bluff and swagger I couldn't figure out what it was that really made him tick. He was in a job he didn't like, living with a woman who was his opposite and keeping himself going with the kind of false energy guaranteed to drag anyone down over time.

He was a bundle of contradictions. His heart was in Ireland but he never lived there. He spent all day making money but he didn't care about money. He'd have made a brilliant husband and yet he'd spent the last twenty years as a bachelor. It was as if everything in the jigsaw pointed to something else, as if he went out of his way to do the opposite of what he wanted. I saw him as a romantic afraid of the romance inside himself. Maybe he camouflaged it inside business deals, inside the childish romance of outlandish profits. He played the performing seal to everyone he knew, treating us all like marionettes as he did his sleight-of-hand routines for us, staving off any real involvements with his cheque books and his charm.

When I got off the plane I felt I'd aged ten years in the time I was away. As a student I thought I knew everything. As a graduate I realised I knew nothing.

Why was I letting Edwin take over my life? Why should his happiness or non-happiness have bothered me so much?

As soon as I got into the house I was pumped for news by my mother. It was as if I'd come back from outer space. I felt like somebody from one of those turn-of-the-century plays where the country boy takes a ship to some foreign shore and nobody ever expects to see him again.

My father was more cynical. 'I hope you emptied that old bastard's wallet,' he said as he poured a pint of Smithwicks for me. He looked at me with that 'Entertain me' expression of his. I did my best to dredge up as many stories as I could but my heart wasn't really in it.

They both sussed that. I didn't tell them about Joleen because I'd been asked not to. She left a gap in many of my anecdotes. My mother sensed something was up but she didn't delve.

At the end of the night she fished a letter out of her pocket. She said, 'Congratulations, you passed.' It was the results of my exam.

I wasn't sure whether to be relieved or not. Passing meant I'd never see the university again. That would be a wrench of sorts. It also meant I couldn't put off thoughts of a career too much longer. That might have been bad enough in the normal course of events but my head was all over the place after coming back from where I'd been.

My mother took in my discomfiture.

'What's the matter?' she said, 'You should be over the moon.'

'I am. I just need time to take it in.'

'From now on it's all downhill,' my father said, 'Welcome to the human race.'

For the next few days I couldn't get Edwin out of my mind. I didn't know if he was just pretending to be happy with Joleen or if he really was. I didn't care what her motivations were. Even if she was using him they could probably still have some kind of a relationship. But I had to try and get my mind off them.

'What do you think you'll do now?' my father said to me one night after tea.

'I don't know. There's nothing special jumping out at me.'

'Well I'll be jumping out at you if you don't pick something,' he said. 'We've made a lot of sacrifices to put you through college. Do you not think we deserve some return on that?'

'Of course you do, and I'll give it to you. It' s just a lot to think about all at once.'

'You've had twenty years to think about it. Have you not come to any conclusions?'

Application forms for jobs came in the post in the next few days but they held little interest for me. I dumped them in the bin when my father wasn't looking. I presumed he was the one who sent for them. My mother, I knew, would have been content to have me round the house examining options till I was ninety.

'You've said very little about what happened to you on your travels,' she said to me one day.

'I told you everything I could think of. I was a fortnight away. How much can happen in a fortnight? I can't think straight at the moment. I wanted to be a university lecturer once. Now it looks like I'll just be a mechanic or a civil servant.'

What would my future be - setting the points on Peugeots till I coughed my guts out with carbon monoxide? Withering into a governmental post and getting the gold watch at 65?

Maybe I'd go back to Edwin, I thought. Or was he just being polite when he said I could work for him fulltime? Maybe he liked me because I reminded him of my mother. He said I looked like her. I thought I looked like him too.

I spent a lot of days working in the garage as I tried to sort my head out. I used to do that in summers gone by when there was nothing else happening. This was different. I knew that by my father's attitude to me. I wasn't just filling in time now as far as he was concerned. I was being apprenticed for a career.

I wasn't a very good mechanic. I got the jobs done but usually the long way round. If I wasn't his son I'd probably have been shown the door. In my privileged position I could probably have made a go of it if he retired and I took over. At least then I'd be able to sit back and let the other people worry about mistakes. He knew I looked down on it. It was something to fall back on if everything else went wallop.

'You're not yourself these days,' my mother said to me one night, 'Is there something bothering you?'

'I don't know. I feel unsettled.'

'We all get like that. Don't worry about it. You're at a crossroads at the moment. I wouldn't make any big decisions now if I was you. Is Martin giving you a hard time in the garage?' That was my father's name.

'To be honest, yes.'

'You're his pride and joy. You know that, don't you?'

'He has a funny way of showing it.'

'He has such high expectations for you. He gets frustrated when they don't look to be coming to fruition.'

'I think he'd prefer me to be a mechanic than a literary scholar.'

'He doesn't mind what you are as long as you're happy at it.'

'I can't agree with you there.'

'I know he can seem tough at times but he's not. He wants the best for you, just like I do. He's worried about your future.'

'He isn't the only one.'

'These things have a habit of sorting themselves out in their own time.'

'I hope so. Sometimes my head feels it's about to lift off me these days.'

'You've had a lot of excitement with Edwin. Now you're plonked back in your old routines again. It's only natural.'

She brought him back into my mind. Maybe he'd never been out of it.

Was he really happy with Joleen? Would she fleece him? Were his feelings about my mother stronger than he admitted to me? The old thoughts kept nagging at me like a drum.

'He has a photograph of you with him,' I said to her out of the blue.

'I know,' she said, 'It was taken when we were going out together.'

I couldn't believe what I was hearing.

'I never knew you dated him.'

'I thought I told you. It was only a few times. Martin came into the picture afterwards.'

'Did you like him?'

'Of course I did. How could anyone not like Edwin?'

'At what stage did Dad come along?'

'It wasn't as clear-cut as that. The three of us were friends. Then Edwin went off to the Navy. It left the way open for someone else to move in.'

I felt there was more to it. The next day I asked my father why he'd never told me about their involvement.

'I didn't think you'd be interested,' he said flatly.

'But he introduced you to her.'

'So what? Are you not glad he did?'

'That's not the point. Did you play fair with him?'

'What's that supposed to mean?'

'Did you scare him off?'

'Where's all this coming from? She chose me, end of story. Are you trying to say you'd prefer to be my nephew instead of my son?'

'How did you win her away from him?' I said.

'I told him I liked her and he slipped into the background. It was as simple as that.'

'Did you not feel guilty about the way things worked out?' My brain was whizzing in my head. Questions formed themselves faster than I could phrase them.

'Why should I have? Edwin was more interested in money than women in those days. It wasn't like we were vying for her. It was more like first man in.'

'So he donated her to you.'

'That's a funny way to put it. He just felt awkward in her company after I got to know her. That's the way I read it. Then the Navy business came up. Before we knew what was happening he was at sea.'

'But Mam was never consulted about which of you she preferred.'

'Did she have to be? Are you trying to say she didn't have a mind of her own?'

Suddenly it dawned on me why Edwin hadn't talked about her since that first day. He was probably afraid of letting his real feelings show if he did.

'No, what I'm trying to say is that I don't think you ever wanted to know how deeply she felt about him.'

His jaw stiffened.

'You're really getting off on this, aren't you? The plain fact of the matter is that Edwin never had the guts to tell her he felt seriously about her.

'But you did.'

'For sure. Your mother was a beautiful-looking woman. She still is. I popped the question to her within the month. If she was waiting for Edwin to propose she'd be waiting yet.'

'How did she take the proposal?'

'How do I know?' He gave me an icy look. 'Actually I've had enough of this. You'd be a lot better off thinking about your future than the what-might-have beens of a tongue-tied uncle. Have you applied for any jobs yet?'

He was going from the sublime to the ridiculous, plummeting me back into a world I hated to get away from his guilt.

'I'm still confused,' I said.

'Well maybe it's time to unconfuse yourself.'

The way he looked at me made the blood boil inside me.

'I think you stole her from him,' I said.

The words were out before I realised I'd said them. I saw the veins jutting out on his forehead. He was incandescent with rage.

He hit me on the jaw.

I fell down. The blood trickled onto my shirt. He was breathing heavily. He looked as if he couldn't believe what he'd done. I couldn't either. Maybe it was a blow that was coming for twenty years. I hardly felt the pain of it. In a way it was welcome to me. It was as if he was finally getting his feelings for me out into the open.

When I stood up he was still breathing hard. He looked as if he might hit me again.

'After all I've done for you,' he said.

'Yes,' I said 'with your brother's money.'

He looked at me with hatred in his eyes.

'I wash my hands of you,' he said, 'You don't belong in my house any more. Why don't you go back to the Big Apple with your high principles? Maybe you'd like to bring your mother with you while you're at it. You're no son of mine.'

I sat on a bunch of tyres that were piled up in a corner. My jaw was starting to throb. I wiped the blood away with a rag.

The engine was running in a car he'd been working on. I turned it off. I didn't feel bitter towards him. In fact I didn't feel anything at all. Maybe that was the saddest thing.

The next few days passed without note. I stayed in the house but I didn't talk to him. Neither of us said anything to my mother about what happened. I knew she suspected something went on between us but she didn't know what. When she asked me why I stopped working in the garage but I told her I just got fed up of it. The three of us covered over the tensions with practical talk about interviews for jobs I had coming up.

I wanted to ask her about Edwin but I didn't know how to broach the subject. Then a letter came from him saying he'd split up with Joleen. It was inevitable but it's even difficult to accept the inevitable sometimes.

She was very upset. I was too but a part of me was relieved.

'She's gone to Hollywood to make a science fiction movie,' he wrote. It was about lesbians on Mars. Somehow I couldn't see her on the Oscar podium for it.

So Joleen was gone. Did it matter? Anyone with half an eye in their head could have seen they were on borrowed time together when I was with them. Anyone except Edwin, that is.

How would he be without her? No doubt he'd jolly on as he'd jollied on from every disappointment in his life up to this, acting as if it hadn't really happened.

'I didn't deserve her,' he wrote, 'not an old fogie like me. The remark was sandwiched in between others about his work. At the end of the letter he said he was thinking about moving to the ranch in Montana that he'd told me about.

'I've made my fortune,' he said, 'It's time I started spending it.' He ended by saying I was more than welcome to come over anytime again and sample the green, green grass of somewhere almost as lovely as Ireland.

'Poor Edwin,' my mother said, 'He brings a lot of his suffering on himself.'

'Why do you say that?' I asked.

'I don't know. I doubt he ever knew what he wanted.'

'Did he ever want you?' I asked her. There was no point in biting my lip any longer.

'What a thing to say. We wouldn't have been suitable for each other. Maybe we were too alike. I thought I loved him when I met him first. Maybe we were too intense for each other. Feelings like that don't last.'

I wasn't sure if she was trying to convince herself of something that wasn't true or if she wanted to hide her real relationship with him from me.

'Did you ever think of contacting him after he went into the Navy?'

'I wrote to him once or twice but I didn't hear back. I thought he'd lost interest in me.'

'That's crazy. He said the same thing about you.'

'How do you mean? Were you talking about me?'

'Once or twice.'

'What did he say?'

'That he thinks the world of you.'

'Oh my God. Now you're embarrassing me.'

I couldn't stop now.

'Did you ever think of marrying him?' I asked her.

She blushed. It was a long time before she answered.

'I didn't think he'd given two thoughts to me after we separated. We were going in different directions.'

'Maybe he was too inhibited to tell you how he really felt about you.'

'That's a possibility,' she said after a moment. 'I remember he used to be too nervous to ask me out. He'd hide outside the door until my father left the house. Then he'd sneak around the back and tap on the window. It was amusing.'

'Would you have married him if he asked you?'

'As I said, it wouldn't have worked between us.'

84

Her eyes misted over. She bit her lip.

'Let me show you something,' she said then. She went over to a drawer that was usually kept locked. There was a key on the top of it. She took out a photograph wrapped in tissue paper. It was of herself and Edwin standing on the pier in Enniscrone. They were both grinning broadly.

'Martin took it.' she said, 'It was the day Edwin introduced me to him. I never saw him afterwards.'

I took it up in my hands and scrutinised it. As I did so, a light bulb seemed to explode in my head.

Edwin looked the spitting image of me in the photograph. Suddenly I knew the answer to everything. The jigsaw had its missing piece.

I was Edwin's son. It was the only way things could have made sense.

It would explain everything: her nervousness, the aggressive tone of my father, Edwin's rapid departure to the Navy to allow the two or them to marry. I was a honeymoon baby. Or rather a pre-honeymoon one. It wasn't too hard to do the maths.

'You're no son of mine,' he said to me that day in the garage.

Did he mean it literally? Was it his way of telling me where I came from?

As soon as the idea presented itself to me I couldn't get it out of my mind. I convinced myself it was true even though I had no evidence for it.

If it was, would Edwin have known? Would my mother? Maybe nobody knew for sure.

I went over to her. Her eyes were still misty. I put my arms around her. She started to cry, her tears falling onto the photograph.

'I don't know why I've kept it all this time,' she said, 'I should have got rid of it years ago. If you indulge your memories too much they stop you moving on. They're bad for you. That's what I keep telling myself anyway. It's not good for either of us to look back. Good things are happening to Edwin now. I hope he's happy in Montana. He deserves every bit of luck that comes his way.'

I wanted to ask her if she'd been intimate with him, if she got pregnant with his child, if I was that child. But all I said was, 'Don't worry, you're not brooding on him. You only have warm feelings for him and him for you. There was no damage done.'

She replaced the photograph in the drawer. Then she wiped her eyes with a handkerchief. She looked at me as if she knew what I was thinking but she didn't say anything. I thought she was probably better off for that. So was I. There was a protection in not knowing. Nothing could be done about it.

'We have to get on with life,' she said finally, looking out the window into whatever past she was pulling up inside her, 'No matter who you fall in love with or for how long, circumstances change. New things take over from the old ones even if they're not as exciting as them or as long-lasting. After a while they make you forget them and that's good for you. It makes you a stronger person even if you're not a happier one. You go on from day to day. Each moment you conquer is like a mountain, a mountain that makes you better able for the next one. Eventually you become serene. You don't even know what was bothering you or why it affected you so much. Life is hard and you need to be tough to get through it. That's all that really matters at the end of the day.'

Apology

I wasn't abused as a child.
I never threw a tomato at a Taoiseach.
I didn't get stoned on drugs
or drive a car into a swimming pool
or throw a television set out the window
as a protest against The System.
Neither did I ever 'come out'
on a reality TV show
or try to take my trousers off
over my head
after a rake of pints
or paint my bum green
on St. Patrick's Day.

At the present time
I have no intentions
of getting tattoos all over my neck
or dyeing my hair purple
or bungi-jumping
across the Himalayas
while cooking chips
on a pan.

Is this grounds for deportation?
Is there a special place in hell
for bores like me?

Promotion

Intense about his lady love
when first they met
he thought she would enable him
to reach the stars.
But later on a building site
with men of pagan thoughts
he realised that this was better after all,
the poker scene in Gaughan's on the *bona fide*,
the laughing eyes of losers marking time.
A graduate,
he looks into the triumph
of a suit of tweed, a banker's card
and Fairyhouse in June.
Next year will bring a trip upstairs
to offices with Super Sers,
a roll-top,
promises of fortnights in the sun.
He'll walk with Sorcha
down the tree-clad groves
where neighbours tip their hats to him
and smile,
saying isn't God good to keep it so mild.
How mild it is he knows at midnight
in the silence of a looking-glass
that says it all too straight
for eyes hungry for the things of a man.
Yet some satanic pride
precludes him still from calling her.
He learns to love his emptiness
the sense of an also-ran.

The Prisoner

The man who's sitting in the cell directly opposite me is going to be executed tomorrow. Nobody told me what his crime was. They brought him in a few days ago. He was as cowed as a sheep when the key was being turned. Sometimes I find myself staring at him through the bars. He never looks back. If he gazes in my direction I feel he's looking through me rather than at me.

The screws are relaxing in their hut at the end of the corridor. Their chairs are balanced on two legs as they lean back against the wall. They scan the latest tabloids. One of them has a revolver in his hand. The other has a truncheon. They seem to be afraid of him.

I heard he escaped from the last prison he was in by scaling a fence. Nobody is taking any chances. He has the same comforts as the rest of us but any time he moves they dart from their base to see what's going on. They rush down the stone floor in their hobnailed boots, creating as much drama as they can muster.

Last night they heard him whittling away at something and they panicked. When they looked inside the cell all they found him doing was making holes in a bamboo stick. He wanted to play music through it. They looked foolish as they watched him scoop the sawdust out.

At the moment it's his calmness they suspect. In a sense they're more his captors than he's theirs. He strikes me as the type of man who could be here one second and gone the next. He has that dormant sense of potency in him. But I doubt he wants to go anywhere any more. There's something sad about him. He's like a wounded animal.

He spends most of his time gazing at the spotlights. They flicker on and off in the courtyard. There are three on the left-hand side and three on the right. They intersect in the centre of the yard like watching sentries comparing notes about what they've seen on their rounds.

Things are unusually quiet in the cells. In normal circumstances a clock ticks noisily. Tonight it's been turned off. It's the clock where the screws punch their cards. Every hour it used to make a sound like a cash register being rung. There are no hands on it, just numbers. A moment ago it went from 9.36 to 9.37. He has about nine hours to go before they take him out.

Every night at this time a woman arrives in to visit him. Tonight is no exception. She's wearing a large woollen overcoat. She has a fur draped round her neck like a snake. I can smell the perfume from her the moment she enters the prison. By the time she passes my cell it's almost enough to make me suffocate. Everybody wonders who she is. Is she his wife? His sister? Maybe she's his lover. He talks to nobody so we can only guess. She seems to be the only contact he has. He's even distant to her.

He looks up when she enters but betrays no emotion. She sits on the blanket and takes his hand. It is the same blanket as last night, the same hand, the same side of the bed, the same greeting. It reminds me of a scene in a play I've already seen. In about thirty seconds she'll begin to utter the same quiet comfort to him. I won't hear the words. The sound won't travel.

When she takes off her coat I see she's wearing a light chiffon blouse. He strokes it absently. Once or twice he looks at her with an intense frown. It's as if he's on the brink of some outpouring but all that comes out is a stutter, a clearing of the throat. She looks at him with a steel-cold glance. It's like a teacher who's just been frustrated by her best pupil. They sit like this for maybe a half-hour, whispering and then going silent as the time passes. Then the warder says it's time up. He leads her out.

The night is beginning to deepen now. The shadows from the nearby town stroll through the bars in front of me. The windows are all an inch thick here. When the screw opens the main door I can hear the sound of bells tolling in the distance. The intonations linger like the after-sounds of tune forks. Elsewhere I hear the petering-out of voices, the dull barking of hounds in an alleyway. Once or twice I think a choir. There's a shrill sound like whistling. Then it stops. The silence is dense again.

Around the middle of the night the screws come for him again. This is a frequent practice now. None of us knows exactly what the purpose is. They lead him to a little room a few yards away. We hear voices and the whirring of some kind of machine. When he comes out he's groggy. Someone told me they give him electric shocks in there. Is it a dress rehearsal for his execution? I don't think they beat him. There are no physical marks on him.

I must have been asleep for a while. The sun is beginning to rise now. It casts sidelong rays across the windows. They're like blinds. When I look into his cell there are people with him – a priest, some jailers, an older woman I haven't seen before. Maybe it's his mother. They seem to have been there a long time. Nobody is moving. Nothing is really going on. He has a cigarette hanging from his lips. Nobody seems to have thought of giving him a match.

A few minutes later they put handcuffs on him. He begins to shake. His teeth clench. He reaches out for someone to hold. He grips the bars of the window so tightly I can see his knuckles whiten. Then they pull him away.

He's led down the corridor by six or seven people. He only puts up a token struggle on the journey. They're still poking at him. It's as if they're afraid he'll turn on them. As he passes me I want to give him some gesture of encouragement or recognition but I don't. I realise how senseless it would be.

After he's gone the day takes on its ordinary delineations for us. We're led outside to break rocks. Cleaners hose down the cells. Everyone is trying to look as if there's nothing unusual. And, maybe, in a way, there isn't.

We crack at slabs of limestone as heat comes into the day. The sun melts the icicles on the drainpipes. I try to think of nothing. It's snowed overnight so we're put to work clearing the slush away. I'm glad of the activity. I watch crows swooping down from a watchtower to peck at hard crusts of bread. We blow on our fingertips to keep them warm.

Somebody else will fill his cell today. They're never left empty. A new inmate with a new crime or the same one, new patients with old diseases. As the morning crawls to noon, the talk will start, morbid or fearful or apathetic. We use any therapy we know to keep calm, any slight escapist trick.

I find myself wondering if his spirit cracked. What way would he have felt in his dying moments? I try to feel emotion for him but nothing comes at all, no empathy or sympathy or even vague human concern. Instead I find myself wondering about my own situation, what I did to be here, the whole sick charade.

When it gets to noon I see a journalist coming into the building. He has a pencil in his hand. He takes notes from a man I know slightly. They jabber into a tape recorder.

There are questions and more questions, the self-important faces of officials. A car wheezes off into the distance.

Afterwards we're led back to the main building for a meal. Nobody speaks about him or anything relating to him. It's a day like any other. There are chores to be performed for better or worse until our own day of reckoning looms up.

The Ravages of Time

Our cousins owned a flour mill
across the river in Bunree.
I loved going down to them.
We used to play tennis
in a court they had
in their large grounds.
We picked strawberries there.
We sold them to Mr Moylett
on King Street.
I played bagatelle
with my friend Michael
in a little room they had
at the back of their house.
The river separated us.
Money separated us.
Their lives seemed so ordered
and ours so chaotic.
But cancer took most of them.
First my Aunt Mary got it.
The following year
her husband was gone too.
His son took over the business.
He used to whizz around town
in his big car.
I still remember the registration:
TIZ 1.
Another son lived in Bohernasup.
He had two sons.
I used to babysit them
with my cousin Ann.
She loved pickled onions.
The fridge was always
stocked with them.
He insisted on driving us home

when he came back
from wherever he was
for the night.
He drove very fast,
screeching around the bend
where the Market Square
met Garden Street.
Then got cancer too.
He died as he lived
in the fast lane.
Two other sons got it afterwards,
and a daughter.
The daughter was my godmother.
She was so kind to me
I used to call her
my fairy godmother.
One of the sons
became an accountant.
I used to see him
around Pembroke Street
after we moved to Dublin.
Another one became a Jesuit.
He worked in a library
in Zimbabwe.
It was the next country to Zambia.
That was where my brother was.
Maybe it was thousands of miles away
but to me it seemed as close
as Bunree was to Arthur Street.
What did it matter where you were
if you were sick?
It was hard to comprehend
such a large family
all suffering from the same disease.
They reminded me of the Kennedys.
That family was decimated too,

by assassination more than disease.
Health is wealth, they say.
We didn't have their money.
We envied them
but then we felt sorry for them.
When I go back to Ballina now
I look across the river
at the empty mansion.
I think of when it once rang out
with laughter
and the sound of young voices.
I look at the disused mill
with its cracked stones
and broken windows.
It seems to be mourning a family
that had so much once
before cancer took it all away.
I remember the frosted windows
at the piano.
I remember the spiral staircase.
and think how sad it is
that there's nobody there
to enjoy these things anymore.
Aunt Mary's husband
had a stomach problem.
I heard he said once
that he'd give all his money
for one good meal.
Great winds blow on high hills.

Reverie

The wind blows softly on my face.
Ships blaze by like ghosts
as the night arrives.
Lights flash
at nothing in particular.
It's Easter.
There are the usual
undulations of the tide
the bobbing of buoys on the quay.
A distant memory hints
that makes me feel unreal.
It's an old man
tipping his hat
to a mermaid.

My footsteps seem
like those of someone else
as I inch towards the horizon.
You could easily imagine yourself
to be those shiply ghosts,
you could be a bird on the wing,
you could be only half alive
as the night sky
burns
burns
burns
to make you feel
both comforted and nervous.

It must be hours later
when I return to a life
I hardly realised I'd left.
Family chores,

shopping,
the car,
promises kept
and broken –
the childish things
that clutter your mind
or what passes for it
as you wait
for something better
or worse
to heal you.

What You Can Salvage

The trees are wet. I sit listening to Joan Baez singing 'Love is Just a Four-Lettered Word' on my fifth-hand hi-fi. It's at maximum volume to drown out the tears of my daughter crying upstairs. My second wife has just served me with divorce papers.

My first marriage lasted the proverbial five minutes. There's not much point dwelling on that. The next time I tried the institution I promised myself I wouldn't make the same mistakes. I held to that. I just made new ones.

Sandy and I had been in college together. I felt that would be an asset but sometimes you can know someone too well. It spoils the mystery of finding out how horrible you both are.

Maybe we weren't horrible, just deluded. We foolishly believed 'Love me forever' wouldn't degenerate into 'Help me make it through the night.'

After graduation we hawked around France picking grapes. I preferred the wine they turned into afterwards. 'You're boring when you're drunk,' she informed me. I told her I was even more boring when I was sober. She tentatively conceded that might be true but she still agreed to marry me. 'It will be an interesting experiment,' she said. It was one that failed. Flying cutlery was the main mood music of that time. We made the Borgias look like Walt Disney.

When she was moving out she used a line that might have come from *Oprah*, 'I need my space.' If we were any further away from one another we'd have been in *outer* space.

We divorced soon afterwards. That shocked me more than anything else. I'm Catholic. We believe in the perpetual state of masochism. Murder maybe, divorce never.

She told me I was in love with my suffering. Suffering, of course, was another excuse to drink. Not that I needed any of these. The fact of being alive was usually enough.

After she was gone I chucked in the job, This was often the way things went with me. Once one part of my life fell apart another one followed. I lost pride in my appearance. Did I ever have any?

I started hanging around the house in clothes a hobo would have discarded. That couldn't go on forever. There was also the small matter of a mortgage to be paid. There were children to be fed. In desperation I started driving a taxi. It proved to be a liberation of sorts. Being on the move stopped me having to think about the fact that I was going nowhere.

I tried to convince myself that each journey I made was more important than breathing. This was necessary for me to give myself a reason to get up in the morning. For a while it worked. I'd always been good at self-delusion.

Deludedly in love with first wife (for five minutes). Deludedly in love with Sandy (for seven years). Deludedly in love with indolence (forever).

I wrapped the taxi around a lamp-post one night after drinking on the job. That was the end of it. And nearly me. The people in Casualty called it a miraculous escape. At the time I could hardly see any escape as being miraculous. Sandy's theory was that I was probably trying to do myself in. That was probably closer to the mark. 'The ultimate loser,' I announced, 'a failed suicide.'

She did flexi-time in a property developer's firm to put bread on the table. Meanwhile I signed on and became a house-husband. 'The New Man,' she snorted, 'bonding with his children through a haze of cocktails.' She had a venomous tongue but I could hardly have blamed her for it. She'd inherited it for me.

She eventually met another man. The first time she came home with him I told him it was way past his bedtime. He looked that young. Or was it me growing prematurely old?

I wanted to hit him. I think she did too. It would have brought some kind of closure to what we had. 'Closure' was another term she picked up from *Oprah*. I refused to give her that luxury. A few nights later she bundled some of her things into a case and bade me adieu.

That was eight months, three weeks, four days, fifteen hours and eight seconds ago. As you can see, I've totally forgotten her.

She muttered something about coming back for the children but she never did. Maybe that threw me more than anything else. She once told me she never had the maternal instinct, that having children was just 'something people did.'

I have our ones now. They keep me sane, at least some of the time. And I keep them sane, at least some of the time. We have better fun when we're not being sane.

How does she not miss them? When I'm with them I think of Meryl Streep from the film *Kramer versus Kramer*, peeping out at Dustin Hoffman and their son from behind bushes after she walked out on the marriage. Does Sandy do the same with me? Sometimes when I'm walking down to the shops with them I get the eerie feeling she's nearby. Keeping an eye on her bewildered ex to see how he's faring out. Or not faring out.

I think she left them with me to punish me. She didn't think I'd want them. I was so much in love with myself for so many years. Yes I mistreated them during those years but kids don't judge you like adults do.

I never want her to think I'm doing well with them. It would make her want them back. And whatever Sandy wants, Sandy gets. She could peddle the image of me being unreliable. A judge might go for it. If he did I'd become a McDonald's dad. I'd be seeing them every second Saturday through groggy eyes and a chocolate milkshake.

'Try to act miserable when she calls,' I advise Cian, my eldest. He looks at me like I'm mad. I probably am. He still pines for her sometimes, as does Sandra. She was named after her. She cries so much for her I feel it's child abuse on my part not to hand her back whether her mother wants her or not.

'What happened mammy, daddy? she asks me sometimes. I say, 'If I knew, darling, I'd tell you.' Cian said to me once, 'Is it because you drink?' 'No' I replied, 'It's because I breathe.' It would probably be easier for me to stop doing that.

A pimply-faced rookie at Free Legal Aid informed me solemnly one day: 'The judge usually goes with the mother.' His tone suggested he'd reinvented the wheel. I'm no lawyer but I know that much. 'What if the mother is Aileen Wuornos?' I enquired. He wasn't interested in following up on that.

The crazy thing is that I still love her - sort of. And I think she still loves me - sort of. We had that kind of relationship in the end: semi-detached, like the house we used to live in. After the property bubble collapsed we lost that too.

Norman Mailer said you never really know a woman until you meet her in court. Is that the next step - her pressing for custody as soon as she gets stability with her new Significant Other I'll meet that bridge when I come to it. For now I function.

I drink too much, love too little and cook boil-in-the-bag curries for two children not yet savvy enough to know the difference between chicken shit and chicken salad. On Wednesday nights they get the added treat of a Simpsons DVD.

The trees grow wetter outside. Stars burn holes in the sky, I sit in a darkened room listening to Sandra crying softly and Baez singing Dylan in that shrill voice she has. Her theme is the end of a relationship. Maybe 'Love is Just a Four-Lettered Word' is a song I should have written myself.

Some things are beautiful even if they're short-lived. Aristotle once said that what's white for a day is just as white as what's white forever. That's what I have to bear in mind. One day at a time, sweet Jesus, even if love is just a four-lettered word. Because life dumps on all of us one way or the other if we hang around long enough.

Some days you're the pigeon, some days you're the statue. What's important is how you deal with it, the crumbs of comfort you sieve from the detritus, what you can salvage.

Degenerate

John Melvin
did press-ups on the bar counter
of the Merry Monk
after a rake of pints
at the age of seventy.
Chatting up the talent afterwards
he poured venom on those
who were spoken for
and reproducing to beat the band.

A bachelor,
he never needed
the things that make life go round
for the rest of us.
The oldest swinger in town,
he was in love with ecstasy
moonshine
and his own mad dreams.

Epitome of all that's nefarious
I envy you, John Melvin.
l am you.
You're all of us
without realising it.
One day maybe
you'll show me how it's done
before l wither into the need
for acceptance by those
whose approval
means death.

Chez Jack

Heffo is standing on the verandah. He looks like the missing link with his three o'clock shadow, his thirty-year hangover. He abuses his body in a way that would make your average kamikaze pilot look timid. And yet he's always there the next morning, hungry for laughter. He spent most of the last millennium in a coked-out stupor but he's still rolling with the punches.

When I say hello he looks up. On his head there's this huge sombrero. In his mouth is a tin whistle. He's smoking pot out of it. In between puffs he's making a pretty good job of 'Fáinne Gheal An Lae.'

'Well,' he says eventually.

'Well,' I say back to him. Then there's a silence between us. We need time to recover from such verbal exertions.

'Are you going to Jack's party?' I ask after a moment.

'Being a masochist,' he says, 'I feel I have no other option.'

I empathise with this. Nothing much happens at Jack's parties except the men get footless and the women get pregnant. In that order. But you have to create illusions. You have to pretend to yourself that this year it'll be different.

'Have the Hards arrived yet?' I ask. Intead of giving me an answer he puts his hand under his arm and scratches it. This is his favourite mannerism since he saw Brando doing it in *A Streetcar Named Desire*.

I venture inwards. Even as I deposit my coat it's clear to me that the night is being given the big treatment. There's enough food for an army and a reverential hush of expectation in the hallway. Jack is standing at the French doors like St Peter admitting us all to our destiny. When he sees me he gives me a big bear-hug.

He's all gussied up in his leather waistcoat, the one he dons this one night each year, the suit he imagines will make him One Of The Boys. Tomorrow it will be stashed away in his neo-Georgian cupboard again behind his 17 sensible suits.

'I see you mean business tonight,' he says, looking at my slicked-back hair, my ersatz punk get-up, 'You must be on the prowl for some filly.'

'All I'm for is someone who can support me in the way I'm accustomed to,' I tell him.

Jack got married in his first year at university. Ever since then he's been apologising to his bohemian buddies for the imagined sell-out to domesticity.

'I know what you mean,' he says, 'Someone with a long purse and a short cough.'

It's hard not to warm to him. Everyone laughs at him behind his back but he remains blithely unaware of that fact. Dolled up in his leather jacket and with a few aptly-chosen witticisms on his lips he thinks all his multiple cop-outs have been forgiven and forgotten.

'Good you could make it, brother,' he says.

I've never been able to figure out why he addresses me like that. It probably goes back to the summer he went to Las Vegas where he spent two nights sleeping rough in a Salvation Army hostel, coming out of it afterwards like a born-again hippie. If you listen to Jack long enough he'll get around to telling you that such a summer was more important to him than the thirty-five others he spent out of it. By this stage of the night the lion's share of the guests will either be strung out on dope or undressing their girlfriends upstairs. Or both.

As I look around me I see the Heavy Metal brigade have arrived, replete with mandatory wisecracks and mandatory supermarket plonk. They stomp their Doc Martens. They shake their greasy dreadlocks in my face. And I think: I'm too old for this.

Fifteen minutes later the decibel level has reached a pitch that causes the man from the bungalow next door to complain. His beauty sleep is being disturbed. He threatens to ring the local copshop before one of our Heavy Metal friends persuades him otherwise. With the gentle aid of a head butt.

A man standing beside me looks like he's going to keel over. I ask him where the drinks cabinet is. When he turns round I see it's Billy Moriarty. Billy is a refugee from my First Philosophy class who dropped out of college to become a subversive. He threw a tomato at a politician once. Ever since he thinks he's Vaclav Havel.

'We're discussing Sam Beckett's literary evolution,' he says. He introduces me to a bald-headed young man with a ponytail and an ear-ring. Billy fancies himself as an intellectual. He loves going to films in the Irish Film Institute, especially those French ones where everyone looks into the middle distance for two hours before deciding life is meaningless.

'What do you think of the early stuff?' he asks me.

'It reminds me of Picasso's blue period,' I say.

It's already apparent to me that there's only one way I'm going to be able to get through tonight. It's the same way as I got through Jack's party last year and the year before. Maybe it's the way I've negotiated every crisis in my less-than-salubrious life thus far. Get drunk.

I retreat to the conservatory for asylum. Jack is already into his rhythm, rabbiting on about his latest pay hike and the extension he's planning out the back. Everyone is bored out of their tree. They're suffering him because of the free gargle. He's performing a familiar function, acting as everyone's light relief until they get tanked up for more ambitious exertions on the other side of midnight.

Aisling watches me watching him. That's his wife. Or as he prefers to put it, his little treasure. They met on a day out with the Vincent de Paul Society a few centuries ago when they were both going through their Social Dogoodery phase. Six months later they were betrothed. Nine months to the day after that a little McCarthy arrived. It wasn't long until Aisling regained the figure that used to drive us all crazy with lust. At the moment, like Jack, she's let herself go in that department. She busies herself these days trying to prove to dissolutes like me that there's life after birth.

'What are you doing with yourself these day?' she says, 'I believe you're still between jobs.'

This is her polite way of saying 'unemployed.'

'It's the recession,' I say, my four-year-old excuse. It's almost like a mantra to me now.

'Don't worry, something will turn up. It always does. Use your freedom while you have it. You'll be working long enough.'

Not if I can help it, I think, but I refrain from depressing her with such decadence. Instead I tell her I'll continue to send glowing CVs to every company in the land as long as there's life in my body until one day I see a light at the end of the tunnel that isn't a train coming the other way.

'How's Tristan?' I ask. She moves into overdrive as she tells me how many words he knows. For Aisling, phonics is the new theology. In my mind's eye I see Jack and herself burning the midnight oil with the latest Ladybird text, going into minor ecstasies when the syllables come out right.

'What about yourself? When are you going to give us all a day out?'

'I'm a confirmed bachelor,' I tell her, 'It's my father coming out in me.' It's my little joke. Only my father is unamused by it.

'What about Fiona Murdoch? Weren't you two going steady?'

You can't blow your nose in this town without someone hearing about it.

'Two ships scraping hulls in the night,' I say.

'From what I hear,' says Jack, appearing suddenly from nowhere, 'that's not all you've been scraping.'

I move into the kitchen. Billy has an intense-looking student pinned against the wall. He's rhapsodising about what it means to be a post-modern existentialist living on the periphery of Europe at the beginning of a new millennium. It's going to be a long night.

Sharon appears at my shoulder.

'Where have you been hiding?' she snarls, 'I've been ringing you off the hook.' She's sporting her trademark time-of-the-month scowl. With Sharon it's that time of the month all month.

'What makes you think I've been hiding? I don't use phones anymore.'

Each time we meet there's this Gestapo interrogation. We've been dating one another off and on for as long as I remember despite the slightly worrying fact that we despise one another intensely. This has put a slight blemish on our relationship.

'You don't use phones? That's like saying you don't use food.'

'Maybe to you, Sharon. Not all of us are surgically connected to the things.'

'I'm surprised you have the nerve to show your face after what you did the last night.'

With Sharon there's always something I did 'the last night.' Sometimes I remember it and sometimes I don't. But she always does. In fact Sharon probably remembers the day she was born. And who slapped her.

'Okay. So what did I do the last night?'

'You deserted me during a slow set, that's what.' A crime greater than ethnic cleansing in Serbia.

'I must have been drunk.' This is hardly beyond the bounds of possibility. It's also a handy excuse to use when you can't think of any other one.

'Either that or lusting after Fiona Murdoch,' she says. Now the penny drops. Fiona paid a surprise visit to our little *soiree* that night, thereby transporting me into all sorts of frenzies.

'I'm sorry. I mustn't have been thinking straight.'

'Yeah, right. Being sorry seems to be one of your favourite hobbies these days.'

'Is there a law against talking to Fiona?'

'No, but when you're dancing with one woman and you start undressing another one with your eyes it's not exactly Sir Lancelot, is it?' With that she's gone. I decided to drown my sorrows in some Southern Comfort.

The music has stopped, the cacophony of an hour ago transmuted into the silent comminglings of couples in corners. Everyone looks out of their brains except Jack. He's going around offering people sandwiches like he's at a Legion of Mary Social. A few feet away from me Billy is lying under the piano with the student. Beside him Heffo is reciting 'To be or not to be' into the goldfish tank.

When he's finished his soliloquy he comes over to me with a joint.

'A friend with weed is a friend indeed,' I say.

'You don't look well. what's the problem?'

'You wouldn't understand.'

'Try me.'

'It's complicated.'

'You're in love, right? I heard your conversation.' He starts singing 'Torn Between Two Lovers.'

'For such a gobdaw,' I say, 'you sometimes exhibit enormous insights.'

'Forget her,' he says, 'Forget the lot of 'em. They're all the same in the Jeyes Fluid.'

This is the extent of his philosophy on relationships. No doubt Julie Birchill would be impressed.

My stomach heaves. I start to feel tragic about myself as I watch the soap operas of infatuation unfold themselves around me.

Fiona is drinking champagne with one of Jack's business connections. Is she falling for him? Does she think I like Sharon more than her? I fantasise about knocking her dancing partner into the potted plants and charging out the door with her. It would be like the last scene of one of those forties farces. But this is real life. So she finishes her bubbly and I stay stagnant.

'How can God exist and still allow parties like this to take place?' Heffo says.

'It's no worse than last year's,' I say, 'and probably better than the one we'll be at next year.'

And so the circle will turn, so many mirrors emulating their own vapidity.

I sink deeper into my shell. Fiona pirhouettes around the floor with her business friend for what seems like an eternity. When she finally gets tired she plonks herself on the floor beside me.

'Don't worry,' she says, looking at my terminally depressed visage, 'it might never happen.'

'It already has,' I say, 'I was born.'

'You know something, Hamlet? I could almost get to like you.' This does wonders for my flagging self-esteem.

'So how did you enjoy cavorting round the floor with Bill Gates?'

'Don't make fun of me. I wouldn't be seen dead with a creep like that. He was only after the one thing.'

'Would you blame him?'

'Are you after the one thing?'

Yes. I'm after the thing called marriage with the most beautiful woman on the planet.'

'Flattery will get you everywhere.'

She puts her arms round me. A couple of seconds later she's planting kisses on my mouth. I'm looking for a part of myself to pinch to convince myself that I'm not imagining things.

'What are you doing?' I ask when I get my breath back.

'I don't know; I feel funny tonight.'

'Not half as funny as I feel.'

I ask her if she wants a drink. She says, 'Make that two. And bring them upstairs.'

'Am I hearing things?'

'Do you not want to?'

'I don't know what to make of you. Every time we meet you ignore me. Now suddenly you're acting like I'm the light of your life.'

'I like it when you don't come on to me.'

'When I like somebody I come onto them. That's the way I'm made. I can't play games.'

'Maybe you should start.'

A few minutes later I'm lying beside her in a child's bedroom. We've dumped a bunch of toys on the floor. My head is spinning. She continues to shower me with kisses. The bottle of Southern Comfort has only a thimbleful left in it now. She watches me amusedly as I empty the last treasured drop down my gullet.

'You'll know all about that in the morning,' she says.

'I know all about it even now,' I tell her.

She runs her hands all over me.

'Are you scared of me?' she asks. When I say yes she laughs.

'You're like every other Irishman,' she says, 'You love chasing women but when we respond you go into a shell.'

As we lie under the quilt I think of how many times I've dreamt about this situation. Now that it's happening I feel almost flat.

Maybe she's right about me. It might be her availability that's dimming the desire.

Sounds die off downstairs. She nestles herself in my arms like an infant. It makes me wonder if she isn't after all the same as the rest of us at base, the same love-hungry soul. Sometimes she mutters comments to me from a half-sleep. I try to piece them together for an insight into her, some porthole into the flotsam and jetsam of her days. Now and again she whispers intimacies to me. When she does I start to think of her as an extension of my own contradictions, my own manic excesses.

'Would you like to be married?' I ask her. She shudders.

'You mean like Aisling McCarthy?'

'There are other kinds of marriages.'

'Is that a proposal?'

'It's just as well it isn't. You'd have no time for the likes of me.'

'Don't be too sure. You care about me. That's the difference from the others.'

'Do I care too much?'

She doesn't answer. Maybe I've hit a nerve.

We lie together in the silence. I listen to Jack embellishing some ancient yarn downstairs, imagine him shambling round with the last of the plonk, offering it to all the cute hoors from work, fantasising about the fact that sometime in the future a promotion will result from these mad nights instead of the soul-destroying job he'll continue to trot into day in day out until they carry him off to Boot Hill.

I doze off. when I wake it seems much later. Everything is quiet downstairs. How many people have gone home? How many have made the easy connections and how many have been rebuffed? How many are now stirring towards the moment that will make the night worthwhile/

Every now and then a car scrunches on the gravel outside. In the adjoining bedroom I hear the gropings of some couple panting like athletes in a race. Afterwards there's the slow fade into silence.

The next thing I know it's morning. She's standing in front of me with a toothbrush in her hand. My heart is beating fast. It always does that when I have a hangover.

'We had a lot to drink last night,' I say, 'I'm blaming Jack.'

'Nice one.'

I look around me at the prams and cots, imagine for a second that they belong to me, to us.

'We seem to have been here a long time.'

'They'll probably have us married by now. When we come out they'll all be waiting for us with bags of confetti in their hands.'

She's baiting me but I'm enjoying it. Maybe this apocryphal night with a dream girl was worth more to me than ten significant ones I could have spent with women I desired less.

'Did I make a fool of myself?' I ask.

'No, but you'd probably prefer if you had. Then all your preconceptions about your shortcomings would be proved true.'

'You look great,' I say. I try to embrace her but she pushes me away.

'Let's go downstairs before they think we've eloped,' she says, tripping out of the room.

I walk slowly because I don't want to run into Jack. I hear his voice in the kitchen. I wonder if he's been talking about me. His voice trails off as I go in the door.

Heffo slaps my back. Behind him Fiona is putting on her make-up. She avoids my eyes when I look at her. It's as if the night never happened. My time with her is over now.

'How's the head?' says Jack.

'I feel like I've just had an argument with a JCB,' I tell him.

'Same here.'

'Never again.'

'That's what you said last year,' he says, wagging a teacher-like finger.

'And the year before,' Heffo chimes in.

'Where did you get that Southern Comfort anyway?' I say, 'It's rocket fuel.'

'Don't play the innocent with me. You've been guzzling it long enough now to know what it does to you.'

I look in the mirror. A face twice my age stares back at me. Who's that man? I know how Dorian Gray must have felt.

'You made me regress to a second childhood last night,' I say to Jack.

'Did you ever get out of your first one?' says Heffo.

I steal a glance at Fiona. I can see how bored she is. She's always been bored by alcoholic Paddies bragging about their hangovers.

'I don't know about the rest of you,' she says, 'but I'm hitting the road.'

'Where are you going?' I say, 'You can't have anything to do at 9 a.m.'

'Did you ever hear of work?'

'I didn't know you went in on Saturdays.'

'Someone has to keep the country afloat. You lot of bozos certainly won't.'

'We keep the pubs in business,' Heffo chirps.

I follow her out the door.

'Would you come for a walk with me before you go?' I ask.

'I can't. I'd be sacked.'

'I need to talk to you.'

'About what?'

'Us.'

'It's too early in the morning for that.'

'What time would suit you?'

'Anytime you can get away from that crowd.'

'I can get away from them now.'

'I mean for good.'

'Oh.'

'I'll phone you,' she says, blowing me a kiss before she goes off.

I go back inside.

'Well,' says Heffo, 'Tell me about last night. Did the earth move for you? Did the sleeping beauty rouse the errant prince?'

'I fell asleep,' I say.

'Tell me the one about the three bears.'

I sit sipping a cup of tea. Jack is across from me trying to look casual. I hear Aisling upstairs making the beds, getting the little one dressed. Such details give me a picture of what every Saturday morning must be like in this household, what every morning must be like. A kind of emotion stirs itself in me, part disenchantment at the ordinariness and part envy. Maybe Jack isn't as laughable as we like to think. Maybe he's the happiest of all of us.

'I'll never forget the look on Sharon's face as you took yer woman upstairs,' says Heffo.

'How was she afterwards?'

'Very good actually. She just went around the place breaking plates over people's heads. Nothing spectacular.'

'Maybe I should ring her.'

'Give her a while to cool down,' says Jack.

'Give her forever,' says Heffo.

The three of us sit in silence. The sun is painting patterns over the fields outside.

'So when's the next bash?' says Heffo.

'In 364 days,' Jack tells him.

We look out at Nephin. Clouds form above it like balls of wool. I fill my lungs with draughts of air to deaden the pain of the night.

'We'll only appreciate it when they bottle it,' says Jack.

'Very true,' Heffo says, 'Heaven's breath smells wooingly here.'

'It's why I bought this place. No pollution.'

I survey the arsenal of empty bottles. They look like metallic flowers on his otherwise immaculate garden.

'Is that all we have to show for last night?' he says, 'Sometimes I wonder why I bother.'

'Don't you start. You above all people.'

'What's that supposed to mean?'

'I don't know. It seems to me that you're the last relic of positivity I'm acquainted with in this lousy world.'

The comment has come out without my intending it. It causes his face to light up like a cherub.

'Fancy a drop of the *craythur*?' Heffo says, pulling a flask of brandy from his pocket.

'Why not,' I say, 'to drown my sorrows.'

'I gather she was playing hard to get,' he says.

'You could say that.'

'There are more fish in the ocean. You might get more out of Sharon.'

'Fiona is a tease,' Jack says.

'And Sharon is a nightmare,' Heffo says, 'Take your pick.'

We walk down the driveway. I feel exorcised of something.

'Goodbye, Jack,' I say. I feel something is ending. I don't know what.

He waves at me. Behind him I hear the gentle strains of Aisling humming a ditty for their five-year-old. I feel a tear welling up in my eye but I hide it from Heffo as he takes a bottle of brandy from under his shirt and slugs it back.

Interlude

The last time I visited you
you were unaware of me.
That helped.
My mother had died.
I watched your face
for a reaction.
There was none.
I became a stranger to you
and to myself.
Her passing clarified things.
I was now the man
of the house.
Crawling out of the womb
at 28.

You had a flat in Swinford.
We listened to the Waterboys
in a room lousy with mice.
The walls closed in on us.
The floor vibrated.
Cats squawked outside.
A 24 hour shop
blinked with all-night offers.

I brought you shopping,
took out the bins.
I acted fatherly to your child.
My friends asked me
if I knew what I was doing.
You had, as they said,
'baggage.'

Reality bit.
Too many people

were in too close a space.
I was The Other.

You said I was a priority
but I wasn't blood.
The tie to the woman
I had come out of
was still there.
Without knowing it
we were both
fighting ourselves.

You cried in the night
for no reason.
Your baby cried too
for every reason.
We grew old
before our time,
our magic dissipated
into this bundle of joy.

We soaked ourselves
in Bette Davis movies
on a TV set
that only worked
when you kicked the floor.
We enjoyed that
more than the movies.

I was in beyond my depth.
I drank and took pills,
the old placebos.
You soaked up the detritus
of my search for emotion.

Ghosts haunted my dreams.
We fizzled out
without knowing why.
We met in town.
You strangled a cigarette,
drank coffee until you shook.
I fumbled in my pocket
for money that wasn't there.
I felt your embarrassment
raining down on me.

You asked me if I was going back
to my old job.
I said 'What job?'
I joked that I might
rob a bank
to make ends meet.
We could be
the Bonnie and Clyde
of Mayo.

I took up with someone
I used to know
before I became me.
You became the mother
you always were
no matter how hard you tried
to be trendy.
There were no arguments now
but that only made me feel worse.
We didn't care enough
to fight.

I search for you these days
in corners of my mind,
I see you

and don't see you.
I care for you
and don't care for you.

I mix desire with fear,
in the middle of nowhere
remembering the stupid things
we did together
more than our declarations
of love.

The Fall

She was from Idaho. He met her at an Irish bar. He'd been a waiter there for the summer.

They were both gone from the bar now. They dated briefly but now they weren't seeing each other anymore. They were sitting in a different bar now. It had been noisier earlier in the night because of some people that had been at a baseball game nearby. Most of them were gone now so they could talk more freely.

'I'm sorry it didn't work out, Walter,' she said to him, 'but that's the way the mop flops. It's not your fault and maybe it's not entirely mine either. You just met me at the wrong time. I know you're going to make some lucky lady very happy in time. You'll have bucketloads of children with her and a pet dog and a white picket fence.'

Walter took a sip of his Budweiser.

'I don't want a pet dog or a bucketload of children or a white picket fence,' he said, 'I just want you.'

'I know. We had some good times but unfortunately I'm with someone else now. He's not as pure a spirit as you are but we seem to be right for one another.'

'You don't love him. I know you don't. It's me you love. You told me that. You told me a hundred times. I believed you.'

'Love is a strong word, Walter. To be honest with you I don't know who I love or don't love or who I might fall out of love with next week or even tomorrow. That's not the way I roll.'

'So you don't care how long you'll be with him?'

'I didn't say that. You can't ask me those kinds of questions, honey. I've never been able to think ahead, it's not in my DNA. Next year I might come back to you, leastways if you still want me. We can have a horse-drawn carriage and flowers and champagne, the whole nine yards. But the way it is now, tomorrow morning I'm going to wake up beside that mother and there ain't a damn thing you can do about it.'

'Do you intend to marry him?'

'Marriage is a dirty word for me. No damn piece of paper is going to tie me to any one man.'

'I wish you wouldn't say things like that. Why is everyone against marriage these days?'

'I don't mean to offend you. I'm just telling it like it is.'

'Does he want to marry you?'

'Goddam it, you sure ask a lot of questions'

The juke box came on. Elvis Presley sang 'Don't Be Cruel.' She tapped her foot to it. She looked at him as if she was glad of the break in the conversation.

When the song finished she went up to the counter. She was chewing a pretzel from the bowl the barman left at their table.

'I'd like some more coins for the juke,' she said.

'I think it's broken, ma'am.'

'Are you dumb or something? I just played an Elvis song on it. Ever heard of him?'

'I might have. Wasn't he a pop singer?'

'So they tell me. Now can I have that coin?'

He gave it to her. She went back to the juke box. She twiddled her fingers on the top of it.

'What about 'Blue Suede Shoes,' she said, 'Or 'Money Honey.' They have that too. That would be a good one, wouldn't it? It might get us in the mood of wanting to be rich.'

'I don't care what you play,' he said.

'Oh come one now, Walter, don't be like that. We're on a night out. You gotta get into the zone.'

She put on 'Money Honey.' She started to jig around to it.

'Sorry, no dancing,' said the barman.

'Jesus Christ,' she said, 'This place is turning into a police state. No dancing?''

'That's right, ma'am. House rules. I don't make 'em.'

She went back to her seat. Walter had his head in his hands. She sat beside him.

'Maybe we'll do our own little dance right here in the seat,' she said, 'Whaddya say to that, Walter my man?'

She tried to pull down the mini-skirt she was wearing but it was still way up above her knees. Why did she wear them that short, Walter thought, when she had to keep pulling them up?

She took a drink of her vermouth.

'Listen, sugar, don't sulk. Come to Momma. Let her give you a big hug.'

'Don't make fun of me,' he said, pushing her away.

'Whatever you say, honeychild. Would you like another drink?'

'No.'

'Okay, well maybe I'll have one. Would that be okay with you?'

'I think you've had enough.'

'What? I've only started. Are you afraid I'll molest you or something?'

'April...' he said.

'Bartender, same again.'

The barman went over to the taps. He poured her another glass of vermouth. She waddled up to the counter.

'Put it on the tab,' she said.

She went back down to the table with it. Walter still had his head in his hands. She grabbed a fistful of pretzels from the bowl.

'Tell momma your problems,' she said. She lit a cigarette.

'I might have one of those,' he said.

'Good job! Now we're talking.'

'Just one,' he said.

'Okey-dokey, one *ceegarette* for the man. Live dangerous.'

She lit it for him. He started to choke when he took a drag of it. She slapped his back.

'It's all right,' he said, 'You don't need to do that.'

'Can I get you a glass of water, honey? We don't want you getting asphyxiated or anything.'

'I'm all right. Don't fuss over me. I'm not a child.'

'Sorry. I seem to be saying all the wrong things tonight.'

'It's not you. My nerves are on edge. I'll be all right. I just wish you'd come back to me. I think we were good together.'

'We were brilliant. We might be brilliant again. You just have to give me some time to get my head together. At the moment I'm freaked out. You're the sensible one. It wouldn't be fair to inflict myself on you.'

'I'll take you any way you are, April, you know that.'

'You don't need a degenerate like me. I'd ruin you. Why don't you find yourself someone else?'

'You're the one I want. Can you not get that through your head?'

'I'm touched that you say that but I don't believe you really love me. You only think you do. In fact nobody in their right mind could love me. I'm like a car crash.'

'Don't say that. You know it's not true. You're drunk. It's the drink talking.'

'No, Walter, I've been around long enough to know what's what. Most men just want to get into my pants. I know you're different. You're infatuated with the *idea* of me. That's different from loving me.'

'Don't keep putting names on things. I just want to be with you. Love grows.'

She let out at laugh.

'Sure, sweetheart, like a fungus.'

'I think about you all day. You're everything to me.'

'That's the problem. I don't *want* to be everything to you. Or to anyone else. It crowds me. That's why I like what's happening to me now with Nathan. He lets me do my own thing.'

'Nathan?'

'Yeah. He's the dude I'm with right now.'

'Nathan. what kind of a name is that?'

He started to think about him, tried to imagine what he might have looked like, what she might have seen in him.

'Does he treat you well?' he said.

'Sometimes he tells me I look nice but that's not his style. Maybe he thinks if he compliments me too much I'll get a big head.'

'I don't think that would happen.'

'You don't know me. You don't know how vain women are. We're not as pure as you.'

'Now you're making fun of me.'

'Look, Walter, what I'm trying to say is I don't want to be adored. Nathan doesn't adore me. In fact sometimes he even insults me. He insults me and I like it. When you praise me you make me nervous. I'm not as good as you think I am.'

'I don't care if you're good or bad. I just want you with me.'

'I'd drive you out of your tree if you lived with me for a week. I'm messy and unpredictable and I can't cook. You need to get yourself a nice Irish girl.'

'Irish girls are boring. You're exciting.'

'It's sweet of you to say that but it's not true. You don't know how boring I am because you never lived with me. If you were with me 24/7 you'd realise how godawfully boring I can be. You'd be screaming to get out of the apartment to see some real life after witnessing all my boring crap.'

'No I wouldn't.'

'I never do anything.'

'That makes me want you even more. That's what I never had with you, just being there. I never wanted those wild dates we were on.'

'You didn't? You coulda fooled me.'

The song ended.

'Let's try a different kind of relationship,' he said.

'Maybe some day,' she said, 'but not right now. Maybe we'll hook up some years down the road when we're both on walking frames. We can stand out on the porch and reminisce about days gone by. At least if we can goddam remember them.'

'That's not funny.'

'I'm sorry. I don't have a very good sense of humour. Maybe I better stop gabbing with you or I'll say something really bad.'

She looked down at her glass.

'That stuff is like firewater,' she said, 'I'm going up to the bar and get me an antidote. Do you want anything?'

'No,' he said gruffly.

She went up to the counter. She was staggering.

'Bartender,' she said, 'Any chance of a cup of coffee?'

'Sure, ma'am. Regular or latte?'

'Regular. And make it black. No sugar.'

'Right on, ma'am.'

'How about you, Walter - you like another Bud?'

'Maybe just get me a Coca-Cola,' he said.

'My, my. You sure are cheap to bring out. Don't you ever need any stimulation?'

The barman laughed. She went back to Walter. He looked at her intensely.

'When I'm with you I don't need anything else,' he said.

'Oh-oh. Don't say we're getting' into *that* again.'

She watched the percolator bubbling over. The barman put the latte in a cup. He came over to her with it.

'Whoa there,' she said, 'I don't like those fat cups. They're for soup, not coffee.'

'I beg your pardon?'

'That there is a soup cup. Give me a coffee one. I don't want it going cold on me in ten seconds.'

'It's actually a coffee cup but I'll give you a different one if you like.'

'Make it snappy.'

He went back to the counter. After pouring the coffee into a thinner cup he came back to her with it.

'Jesus,' she said, 'It's like getting the Crown Jewels in this dump if they give you a cup of coffee.'

Walter sipped his Coca-Cola.

'First the juke,' she said, 'and now this. They act like they're doing us the favour. If it wasn't for our business, this joint might as well close down for keeps. Have you seen anyone come in since the game crowd left?'

'No.'

She took a drink of the coffee.

'A few of these and I'll be sober as a judge. Or as jober as a sudge.'

She looked at Walter to see if he'd smile at her joke but he didn't.

'Nathan hates me to come home drunk,' she said.

'I wish you wouldn't keep talking about Nathan.'

124

'Jesus, Walter, I live with the man. What am I supposed to do, forget he exists?'

He gave her another intense look.

'I have a favour to ask you,' he said.

She threw her eyes to heaven.

'What is it?'

'Would you come out with me one last time?'

She banged her fist on the table.

'Judas Priest! Tonight was meant to be closure, right? You admitted that yourself. That was the only reason I agreed to see you. Are you going to go back on that now?'

'I just felt if we got to know each other better...'

'No, Walter, no.'

'I mean, this Nathan guy, who is he? To be honest with you, April, he. sounds like a jerk. Does he even respect you? It doesn't sound like it.'

'Of course he respects me. He spoils me half rotten. In fact he would have brought me to the game tonight if I wasn't seeing you. He's cool.'

'It seems to me you're trying to convince yourself you like him more than you do.'

'Don't try to be a psychologist. We've been through this so many times before it ain't funny. We're not really getting' anywhere, are we?'

He grunted.

'Now listen carefully to me. I know you're a sweetie but I don't really think these types of discussions are doing us any good - you included. So I'm going to cut this meetin' short. Does that sound cruel to you?'

She put on Elvis' voice. She started singing 'Don't Be Cruel.' Walter tried to smile.

'Could you not stay even a little while longer?' he said.

'There'd be no point. I love talking to you but you're not listening to me.'

'Okay,' he said, 'Go.'

'Now you're making me feel guilty.'

125

He slugged back the last of his Coke.

'Can I ring you?'

'No. Nathan would go batshit. He's like that. If you don't like my temper you should see his. He makes King Kong look like Daffy Duck.'

'What if you gave me a special mobile number he didn't know about? Or maybe I could email you.'

'He knows my cell number. I can't get a second one. Don't keep pushing it. You need to go home to Ireland. Find yourself a red-haired lass who does Irish dancing. She'll put on some home cookin' for you. Forget this mad Yankee lady who nearly destroyed you.'

'You didn't destroy me. You fulfilled me.'

He tried to remember how many times they'd been out. Was it ten? Twelve? He'd been in a daze most of the time. He remembered the early nights when they left work together and just went for a drink or to a film. These were the best times.

The nights back in her apartment weren't as good. He wasn't on neutral ground there. He felt intimidated. Sometimes he even felt in the way. It was her turf, as she put it. Being with her there made him feel he was out of his depth.

Then there was the night when they slept together. He thought he disappointed her. She didn't say anything but he knew by the way she looked. It was as if she wanted him to be rougher. Maybe she even wanted him to hit her. There were women like that. He'd heard about them in books.

He'd never been intimate with a black woman before. It was different to anything he'd ever experienced. The morning afterwards as she put on her clothes she winked at him and said, 'Once you've had black you'll never go back.'

'I'm going now, Walter,' she said. She stood up, 'What time you got?'

He looked at his watch.

'It's ten after nine.'

'Ten after nine!' she said, mimicking his voice. He didn't know why he said it like the Americans.

'It sounds real trendy the way you said that,' she said, mussing his hair. 'When you get to Ireland they'll think you've lost your accent.'

'There'll be lots of time to get it back,' he said. There would be fifty years.

She buttoned up her coat.

'Give me a holler when you get there. You won't forget me now, will you?'

'How could I?'

'You might even buy me one of those Aran sweaters if I'm lucky.'

She kissed him on the cheek, smudging his face with her lipstick.

'I'm going now,' she said, 'Ask that nice barman to fix you a drink. Then play some more Elvis for yourself on the juke.'

She went up to the bar. He heard her whispering something to the barman. When she turned around she put her hands on her hips. She did a little dance for him.

'Like that, huneybunch?' she said.

He didn't know what to say. His tongue stuck to the roof of his mouth. She thought she'd liberated him from the nervousness he always had around women but she hadn't. It was all coming back.

'I gotta go,' she said. There was no point asking her not to anymore. He was spun out.

She gave a little wave to him as she went out the door. He watched her walking down the street. She looked around once but she didn't wave. Then she turned a corner.

She was gone. He kept looking out at the street in some mad hope she'd come back but he knew it was ridiculous.

He went back to his seat. He started fidgeting with a matchstick and then threw it aside. After a few minutes he went up to the bar. The bottles around him looked funny. He wondered if he was seeing double.

He drummed his fingers on the counter.

'Yes?' said the barman.

He wasn't sure what he wanted. The first bottle he saw was a Jack Daniels so he ordered a glass of that.

'Jack Daniels,' the barman said, 'Frank Sinatra's favourite.'

'So I believe,' he said.

'Coke not doing it for you?' the barman said.

'And a pack of Marlboro,' he said, ignoring him. The barman turned around. He watched him pouring the drink.

'How much do I owe you?' he said.

'Nothing,' the barman said, 'The lady took care of it.'

He should have been grateful but for some reason it made him feel worse.

'She's something else, isn't she?' the barman said.

'Yes.'

He took the drink and went back to his table.

'Give me a holler if you need any change for the juke box,' the barman said.

'It's okay,' he said brusquely. He was hoping he wouldn't keep talking to him. He felt he was mocking him. Maybe she'd mocked him too.

He didn't want the drink. What should he do now? There was no point going back to the hostel. The Filipinos would be there. They'd be on their computers or playing chess. It was easier to stay out till bedtime and then just wander in. That way he wouldn't have to talk to them.

He knocked back the Jack Daniels. Then he called for another one. He drank that too. It tasted sweeter, That was the thing about whiskey. The more you drank, the easier it was to get down.

He wondered if she'd got back to Nathan yet. He imagined her going in to her apartment in the all-purpose complex where she lived. She'd walk up the narrow stairs with the criss-cross carpet pattern on it. After a minute she'd get to the heavily-padlocked door. Once inside she'd let Nathan do what he wanted with her.

He imagined him as someone who'd have his head shaved. He'd probably have tattoos and sing rap songs and not be too bright. He imagined the two of them dancing round the floor together, imagined Nathan putting his hand up her dress.

He started to feel sick. He'd been drinking too fast. It wasn't good for him. He thought he was going to throw up.

He ran to the rest room, barging into the first cubicle he saw. He knelt at the edge of a toilet bowl expecting to vomit into it but nothing came up.

He walked over to the washbasin. His heart was beating fast. He looked at himself in the mirror. He thought he looked old in the light. He wiped her lipstick off his cheek with a tissue. There was a man waiting at the door with a towel but he ignored him. He assumed he was expecting a tip. One of these days they'd expect to be tipped for the air you breathed.

His feet were unsteady as he walked back to the bar.

'All right, my friend?' the barman said.

'I'm going now.'

'Not enjoying your evening?'

'I had a great time.'

'Good night, sir. Thank you for your business.'

He went back to his table. It looked dirty. Her half-drunk coffee and the vermouth glasses and the pretzels were scattered all over the place. He remembered her saying she was messy. Maybe that was another example of her mocking him, mocking him for being too tidy. He doubted Nathan was tidy.

They were welcome to each other. He found himself getting angry with her, angry with the way she'd manipulated him, angry with her jibes and her patronisation. He could have hit her if she was standing in front of him now.

He started to walk down the street. Taxi cabs honked around him. The night was beginning. He pulled up his coat against the cold, his breath fogging the air. As he inhaled he smelt the whiskey from himself. He felt pleasantly dizzy.

She was right, he thought. They wouldn't have suited each other. They were from different cultures. Besides, his parents would have found it hard to deal with if he got serious with a black girl. They weren't racist but it would have been strange for them. He probably wouldn't even tell them about her.

He'd like if it had gone on longer but that was life. He'd had a few months with her. He couldn't complain. If she continued to go out with him it would only have been out of duty. What good would that have been?

He would go back to Ireland. He'd attend interviews for a job in the IT sector in his firm in the Ridge Pool. He'd do his studies and try not to think of her, try not to think of her beauty and her figure and that personality that made every minute he was with her seem like the Mardi Gras.

It was stupid of him to think the two of them could have made a go of it. Nathan probably relaxed her. He wouldn't talk much to her or ask her serious questions about life or love or how long they might last. She'd like that.

He couldn't forget the image of him putting his hand up her dress. He thought of her in her micro-mini, her sexy legs, the low dresses she wore that left so little to the imagination.

The whiskey was making his mind go faster. Everyone around him seemed blurry. His feet felt weak. He stood up against a fire hydrant and tried to collect his thoughts. A policeman passed by.

'Everything okay, buddy?' he asked.

'Fine, officer.'

He walked down by the poor end of town. The lights got grimmer, the buildings more dilapidated. He passed some hoboes. They were sitting in an alley, passing a wine bottle between them inside a paper bag. He caught the stench of it as he passed by them. And the stench of his own breath.

What would he do now? He didn't want to go back to the hostel. April had created an appetite in him for talk, action, anything. His mind was on fire. He'd never drunk so much beer before. It was making his insides feel like jelly. He thought he might throw up again. Why had she forced it on him?

He passed by the Irish bar where he first met her. There was a fiddler playing inside. For a moment he wanted to go in, to recapture some of the magic of the early days of the summer when he watched the GAA matches and drank with the emigrants.

He remembered the first time he saw her. She'd walked up to the counter and said, 'Hey, Irish, what do you say I show you a good time?'

She'd done that all right but now it was over. It ended as all things end. Now he was back to the person he was before he'd met her, the gawky adolescent who thought he was different because he was in a different country. But he wasn't. He never could be. Maybe he could never be anything.

He didn't know what to do. He thought of going in and drinking some more. That would kill a few hours. Then maybe he could go back to his place and sleep.

Maybe if he went in he'd get talking to people. Maybe he'd even meet a new girl. But he doubted it. He didn't have the energy for that kind of thing any more. April had taken it out of him. They all took it out of you. Maybe they weren't even aware of it. People said men were cruel but women were worse. They were worse because they always excused themselves. They found ways to make themselves look good even when they were putting a knife in your back.

He decided he'd go down to the red light district. At the docks he'd be able to pick up a hooker for the night. He'd passed them off and on over the summer and been tempted by them, tempted by their long boots and short dresses, by the way they swung their hips at him and promised to melt his heart. He thought of going in to one their seedy rooms smelling of smoke, thought of lying under a cover with them and telling them what he wanted them to do.

He tried to imagine April standing there as one of them, her dress hoisted up above her knees as she propositioned potential customers. He imagined himself asking her if she was doing business. He imagined himself bringing her back to his hostel and having sex with her for a fee. It was the only way he could get the memory of her out of his mind.

Zoning In

Crawling through customs
on a bad hair day
she guards the Waterford
like an extra child.
Outside, the taxi-men hover
like so many cormorants
stuck in a black hole,
biting nicotine-stained fingers
as they wait on fares.

Some things never change.
Dear, dirty Dublin looks like
an old pair of shoes to her,
a bad habit she can't kick,
unlike the hellholes of Soho
where only the barmen were friendly
and only loan sharks smiled.

Back home her vodka speaks to her.
She lets the city speak as well.
It makes the tired deprivation
somehow bearable.

Her mother called her classy.
That was before
her life caught up on her
and marriage made crassness
somehow acceptable.

She guards her family bonds
with loyalty these days
fends off the charge
of irresponsibility
as vodka does its work on her.

She contemplates a year
of squaring accounts,
accepting the inevitable
as the illusion of new pastures
enmeshes itself
inside the steamy arabesque
of Collinstown
in the rain.

Alone

It's like nobody was ever born
or died here.
The waves break
over my isolation.
A tear falls somewhere
as the birds shriek.

It's like the beginning of the world
or the end of it.
No cars or people move.
The sky is cobalt black.
Nothing intrudes
on the silence
as another day,
another year,
drifts into a spire of white.

You're gone from me
but your image remains
breathing through the trees
that hover around me
like obelisks
as the night comes down.

Where Love Stories Begin

It's weekly pubcrawl time.

Yours truly and three other would-be geriatric trendies are trading ferociously witty ripostes about life, love and the whole damn thing. The beer is flowing freely and so is the toilet humour. We eyeball the Smartphone brigade, pinstripe-suited refugees from the inner bowels of Dublin Four and beyond. They're all having a wild time as they engage in the yuppified pursuit of trying to out-glitz one another with the latest Paul Costelloe creations.

Their dialogue is the hot-to-trot variety beloved of such a breed. As I earwig it I find the vomit rising to my throat. You can take just so much of psychobabble about the immanent destruction of civilisation as we know it.

In our own slightly more minimalist corner, Les wears his familiar 'This is the pits' expression. He wants to hightail it home to Donnycarney to catch the late night porn movie on Channel 4. Robbie, on the contrary, is getting ready for that part of the night where he contemplates the meaning of existence – or, to be more precise, how come some cowboys in Kildare Street are making megabucks while he malingers like John Lennon's Nowhere Man in flatland. Anto, for his part, is in the bog busily throwing up the last quarter of his spaghetti bolognese. He's making noises that sound like special effects from the climax of a Roger Corman film.

We're joined by Fran, our local friendly egghead, a legend in his lunchtime. After he deposits his carcass he starts this po-faced discussion about some abstruse Scandinavian writer probably about five people in the universe have heard of. The ulterior motive in such an exegesis, which it wouldn't take Einstein to work out, is the fact that there's an impossibly beautiful woman reclining at a table adjacent to us giving him the eye. So, at any rate, he believes. 'Next stop the luxury suite in the Hilton,' he beams, seriously thinking she's going to become smitten with him on the basis of his mind. (What mind?)

Instead of falling headlong for his charms she gives him a withering look. At which point he dips his head like a pimple-faced boy who's just got sand kicked in his face at a beach.

'Nice try,' says Robbie

'Did you think I was interested in her?' Fran rasps back, 'She's so ugly the sea wouldn't take her out.'

As for now, there are other pastures. 'Listen, honchos,' he says, 'Are we going somewhere or are we going somewhere? Let's get out of this toilet.'

I suggest a late night meal at one of the ritzier restaurants in Grafton Street. Premature middle age is turning me into this robot-like creature that suggests midnight fry-ups in classy eateries.

'Shag the meal,' says Robbie, 'Why not hit a club.'

Anto comes back from the bog. I ask him how his stomach muscles are. He tells me he thinks he left a few hundred of them on the urinal floor but apart from that he's okay.

'So what's the decision then?' I ask, 'Where are we off to?'

'I just want to go home to kip,' says Anto. Robbie tells him he'll look for a soother for him. Fran tells us all to cut the crap, that the night is getting on.

As the shutters come down, Robbie makes a pass at the girl he's been eyeing up.

'Where have you been all my life?' he says.

'Listen Mr Shit-For-Brains,' she says 'Why don't you get a personality transplant?' Robbie tries to smile but it comes out like a grimace.

'Jesus,' he says, 'there was a time you got ladies in this town. A couple of minutes ago I thought I might entertain you with my wit. Now I wouldn't piss on you if you were on fire.'

Romeo and Juliet it ain't.

It's past the witching hour. We discuss options. Anto has suddenly decided he wants to head for a massage parlour. 'To have my hamstring seen to, you understand.' And of course, we do. Les is still thinking of moseying back to his old lady's gaff for a nosh. Fran tells us he's freezing his nuts off, that we better come up with something sensational pronto.

'Come on, lads,' says Robbie, 'This is Dublin, remember?'

Yeah, this is Dublin all right. The metropolis. Where all love stories begin. And end.

Now that Robbie has got the bum's rush from his female friend, Fran's confidence has been restored to its customary pinnacle. He starts yammering on about this snazzy new nightclub that's just opened in Leeson Street. 'The chicks down there,' he propounds, 'would eat you up and blow you out in little bubbles.'

We amble vacantly into Earlsfort Terrace. Anto is coughing like a consumptive. Les suddenly gets the wind up about being attacked by muggers. He goes pale as he tells us of an acquaintance of his who had his nose bitten off on this very street last week after telling some yobbo to bugger off when he asked him for a few bob.

'Dublin is a jungle,' he says.

We walk around in circles. Fran tells us that we better get our act together, that another night is slipping through our fingers.

'I'm going to have it off tonight if it's the last thing I do,' he says.

'Knowing your luck, it probably will be,' Anto says.

'I'm serious. Even if I have to rape someone.'

'What other way did you ever get laid?' Les enquires.

Fran turns round. He fixes him in a glare. 'Are you still here? Someone told me you fell into the Liffey about a half-hour ago.'

'Leave my mate alone,' says Robbie, 'unless you want a dig in the snot box.' He puts his arms around Les, giving him this big fat smackeroo on the cheek.

'Faggot,' Fran snorts.

Anto stays on the road clutching his sides. He's getting sick, so sick he can't move out of the way of any oncoming cars. A taxi screeches to a halt ahead of him. The driver gives him two fingers. Anto starts blowing kisses at him. You can tell by the taxi driver's face that he'd like to come out and do a job on him that would require a lot of plastic surgery to repair.

'I'm pissed off,' Fran says, 'Let's hit Rasputin's.' I haven't had the pleasure of entering this emporium but it sounds promising. The only problem is that it entails bringing the car. That means breathalysers. At this point of the night, I imagine any one of us would turn that bag into all the colours of the rainbow.

We reach the car. Robbie and Les pile into the back. They're squashed beside two gigantic loudspeakers that Fran put there. Anto insists on driving. I'm in the passenger seat with Fran on my lap. As we set off he takes the opportunity to engage in a bit of horseplay with Robbie and Les. This pushes my pancreas somewhere up around my Adam's apple.

We take a corkscrew bends on three wheels. I say a silent prayer to the patron saint of Confused Motorists, whoever that is. There's also a general Act of Contrition. This is called hedging your eschatological bets.

As we swerve round Stephen's Green, Anto narrowly misses a pedestrian. I tell him to be careful.

'Fear not, my man.' he assures me, 'I did that for a mess. The situation is under control.'

'You know something?' Fran says, 'You're a cocky bastard when you're behind the wheel, aren't you?'

'You're going to kill us all,' I say.

'If I do, you have to admit it's a helluva way to go.'

'What if we all end up as veggies?' says Les.

'Are you nuts? At the speed I'm going, if I hit something, nobody walks away.' If nothing else, you have to give him credit for consistency.

At Pembroke Street a cop pulls us over the kerb.

'You've had a few, lads?' he suggests.

'One or two, guard.' Anto says, 'You know yourself.'

He shines his torch onto the back seat. Robbie and Les go into a sepulchral silence. I'm reminded of a pair of Holy Joes on their first Communion day.

'Is there any particular reason you're not wearing your seatbelt?' he asks me. I'm tempted to tell him Fran is my seatbelt.

'Don't travel too far,' he says.

I pinch myself to make sure I've heard him properly. 'Don't travel too far'? I thought he was going to lock us all up and throw away the key. There must be a God.

'That blind pig has to be a good omen,' Anto says when he's out of earshot.

Our collective mood lifts.

'I really feel I'm going to score tonight,' Anto announces, He tells us he plans to take some lucky female up into the Dublin mountains in the wee hours. Les isn't too sure going up the Dublin mountains in the middle of the night is such a good idea in view of Dublin's present crime statistics. Anyone who does that, he says, is looking to wake up with a crowd around them. Anto tells us he has a fantasy about dying after sex. I tell him he's welcome to that one.

We reach Rasputin's. The car is parked about three feet from the kerb. Anto is on cloud 37. Les is doing his best to act cool but he looks like he's done a number two in his pants.

Anto puts a coin in the traffic meter after we get out of the car. It's 12.30 a.m. and he's feeding the meter.

As soon as I get inside I start to feel woozy. The room is moving around like a ferris wheel.

Robbie comes up behind me with a pint. We've been in the joint about two minutes and he's already organised replenishments.

'It's one of those snobby places where they charge you twenty euros for a bottle of plonk,' he says, 'You're safer with the tried and trusted.' I'm in no condition to argue.

I watch couples in various stages of undress dancing in a manner that makes them look as if they're having sex standing up. Whatever happened to foreplay? Some of the women look as if they're dressed for the beach.

'If you've got it, flaunt it,' Robbie says. The trouble is, even the people who haven't got it are flaunting it tonight.

I ask a girl onto the floor. I try to be casual as I swing my arms around but I don't make a very good job of it. She tells me I look like an antelope. Her own movement reminds me of someone undergoing electric shock treatment.

'I think I know you from somewhere,' she says.

'We've probably met in a previous life,' I say, 'as dinosaurs or something. This sort of thing is always happening to me.'

My hands start to move around her body. A few moments later we're locked in Close Encounters of the 77th Kind.

Over a drink afterwards she tells me the story of her life. It's actually a very short one. She's a single mother. She's living on the dole and she hates both of her parents. Oh, and life's a bitch. Almost already I know we're made for each other.

Robbie arrives at our table. He starts to rabbit on about a woman he's met, someone who makes Kim Basinger look like the Elephant Man.

'I think I'm in love with her,' he says, 'I've proposed marriage but she thinks it might be a bit hasty.' He's so happy he wants to do a somersault on the table. I tell him I doubt the bouncer would be amused. Then he starts into an atonal rendition of 'Auld Lang Syne.' It's March and he's singing 'Auld Lang Syne'.

Fran is dancing with an arty type. Anto is dug into this debutante in leotards. Les is leaning on the bar being smoked by a cigarette. In the middle of the floor two men are fondling one another. Or is it two women? How can a woman have a moustache?

I retreat to the toilet. It smells like a sewer. I try to get sick but nothing comes up. Anto arrives in after me. He's chortling merrily. 'It's easier to get it in than get it out,' he says, standing up against the urinal. He must have enough for a brewery inside him.

'I'm dying, Anto,' I tell him, 'I'm too old for this.'

'I'll inform your next of kin,' he says.

It's time to go. I don't go back to where they're dancing, making a detour for the exit instead.

The pain is like a chainsaw through my head as I step out into the street. I watch taxicabs come and go like gigantic beetles stalking their prey. A couple of yards from me a pair of punks are scuffling over a girl. One of them has the head of the other in a nelson. He's ramming it up against the railing. The girls looks on bemused. He falls down like a sack of potatoes.

I arrive at the corner of Mount Street. A woman in a mini skirt approaches me. She's caked in make-up.

'Doin' business, luv?' she enquires. I shake my head.

'We could do anything you want,' she says.

We stand in the silence.

'Why do you do this?' I ask.

'You patronising bastard,' she says, 'Who the hell do you think you are?'

My heart is going like a pump. I think she's going to hit me but instead she just slinks off. I slump down on the pavement.

Already I know that today will be a total write-off for me. I'll do everything wrong because my brain will be on fast forward and my nervous system on pause. On days like this I feel I'm losing my mind. It's as if a strange person is inside it, making decisions I have no control over. Is it my fault or should I blame the Man Upstairs? He's been dealing me cards from the bottom of the deck for many months now. Maybe he's paying me back for some of the bad things I did in the past.

I shamble down empty streets to kill my thoughts. The dawn hints. I wonder where Fran and Anto ended up. Down the road from me a hobo cradles a bottle of vodka in a doorway.

I need to go home and get some sleep. When I wake up I'll make some decision about my life. Maybe I'll carry through on that and maybe I won't. As for now, all I want to do is forget. When you forget you become clean somehow.

I need to become free of this cesspool that's bleeding me white.

Enniscrone

The fields are nakedly green
the sheep looking up at you
as if nothing could bother them.
The sun beams down on you
making the day endless,
encouraging you to do nothing
on this mound of earth
where the air is still
and you feel suspended
outside time
outside space.
Nothing can bother you,
not events or people,
not even the sun on the hill
beckoning you to a future
so different
from the world you know.
Shadows lengthen
on the foam of the sea
as it tumbles towards you
daring you to mesh with it
in its silent world
of midnight
where your heart resides.

Memories of Being Eighteen

Yesterday I celebrated
my eighteenth year on earth
with sea food, cottage cheese,
a knickerbocker glory
for dessert,
some mutton for the gluttons
after eight
and an examination,
witnessed by all
of my bellybutton at the gate.

Drink was consumed.
I woke up in the cabbage patch
at dawn
dazed and confused
and blaming the booze
for making me a pawn
in the game of life,
a young man
with his brain eroded
like his wits
in the fast decaying ratpits
of the sticks.

Gravitating afterwards
to the dole office
for my unemployment cheque
I banter with my buddies
on the burning economic deck
before being presented
with my bounty
by a cashier
who's also been in the inferno

one time
who advises me
of better things to do
than wither
under unemployment blues.

It's Tuesday once again
my friends
and with a dozen crispy greenbacks
in my hands
the taste of undrunk Smithwicks
in my head
I inhabit, once again,
on grass amoral beds
the cosmos of the temporary undead
reclining sybaritically
 in the town square
with nothing but poverty to share
as free as the elements or the sun
with prospects of more parties
to come.

Dad comes on the line
sometime around
the bewitching hour of nine
talking of promising futures
in the gilt-edged land of computers.
Unfortunately
I don't want to know.
The call lasts all of ten seconds
before I go.

Mum's saintly patience is running out
I'm sad to say
and Dad's bank balance
isn't what it used to be

in his heyday.
Both of them affirm
in no uncertain terms
I'm on my own
in this welfare *shtick*
and if something pensionable
doesn't happen real quick
then someone near and dear
is going to die,
thereby increasing
the already increasing
crime epidemic by one.

'No mon no fun,' my father says,
'Your race is run.'
His words depress me,
clashing, as they do,
with my attempts
to get away from it all,
to have a ball
with fellow decadents
and spend my adult years
without doubts and fears
in Torremelinos
in the sun.

Love and Apricots

Andrew was one of the first big casualties of the recession. After graduating from college he bought a shop selling golf equipment. He was going a bomb till the bubble burst. He thought he'd be able to hang on because he had so many rich friends (chief among them his father) but one day he wrote a cheque for the (to him) relatively modest amount of €35,000 and it bounced. He presented himself at the bank the next morning with the rubber cheque.

'So what's the story?' he said to the bank manager.

'The story is that you're out of business,' the bank manager said.

Andrew felt like throttling your man on the spot. He'd been a good customer of banks all his life and conscientiously paid them their extortionate interest they demanded of him at the end of every month. And now this. Once voted 'Most Likely to Succeed' in the College Yearbook (and a possible place-kicker at Lansdowne in his spare time) Andrew Chisholm Hennessy now sat in a Stillorgan bank in front of The Most Reprehensible Man In The Universe.

'It's just a cash flow problem,' he said, trying to keep cool, 'I'll be back on my feet next month.'

'There won't *be* a next month,' the bank manager said, 'We're pulling the plug.' And they did.

Andrew didn't just lose his shop. He also lost his poise, his dignity, his self-respect. Oh, and his fiancée.

Chloe was a past pupil of Mount Anville, a beautiful girl he fell in love with almost before he even saw her as he liked to tell people. They were childhood sweethearts. They ate each other's food. They finished each other's sentences. They were so much on the same page it wasn't funny. Dammit, they almost went to the toilet together.

But Chloe was never going to be a fan of love on the dole. As soon as Andrew's cash pile disappeared and he wasn't able to bring her to Paris any more for rugby matches (or, more importantly, shopping on the Champs Elysses), she did a runner.

'I still love you,' she told him over a cocktail one night in the Westbury, 'but I think we both need time to think things over.' By

146

which she meant 'I still love you but I need some time to find, and get engaged to, my next millionaire.'

Andrew burst out laughing.

'So this is what it all comes down to,' he said, 'the do-re-mi.' He was almost relieved. 'Imagine if I found out after 30 years of marriage,' he said to her, 'Thanks for saving me.'

'I'm sorry you see it like that,' said Chloe, managing to keep a totally solemn face, 'but it's really not about the money.'

Afterwards he took to high living. He went to Chepstow and blew a stack there. Then he took a holiday to Croatia (*sans* Chloe). When he came home he spent the remainder of his cash in Madigan's buying drinks for everyone he'd ever met since the day he was born. Well, almost.

'I'm not letting those bastards in the AIB get their hands on a cent of it,' he said. When they came in with their heavy hitters a few weeks later he made sure there wasn't enough for them to buy a match for one of their fancy cigars. Andrew had the grand sum of 38 cents in the bank.

'It was much easier becoming poor than rich,' he told his father, 'and much more fun too.'

'What do you intend to do now?' he was asked.

'I think I'll live on the streets,' he announced.

The following week he looked up Amazon and bought the most expensive Afghan coat he could find.

If you're going to do something, he thought, do it in style.

He rooted through his mother's wardrobe. After some deep digging he found a woolly blanket at the end of it. He got his gym bag and put a Walkman in it and a book by Gunther Grass that he'd last read when he was a student in Trinity. A few days later he sat in an alcove in Aungier Street wrapped in the *Evening Herald*. He was fighting a hard wind.

Was it a good idea? Andrew thought so. His parents didn't. his father put his head in his hands and wept. His mother ended up in John of Gods dosed up to the eyeballs after being diagnosed as being bi-polar.

'I don't believe that diagnosis,' he said, 'She's just a bitch.' His father, meanwhile, developed angina. And a stoop.

'Was this what we scraped for to send you to Gonzaga?' he said when he tracked Andrew down, 'To see you examining your bellybutton in the inner city with a Styrofoam cup in your hand?'

'It's not Styrofoam,' said Andrew, 'it's plastic.'

His father groaned.

'Look,' Andrew continued, 'I'm fed up of capitalism. Poverty cured me of it.'

'That's all very well,' his father said, 'but who's going to take over the firm now? I'm about to call it a day.'

A position in the old man's locksmith business was being kept warm for him. Now it would have to go to someone else.

'Maybe you could hang on a few years longer,' Andrew said, 'I can't really be worried about things like that.'

'Come home, please,' his father said, 'Apart from everything else you'll freeze to death here.'

He didn't think so. For some reason the *Evening Herald* was warmer than most duvets he'd sampled back in the days with Daddy and Mammy in The House That Jack Built on Clyde Road. They called it that because his father made most of his dosh from his job during Jack Charlton's glory days with the Green Army. He found the *Evening Herald* much more beneficial as a blanket than as reading matter.

'Would you not think of me?' his father continued, putting on that pathetic face he was so good at.

'How do you mean?'

'I don't want to end up in John of God's,' he replied, 'like herself.'

His mother thought he was on drugs. How else, she reasoned, could a 'normal' person end up like this? The funny thing was that it was herself that was on drugs. She'd been dosed up to the eyeballs on Valium. His father blamed Andrew for her decline but that wasn't fair. The pair of them had seen her popping pills for yonks now. He refused to take the rap for that one to placate the old man.

'Herself was on drugs long before I became a social crusader,' he said.

His father ignored the comment.

'Harriet is in bits without you,' he said, 'If you come home, she said she will too.'

Andrew felt he was a victim of emotional bribery. They'd always been at that together to get their way with him. This time it wouldn't wash.

'I'd only be back a day when I'd be gone again,' he said.

'Why?'

'I can't explain it. The son you brought up doesn't exist anymore. I can't bring him back.'

'Do you want to?'

'Not really. Look around you. Ireland is going down the toilet. It isn't just me.' Yesterday he'd seen a piece of graffiti on a wall in North Strand: 'Will the last person leaving the country please remember to put out the lights.' It seemed to say it all.

'That's just an excuse to do nothing,' his father snapped, 'If we all dropped out, are you saying things would suddenly get better?'

'Do you not see what's going on? I'm not the bad guy here, the government is. I didn't cause the bust, the bankers did. We're paying for their gambling debts. That's something I intend to bring up with Sour Kraut the next time I see her.' That was his nickname for Angela Merkel.

His father stood up.

'Is that the nonsense your buddies feed you in Madigan's? It's probably some kind of bolshie thing, apologising for the fact that we're well off. Are you trying to join the lower orders to 'make up' to them?'

The old codger couldn't understand how Andrew could live without a roof over his head. Maybe a few months ago he wouldn't have been able to himself. The thing was, the middle classes were becoming homeless too in post-boom Ireland. They were getting turfed out of their houses because they couldn't meet their mortgages.

What was the difference when you boiled it down? People who worked their butts off for thirty years were now in the same boat as him. Or even a worse one. After being kicked out on the street they were told they still owed big-time on the kip they weren't allowed to live in.

It was like something you'd see in a surreal movie. There was only a slight difference between the homeless who were poor and those who were rich. The poor homeless sat inside their trusty *Herald* while the rich homeless went mad. Or shot themselves. Or jumped out windows. Or dosed themselves up to the gills with cocaine and moved back in with the wife (or husband) they'd recently divorced and still couldn't stand but who happened to own half a house, thanks to the divine God and his blessed mother. Now they could hang their hat in it without speaking and pretend they were still in love. Or maybe not even bothering to pretend. Either way it avoided having to sit in a doorway in Aungier Street in an Afghan coat that looked like you could house bees in it.

In Gonzaga they called him The Designer Hobo. He didn't mind. There were worse things you could be. Some of his friends couldn't get their heads around the fact that he appeared to be enjoying the Arctic temperatures of a wind-hit doorway when a state-of-the-art central heating system was waiting for him back in Clyde Road. He could see their point but he didn't agree with it. Sometimes it was important to do without.

'Are you a saint or a masochist?' one of them asked him.

'Neither,' he said, 'I'm just a fat slob bored out of his tree with comfort.' The fact that Pleasantville (as he called his house) was always available to go back to helped.

'This is some kind of warped intellectual protest,' his father said, 'You're trying to tell us you're going to solve world hunger from your little perch.'

'Stranger things have happened. Maybe Richard Branson will pass by some day and drop a few million quid into my cup. Or take me off in a balloon somewhere.'

'It's only a matter of time,' his father said, playing along to try and keep his sanity.

'Well he's going into space, isn't he?' he continued, 'The man gets around.'

His father was at breaking point now.

'What's the story on Chloe?' he asked him.

'Kaput, finito, history.'

'No hope at all of a reconciliation?'

'There's less than no hope. There's a *minus* hope. But I wouldn't want her anyway. She was a gold-digger.'

'Your mother liked her.'

'She was a good actress. Like most gold-diggers.'

There was nothing else to say. He wished her well with her next victim.

'What about that other girl you used to go out with?' he said then.

'What about her?'

He was referring to Bernie, someone he knew from college.

'It might do you good to see her.'

'Why?'

'Don't they say that if you break up with someone it's advisable to fill the gap?'

'The timing isn't right at the moment. At the moment the whole female species stinks for me.'

'That's a bit harsh.'

'It's a harsh world, Dad.'

'Are you still interested in her?'

'I don't know.'

'What's that supposed to mean?'

'It means I don't know.'

'That's ridiculous. Either you are or you're not.'

'Maybe in your world that's the case.'

He'd known her from the old days, taking her out a few times after he broke up with Chloe. He even brought her to his house one night. But then they fizzled out.

Dating. What was it but the postponement of a permanent love gloom.

'Why do you want me to see her?' he said, 'Do you think she might persuade me to put locks on people's houses for the rest of my natural? Or save me from myself?'

'I'm just making conversation. There's no need to bite my nose off.'

'I'm not biting your nose off. I just feel you're missing the point. Do you have even the tiniest clue why I'm here?'

'In all honesty no. We gave you a good upbringing.'

'A good upbringing. What does that mean? A five-bedroomed house and march to the beating drum of a corrupt bureaucracy?'

'Have you anything better to offer? Maybe you'd like to go off to a leper colony. You could take up where Mother Teresa left off.'

He felt the blood rising to his throat.

'You bastard,' he said.

'Sorry. That just came out.'

He lay back on the blanket. Sometimes he didn't know why he bothered talking to the old fossil. It might have been better to let him rot in his corrupt mansion.

'Let's put it this way,' he said, 'Bob Dylan protested against injustice even though he was from a middle class background. Elvis Presley didn't even though he was born poor. He was too busy trying to get out of the poverty trap to see beyond it.'

'Are you saying Elvis had no interest in the poor? I heard he gave cars to people for presents.'

His father was big into Elvis. He'd done the whole leather and winkle pickers thing then, like most fifties rockers.

'Not on a collective level. He helped individual poor people by giving them presents but that was probably just to take away his guilt over being such a rich bastard.'

'If you feel that strongly about the unequal division of wealth in the world you should become a politician.'

'Are you joking? That shower are only making things worse.'

'I'm talking about the idealistic ones.'

'An idealistic politician is as rare as a Hollywood virgin.'

'You have all the answers, don't you? Well let me tell you this, bucko, I wasn't born rich. I pulled myself up by my bootstraps to get where I am.'

'That's my point. Once you did you forgot about all the other poor buggers that didn't get there.'

'What am I supposed to do, break my heart over them? Do you think they'd have done anything for me if they were in my place?'

'Probably not. Which is why I'm here. Everyone is out for Number One.'

'Including you.'

'How do you make that out?'

'I don't know. It seems to me you're on some kind of attention trip. Maybe we didn't give you enough when you were a child.'

'Oh so we're on to Spock now, are we? Or is it Freud? Look, Dad, I think the best thing for you to do is go back to mother. Ask her to make one of her tasty *salad nicoises* for you. We're not really getting anywhere here I'm afraid.'

'I just want you home, that's all.'

'Don't push me.'

The conversation was going nowhere. It was always the way. They'd go round the mulberry bush until he became bored with the sound of his own voice.

'All I ask,' said his father, 'is that when you come back to us, whenever that is, it's not with your insides hanging out from some druggie attacking you.'

'Don't worry about that.'

'I won't argue with you anymore because it's pointless. I'll just say one final thing. You're sitting there in front of me looking like someone I don't know. I fear for your future. I fear for it because there may not be one. Because you don't seem to have any plan in life.'

In a way he was right. He didn't have a plan. That was what he liked most about his life now. That's what was wrong with most people in life, their plans. Fianna Fáil had a plan. The bankers had a plan. Ireland had a plan. Even bloody Angela Merkel seemed to have a plan – though she didn't seem to like telling anyone what it was.

And all the plans invariably ended up as a joynormous pile of crap.

'Look,' he said, 'If you go home now I promise to look up Bernie. Maybe we'll both apply to do a business course in college. We'll get rotten rich and earn more than the Gross National Product of a small South American country. Would that make you happy?'

'Deliriously,' his father said.

Deliriously. That was funny. They both started to laugh. Suddenly he thought the old lad wasn't so bad. At least he had a sense of humour. That was reassuring, especially in a crisis. Maybe they could have a pint together some night when it was all over, at least if Mother was off the tabbies.

'Okay,' he said, 'You bugger off home and I'll check Bernie out. When we're sorted I'll give you a shout. Deal?'

'Deal.'

Before he went off he fumbled in his pocket for some money.

'Take this,' he said, 'it will get you a roll or something.'

'It's okay,' he said, 'I won't starve. You just get home.'

'Okay.'

He put the money back in his pocket.

'And give my love to herself.'

He started to walk away. Then he turned back.

'Don't get hypothermia,' he said, wagging a finger.

'Don't worry,' he said, 'I'm tough. Think Clint Eastwood. Think Arnold Schwarzenegger crossed with Dolph Lundgren.'

His father shuffled off. He wasn't the worst, Andrew decided, looking at his tubby little shape waddling around the corner.

He put on his Walkman. There was a Bob Marley CD in it. It gave him a headache so he turned the volume down. Then he took out his Gunther Grass book. He started to read it but he couldn't concentrate.

What now, he wondered. Bernie?

He remembered her ranting on about the rugby crowd he belonged to one night in Madigan's. 'They should all be put in a boat,' she said, 'and shipped off to Siberia.'

Another night she told him she was thinking of gathering her savings together and putting them towards the purchase of an ostrich farm in New Zealand.

Andrew was all for it. At first glance it didn't sound like too bright an idea but when he thought about it he thought: What is there not to love? Out in the fresh air without having to listen to Merkel (or his mother). Lots of colourful birds gambolling around the fields with Bernie beside him. On the clear days they'd be able to wave to all the bankers standing in the dole queues in Melbourne.

Bernie was living somewhere in Maynooth. He decided to go down there and look her up.

What could he bring her as a gift to sweeten her up? What had a poor bastard sitting in a doorway left in the world?

There was one thing – an apricot. He had it tucked away in an inside pocket of his Afghan. A passer-by had given him a few days ago outside TCD. Some people were indeed kind.

After handing it to her, maybe he could follow up with a proposal of marriage. That should be the kind of thing that would appeal to her: an apricot-encrusted engagement ring.

Why not do things in style? They could honeymoon on one of the ghost estates in Kildare, at least if it hadn't been bulldozed by Enda Kenny's henchmen. In his mind's eye he saw them living on wild berries in the Golden Vale. He filed the idea away for future reference.

The evening darkened. His mind started to race. He tossed and turned in a desperate effort to keep warm. He wondered what Chloe was doing on a night like this. Probably tucked up in her apartment with the latest Cecilia Ahern novel.

He'd owned half of it when they were kipping up together. (That's the apartment, not the novel.) After the crash she bought him out. What a time. It hurt him to even think about it. Those NAMA bozos threatened to put him in the clink for unpaid debts if he didn't cough up. He used his share to sort out the IOUs.

Now it was hers. The pad he should have been living in tonight. Cooking up some Taiwan food and settling down to a DVD on their plasma screen. Why had he not seen it all coming down the tramlines. It was gravity, wasn't it? What went up had to come down. A no-brainer.

All the economic experts were now telling us why it happened. Experts always knew everything too late. In that they were like the politicos.

He pulled his blanket over him. It was still bloody cold. He put on a second pullover It didn't do much for him even though it was an Aran one.

He began to shiver. Was he coming down with something? He had a tendency towards bronchitis. His mother said it went back to his childhood, some weakness with his lungs. Suddenly he felt a long way from Bob Dylan.

Did Dylan ever get the flu? Would he freeze his arse off in a doorway to make a point? Not bloody likely. He'd be too busy getting rich.

He thought about Bernie, about the ostrich farm. Would it work in the long run? Maybe she'd laugh in his face if he suggested going down there with her.

What did the pair of them have in common when he thought about it? He was a rugger bugger. She was a free spirit from the bad end of town. They'd probably be at each other's throats within the week. Maybe she'd set one of the ostriches on him. He imagined himself climbing a tree with his trousers being nipped off by this crazy bird. It would have been nicer to have them ripped off by Bernie, another crazy bird.

The night became black. Pubs started to disgorge their drinkers. He hated these supercilious slackers who sprouted at this hour every night. Most of them were pretentious TCD students with plummy voices and non-existent minds. Not too long ago he probably sounded like them himself, passing facetious comments about this and that before getting on the Luas with their Leap cards.

A few of them started singing as they passed by him. One of them gave him the fingers. Another one put on a Northside accent. He said, 'I'll give you a euro, head, when me dole comes through.'

They started laughing. Obviously they though this was uproariously funny. Was it funny? He didn't think so. But you'd laugh at anything with a few jars in you, wouldn't you? He missed his few jars. Jesus he'd kill for a hot whiskey now.

He felt ridiculous sitting there. Maybe it was time to give up his protest. Why prolong the agony? He'd made his point. How many of the Madigan's crowd would have lasted this long? Gareth Keegan had stayed up all night for Trócaire once when he was in First Eng. The way he went on about it you'd think he just cut off an arm to give to the Black Babies.

He was hungry. So hungry he could have eaten a pig through a tennis racquet. He took the apricot out of his pocket. He started to nibble at it.

It looked pathetic with the skin hanging off.   How could he give it to Bernie now?

He saw himself down on one knee in the arsehole of Kildare: 'Bernie my darling, wilt thou be my wife? I pledge my troth to thee with this apricot. Sorry, half apricot.' No, it wouldn't work.

It started to rain. He let out a few curses. People started to look at him. It was all right for him to starve to death but don't burn our ears with your expletives. The New Irish Charity.

He pulled the blanket over his head. There was a hole in the top of it that was letting in. The rain was dripping onto his body. He felt like a drowned rat.

His father was right. He'd probably get hypothermia if this continued. Where would that get him? He could see tomorrow's headlines: 'Dublin Four Rebel Succumbs To The Elements.' Was it for this the wild geese spread their wing on every tide?

The rain got torrential. He huddled up like an embryo but he couldn't keep it out. When he pulled the blanket over his head his toes were exposed. If he put it over his toes his stomach got the brunt of it.

He started to cry. Suddenly all the emotion of the last few months hit him. The hatred of himself that brought this mad idea on. The fear of bankruptcy. The big hole of apathy he was in now that all his dreams had crumbled into dust.

Was there was any hope for him? Maybe there was still a way out. He owed it to himself to stop this insanity, to get to know his real self. You couldn't disown your past just like that, could you?

He was a child of plenty, not Gandhi.

It was as if a light went off in his brain. He didn't belong here. It wasn't just the hunger or the cold. There was something inherently wrong with it.

He stood up. The rain stopped. The sky looked clearer. As he looked up at it he felt purged of something.

His blanket was in bits on the ground beside him. He took it up. He started to talk to it.

'Look at you, pathetic blanket,' he said, 'A few weeks ago I thought you were my saviour. Now I'm more inclined to see you as a traitor.'

What should he do with it, he asked himself. Keep it in a glass case? Donate it to the museum? Put it in the attic until he became famous and then dig it out for his fans as Exhibit A of his regeneration?

None of these courses of action would be appropriate. He lashed it over a wall onto some waste ground. 'Farewell wasted cloth,' he extolled, delighted to see the end of it.

He stood up. His limbs ached as he drew himself up to his full height. He looked around him. The streets were deserted. He was a lone wolf in the darkness.

He could have died there and then. If he did, who'd have cared? What was it Dylan said? 'Only a hobo but one more is gone.' It would probably be good riddance as far as those latchikos in Dáil Eireann were concerned. Maybe they'd be his next target. Put a bomb under the whole fucking lot of them.

He started to walk, slowly at first but then picking up speed as he got going. He threw Gunther Grass into a bin at Leonard's corner.

Good old Gunther, he thought, but you're a bit *deja vu*. He was already starting to feel back to his old self.

What would his next move be ? Maybe the locksmith shop. He wasn't sure. Enda Kenny said the economy was picking up. You'd never know. He still had a few golf clubs hidden up in the attic. Ha ha, those extortionists from the IMF wouldn't get their hands on these. Maybe he'd put them up on eBay now, get a few bob to start him on his road to recovery. The first step was always the hardest, getting on that ladder.

First he had some scores to settle. With the 'friends' who said they'd be there for him come hell or high water.

Now it was payback time. As soon as he got on his feet he'd let them know what was what. You had to fight dirty to beat those bastards.

Enda was talking about burning the bond holders. He knew where he'd burn them. In a vat of hot oil.

A taxi passed him by. He thought about hailing it. Pity he didn't take the few quid from his old lad. It would have got him home in jig-time.

He was looking forward to seeing him. He was even looking forward to seeing Mammy Dearest. Both of them would give him major league hugs. They'd welcome him back into the bosom of home. That was one thing he knew he could count on.

Love meant letting go of the past. What right had he to judge anybody? We were all just trying to make our way in this crazy world.

The first thing he was going to do when he got in the door was put on the immersion for a nice warm bath.

Departure

Where memory ends
and dream begins
the light slants
onto purple days.
Sitting under
a hawthorn tree
I wait for you
with a flame in my heart.
Time scatters youth
to the winds.
Clutching at straws
as the sun sets
and the river
floods its banks
I wake to change.

Apartment

There's always someone sick
downstairs.
At the end of the corridor
is a room
no one enters.
The bathroom betrays fragments
of lives I'll never know,
the bottles and sprays of those
who lead hygienic lives.

My life is separate from theirs.
All I see
are faces on the stairs
phone messages
about burst pipes,
love notes from absent Romeos.

Next door I hear a switch
that tells me somebody
is going to bed
or getting up.
Downstairs
the landlady wheezes
into her nightly drink
content
that another day
has passed without event.

I watch a news report
that tells me
39 have died in Mexico,
that the government is unstable
that tomorrow will be rainless.

I switch to the late night film,
light a cigarette
as I reflect
that nothing has made this day
different to yesterday
or all the yesterdays.

No thoughts go through my mind
as the night comes down.
No visions penetrate my senses.
All I hear are the trains
that pass interminably
above my head,
car sounds dying
like the day just gone.

The after-image of an erotic film
spins through my subconscious
as my head drops
into a fallow time I half invite,
as my future clarifies itself
in front of me
like a pre-recorded text
and I make a kind of covenant
with the ordinary.

Driftwood

It was one of those parties you attended to get drunk at. She stood under a street sign that said 'Gortnor Abbey, 18 miles.' She was drinking whiskey out of a teacup. Her cardigan was frayed at the edges. Outside it was raining.

When we fell into conversation I started to stutter. I was nervous with her. She told me to relax. 'You're not used to talking to women, are you?' she said. I had to admit it was true, particularly women as alluring as her. She offered me some of her whiskey. As I drank it she started talking about her chequered history with men.

I couldn't take my eyes off her. I said, 'How is it that someone as beautiful as you isn't married?' She started laughing at that, not only because it was so old-fashioned but because it sounded like a chat-up line. I can't remember what happened afterwards. She was dragged away from me by a posse of other admirers.

I didn't see her for the rest of the night. I stumbled home only half-remembering her. When I woke up the next morning I found a photograph of her in my pocket. It said 'Enniscrone Beach' on the back of it. Underneath it she'd written her phone number.

My hands trembled with anticipation as I rang her but when I asked her to go out with me she agreed. I called around to her flat in Ardnaree that night. It looked like a bombsite. There were beanbags instead of chairs. She had a bollard in the corner. I presumed it was stolen by the same person who got the Gortnor Abbey sign.

After that I met her almost every night. At the beginning I said little, content merely to be with her. We used to meet outside Gaughan's pub. When we didn't have anywhere else to go we rambled in there.

She told me about her life. It excited me because it had no plan to it. She was an adopted child. That seemed to give her the freedom to roam wherever she wanted. She'd been all over the world even though she was still only in her early twenties.

In the next few weeks I became more attached to her than I felt she wanted me to be. I tried to act casual even though I felt I was falling in love with her. She was seeing other men as well as me but that didn't seem to matter to me. Or to her.

When I felt I couldn't do without her anymore I asked her if I could move in with her. I thought she'd laugh at me but she didn't. She just shrugged her shoulders. 'If you want,' she said. I thought she was joking. At times it seemed to me as if her whole life was a joke. 'Let's play it by ear,' was her favourite expression.

Most nights we didn't go anywhere. We sat in watching mindless films. We usually split a bottle of wine between us. She had no trouble out-drinking me. It was another thing she was good at. In the mornings she'd be slow to come to life until she had a few black coffees. Then she'd be in a party mood again.

As the summer approached she said she was giving up her job. She'd been working as a barmaid in the Downhill Hotel.

'Why?' I said.

'Because I want to go to Europe with you,' she said.

The fact that I'd never mentioned wanting to go there didn't seem to enter in to it. 'That's like the other side of the moon to me,' I said. I'd never been out of the country before. I'd just finished three years in UCD examining my navel. I was expected to go back to Ballina to teach. The idea didn't exactly enthral me.

The excitement of being with her merged with the thrill of the trip. Over the next few days I convinced myself it was all I wanted. She was amused by my fussing as I searched frantically for an old passport I had. 'You worry too much,' she said.

I didn't tell anyone I was going for fear they'd put the kibosh on it. One rainy Tuesday we drove to Rosslare in a friend's battered Fiat. I was intoxicated with her presence. Afterwards we got the ferry to France. I kept going through my pockets wondering if I had all my documentation. She was doubled over laughing at me.

I gave her the wheel at Le Havre. She drove like a mad woman down the motorways as I proceeded to get multiple minor coronaries. The worse I got, the faster she drove. At one point we veered off the road into a wheat field. She screeched to a halt and turned off the engine. She got out of the car. 'I'm waiting for you,' she said. Her blouse was half off her. I followed her into the field. She started getting passionate with me. I couldn't breathe.

After a while she went back to the car.

'I'll let you off this time,' she said.

We zoomed off. Drivers were going crazy all over the road as they tried to avoid crashing into her. I feared her foolhardiness.

After we got to Paris I sent a postcard to my parents. I imagined them getting apoplexy as they read it. I felt I dodged a bullet by taking French leave of them (in Paris). 'See how easy it is?' she said, digging me in the ribs.

We went to Florence. I felt my personality turning into hers. She hypnotised me with her recklessness.

I thought of the pair of lovers in the film *Elvira Madigan*. They lived on berries in the middle of nowhere. Were we like them or just pretending to be?

We told ourselves nothing was beyond us. We threw ourselves into experiences that already seemed to be half fading even as they happened. I tried to shred my past, to make her my prized accessory. She was amused at my awkwardness as I surveyed the benchmarks of my other life back home. The Fiat rumbled along, carrying us through Rome, Milan, the dark recesses of Genoa. .

In Turin we thought we'd opt for a a longer stay. We became practical there. You could always become practical when there was something in it for you. Suddenly we weren't tourists anymore. We started to think of things like money, accommodation.

She got part-time work translating business reports for a politician. In the evenings she served in a bar. From what I could see she imbibed more alcohol behind the counter than most of the customers did outside it.

'Why do you drink so much?' I asked her one day, 'Are you trying to escape something inside yourself?'

'Spare me the psychology lesson,' she said, 'You sound like a Sunday school teacher.' When I asked her if she thought we could go the distance she said, 'I've never understood terms like that. Does it matter?'

The Turin experience didn't last. Neither did our brief approximation to something approaching an old-fashioned life. Neither of us were good at being bored. Time passed too slowly that way. We'd be old long enough.

We hung our hats in any city we could think of for no other reason than that it existed. I pretended this was what I wanted for fear of losing her. Eventually we settled in a place called Livorno. It was a naval base. We watched the sailors walking along the pier every morning in the scorching heat. I grabbed whatever casual work I could. It was my turn now. She'd supported me mainly up to this. We were living in a one-room apartment on the edge of the city. It didn't cost much. It smelt like a slaughterhouse but it was all we could afford.

When we ran out of money we sold the Fiat. We got enough for it to tide us over a few months but we weren't thinking in those terms. We drank most of the proceeds. When we thought of it we phoned our parents. They were relieved to know we were still in the land of the living. We guffawed down the line with contempt for a world we felt we'd outgrown.

My possessiveness of her was our main problem now. Some nights I watched her flirting with other men in nightclubs. I was jealous but I said nothing. I knew what her temper was like. She seemed to enjoy testing me. Or maybe it was herself she was testing. She could have been trying to find out what worked best for that convoluted mind.

A man she danced with one night said to me in broken English, 'Your girlfriend, she is *crazee*.' When I asked him what he meant he put his hand to his head, pulling an imaginary trigger.

She started going out without me. I wondered if she was having a relationship with him. I never saw them together but she mentioned his name a lot. When we were on our own she seemed nervous with me. It made me think she was hiding something.

One night when she came back to the apartment she was crying. Her blouse was torn. She had a bruise on her face. When I asked her what happened she said, 'It's nothing. I fell.'

When I pressed her for more information she started screaming at me. She stormed out of the apartment. I ran after her. When I caught up with her she pulled herself away from me. She went into a restaurant and sat down at a table. I wasn't sure if I should join her or not. A sad old man with a bald head played a violin in the corner. I sat down beside her but she didn't acknowledge me. Then she started to cry again. I asked her if she wanted something to drink but she just nodded her head.

She stayed quiet for a long time. Then she said, 'Where are we going?'

I said I didn't know what she meant, that she'd always said the whole point of us being together was that we weren't going anywhere. She went quiet at that, her hand running up and down the grease that poured from a candle that was on the table.

'That's not enough for me anymore,' she said then. Her words startled me. They were what I'd wanted to hear from her almost from the night I met her. Now there seemed to be something wrong with them. It was as if someone else was speaking. She was saying them from an unreal part of herself.

Afterwards she burst out laughing, that wild laughter I could never decipher. She called the waiter over to her and asked him for a bottle of wine. She spent the rest of the night slugging it back, telling me she wanted to have 'ten bambinos' with me. For once I didn't join her.

The next morning she was back to herself. When I questioned her about her behaviour she laughed it off as if it was nothing.

Over the next few days I grew uneasy in her company. Our lives went on as usual but there was something wrong. I tried to forget her words but I couldn't. I knew she was thinking about them too. She spoiled me with little treats but that only made things worse. I grew afraid of her. We tiptoed around one another like strangers. I knew she was being untrue to herself. She was losing her nonchalance, the thing I first fell in love with.

She suggested moving to another town. I thought I knew the reason. She wanted to take away the tension. When I asked her if she slept with the man she was dancing with that night she hit me.

The arguments between us got worse. Often they were about nothing. We started to resemble a boring old couple, something we promised ourselves we'd never become.

She became involved with some shady characters. One night I found her in the apartment with one of them. I threw him out but when I came back to the room the door was locked. I thought she might have been crying but I didn't know for sure. I spent the night in the other room.

When I got up the next morning we didn't seem to have anything to say to each other anymore. I wanted her to flare up at me again but she didn't. She became indifferent to me and I towards her. Three months earlier I would have cut off my right arm to be with her. Now I felt nothing. Over the next few weeks we moved in different spheres. I got a job in a trattoria. She'd left her own job by now. When I told her I was thinking of going back to Dublin she just shrugged her shoulders.

'Would you come back with me?' I asked her.

'I can't,' she said, 'Ireland is like a living death to me.'

I felt that was an excuse. She wanted me to be gone. We still did the same things together in the next few weeks but without conviction. I was a different person to the man who fell in love with her. She was a different person too. Neither of us admitted this. It was easier to play the blame game.

The clock ticked down to my departure. I was nervous waiting for the flight date. It couldn't come quickly enough for me. As I was leaving her I thought I sensed some emotion in her.

It wasn't backed up by words. The hug she gave me at the airport was like one you'd give to your sister.

When I got to Ballina I moved back into my parent's house. Returning to my old life I felt like an orphan seeking approval from a world I thought I'd disowned.

I wrote to her a few times but my letters came back unread. When I phoned her she didn't answer. Then one night she did. I heard a man's voice cackling behind her. She seemed drugged. I wasn't even sure if she knew who I was.

She never picked up again. Neither did she acknowledge my letters. They didn't come back anymore. I imagined her throwing them in the bin. I tried to get back to my old routines but it was difficult. I was older; they seemed banal.

I went back to see her once. My parents thought it was a bad idea. I did too but I still had to go. There was something to exorcise. I didn't care if she ignored me. I didn't even care if she hit me. I wanted closure.

I made the journey almost without being aware of it. Too many things were crowded in my mind. It was only when I got to Turin that my brain told me what I was doing.

I was nervous knocking on her door. I wasn't sure if she'd answer. It was a while before she did.

'I don't believe it,' she said.

She looked older. She was dressed in a kimono. There was no sign of a man being there. The room was dishevelled.

She made me an espresso. We sat without speaking for a while. She smiled sadly.

'I don't know what you're doing here,' she said. I said I wasn't either. After a few attempts at conversation I realised she wasn't going to give me anything. Her eyes looked glazed. I presumed she was on something. I knew better than to ask what.

I begged her to come back with me but she wouldn't. We went walking by the canal. She threw bread at the ducks.

'Why does life have to be like this?' she said.

'It doesn't,' I said.

The sun died over the canal. We went into a café. It had a tablecloth like a chessboard. There was a winding plant in the corner.

'I've never loved anyone but you,' she said.

'Then come back to Dublin with me.'

She laughed.

'You never give up!

Back in the apartment her eyes started to droop. She went into her bedroom. When I followed her in after a few minutes she was already asleep. I sat looking at her as she lay half in the bed and half out of it, the sheet strangled around her like a rope. I left the next morning before she woke.

She rang me after I got back to Dublin.

'You left as suddenly as you arrived,' she said. I told her I learned that from her. She asked me about my parents, my life.

'Why didn't you ask me these kinds of questions when I was with you?' I said to her.

'I wasn't myself,' she said, 'I'm sorry.'

I had nothing of any significance to tell her. It was too late. For a second I thought she wanted me back. If she did I wasn't sure I could go.

Coming up to Christmas a person who knew her from the past told me he heard she was dating an ex-convict. A few months later the same man drove his car off the pier in Livorno with her in the passenger seat. Both of them were out of their minds with booze at the time. By the time the emergency services arrived it was too late to save either of them.

I tried to react to the news but I couldn't. She'd already died for me the night she told me she couldn't be with me. I was relieved for her. Maybe it was the only way it could have ended.

When her body was flown home to Dublin I met her parents for the first time. They were surprisingly ordinary, surprisingly nice. At the funeral I showed them the photograph I had of her, the one that she'd written her phone number on the back of that first night, her hair blowing in the wind on the beach at Enniscrone. Her mother cried when she saw it.

'We never knew about you,' she said, 'She wasn't inclined to share things like that with us.' We didn't talk about anything that happened afterwards, freezing her in the moment.

Sometimes I blame myself for what happened but more often I tell myself there was nothing I could have done. I don't think about her much now. I remember a day towards the end of the summer when she was sitting in a field overlooking the sea at Livorno. There was a lighthouse behind her, angled by the sun. Her face seemed to foretell something - the end of me, maybe, or the beginning of someone else.

I've gone back to the place we stayed many times over the years. The streets still look the same. People look at me as if they know me. Even though we didn't last together I'm grateful it happened. I can look back on a summer where I lived with a goddess for three months, three months where we tried to work out what kind of future we wanted without knowing why we'd come together in the first place.

What I can't get out of my mind is that first night at the party when she stood in front of me with her cup of whiskey and her cardigan frayed at the edges, her laughter cascading into my sad and lonely heart.

View from the Lighthouse

I sit on the balcony of the apartment
like Henry Fonda
from *My Darling Clementine*
dangling my legs on the rail.
The moon looks like it was slashed
in half by a knife.
Lights necklace Bartra Bay.
A straggler chats across the sands
of Enniscrone
reviving old memories.

I was here before my father died
before everything went wrong.
Was it a honeymoon
or a summer holiday?
Life was easier then.
We lived it
without consequence.
He came here too.
Then he died
and the world stopped turning
for a day, a week,
forever.

The pier is deserted.
Strobe lights
pierce hearts like mine
in a discotheque,
a shopping centre, a mall.
All of us hang on
to the dead wood of our lives
because nothing better
presents itself.

We piece together the trivia
that keeps us going
from day to day.
He couldn't do that.
We wouldn't let him.
He went from us
on a day we least expected
when too many other things
took precedence for us
over the hazy allure
of a past we craved
just as he had
in another time.

Bad Luck Charm

'How is the house-hunting going?' Tony asks me as we settle into one of the cubicles beside the bar counter. We're about to move out of the poky flat we have in Morrison Terrace.

'Not too bad. We have our eye on a semi-d.'

'What's the price like?'

'A bit out of our range at the moment but the auctioneer says the seller is desperate to get rid of it. We'll probably drag him down a bit.'

'That should do you nicely. Of course you've got the few extra bob coming in now that you've got that plum job.' He's talking about a recent promotion.

'I won't get far on that. Anyway, no matter what you get on Friday it's gone again on Monday morning.'

'You can say that again. It walks, doesn't it?'

The television is on in the background. We're watching Manchester United getting yet another goal in Fergie time. The beer has numbed my brain, numbed even the need for more. The bar is full of people even drunker than ourselves. They scream madly at the screen as the game ends.

The barman changes the station. A Hugh Grant film comes on.

'The only thing I ever liked that bollox in, 'Tony says, 'was Liz Hurley.'

He looks at a woman sitting across from us.

'Good pair of headlamps,' he says, 'She was here last night as well. Maybe she has her eye on me.'

'Don't make a fool of yourself,' I tell him, 'Remember what happened last Friday.'

''Have no fear, my friend. In matters of the heart I rarely lose. She's been eye-faxing me all night. I feel it would only be the decent thing to reciprocate the gesture.'

'Don't presume too much. She could be a tease.'

'What about yourself? Are you on the prowl?'

'Not tonight. I told Pauline I'd be back early.'

'We can't go yet. The night is young.'

'Maybe, but I'm not.'

'I was thinking of hitting that new club on the Quay.'

'Pauline would suspect something if I was late back again.'

'Jesus, she's not going to kill you for one night. There are some women I'd like you to meet.'

'No, Tony.'

'You have to live sometime.'

When he's in this mood he's impossible to say no to.'

'I'll go with you but I won't do anything.'

'Good on you.'

'I don't know why you want me.'

'For moral support. Or even immoral support.'

I contemplate an excursion that has become hauntingly familiar in recent times, one which I seem powerless to resist. My suggestion that we walk instead of drive is dismissed with a wave of the hand, the drink making him even more gung-ho than usual, 'Ladies get turned off if you don't got the wheels,' he informs me.

When we're in the car he starts telling me details of his last sexual experience. His anecdotes both fascinate and repel me. I envy him his confidence and feel sorry for the fact that he can't ever form a relationship with a woman that's longer than a month.

'I feel lucky tonight,' he says, 'Maybe this is my night, Charlie.'

He guns the engine. He's taking the two sides of the road.

'Shut up,' I say, 'or you'll kill the two of us.'

'Chill out,' he says, 'That's your problem.'

I get a rush of adrenalin as we reach the club. I want to be here and yet I don't. Guilt and excitement mix inside me. He tells me to relax, that I look too married. It's easy for him. He isn't.

A bouncer at the door smells the drink off us. He doesn't want to let us in but Tony slips him something and we get the nod. As soon as we get inside he gets us a bottle of wine each. I try to pay my share but he won't let me. 'Today is payday,' he says.

He eyes up the women around us, making sexual gestures to me as any potential conquest hoves into view. I look around me at the bodies on the floor. They're dancing close. 'Get a room!' he calls out to one couple.

175

'Do you see that one leaning against the pillar?' he says after a minute, 'I think I know her from somewhere.'

'I hope you're not planning to use that as a chat-up line.'

'I'm serious. She's like Sorcha from work.'

'If she's Sorcha, I'm Yehudi Menuhin.'

'Salud, Yehudi,' he says, knocking back another glass. He's getting high already.

My conscience is starting to kick in.

'I'm not sure if this is a good idea,' I say. His face hardens.

'If you want to be a Boy Scout, leave now. I'll organise a soother for you. But if you stay I don't want any more bellyaching.'

I take his point. If you don't like the heat, get out of the club. Back to boring suburbia, to the pregnant wife and the dead-end life. Or, alternatively, atrophy here. What fresh hell is this? Maybe it's just the old one in disguise.

'Give me another drink,' I say to my Mephistopheles. He grins as he pours it for me.

'With a bit of persuasion I might even get you out onto the floor,' he says, 'at least if the right woman comes along.'

'I'm not Michael Flatley, you know that.'

'It's not what you do but who you do it with. I have two left feet myself and look at me.'

'Do I have to?'

He flicks his finger at a barmaid to indicate he wants another bottle. At this point of the night it's futile to argue with him. He goes up to the counter to pay. I see him talking to two women I half-recognise. He comes back to our table with them.

'I'd like you to meet some old friends of mine,' he says.

. One is a blonde and one a brunette. He's decided on the blonde for himself. She has so much cleavage, when she bends over you can almost see her ankles. The brunette sits beside me. She smiles. He winks at me as if to say 'She's yours if you want her.' Such are the nuances of his foreplay techniques.

I sense she's been expecting me. I wouldn't put it past him to have set up something like this. He's been threatening to long enough. Since his marriage broke down he's been like a child in a toy shop trying to make up for lost time. In me he seems to have found a Sancho Panza.

She tells me her name is Nicola. I say that's a nice name. She says thank you. Then she gives me a kiss.

'I'm elephants,' she says. 'Promise you won't tell anyone. We've been on the lam since lunch-time. Isn't that atrocious?' I say her secret is safe with me.

'You're cool.' she says, 'You know that? I've seen you here a few times before but I never had the courage to talk to you. Tony says you're quiet but a bit of fun when you get going.'

She suggests we go onto the floor. I allow myself to be led out. A rap number belts out of a speaker that's hanging off the wall. She puts her arm round me.

'We shouldn't be doing this,' I say, 'I'm married.'

'That's the fun part.'

She does a weird dance. People start to look at her. Tony gives me a gesture from the far side of the floor that says, 'Go for it.' She puts her arms around me in a way that makes me uncomfortable.

'Relax,' she says, 'You're like an elastic band wound up. Smile and give your face a holiday.'

Out of the corner of my eye I see Tony getting his coat and walking out of the club with the blonde girl. The room revolves around me. I ask her if she minds if we sit down, that my head is feeling light.

When we get back to the table I see Tony's coat is gone.

'It looks like the bird has flown,' she says, 'That means we can have more privacy.'

She starts singing a song I don't know. I tell her to keep her voice down but she's too drunk to care.

'What you need is a refill,' she says, emptying more wine into my glass.

'If I drink that I won't wake up tomorrow.'

'That's the general idea.'

As the dancers filter off the floor she says Tony told her I had a bad marriage.

'Is it true?'

'Do you want it to be?'

'I like you. Is that a crime? Tony told me all about you.'

'So he set this up.'

'You came to the club, sunshine, don't forget that.'

'You're right, I did.'

'You're confused. Isn't that it?'

'Something like that.'

'Don't be afraid. You're not doing anything that's grounds for divorce.'

She puts on a funny face.

'I'm sorry,' I say, 'I'm not much fun tonight.'

'Stop mugging yourself off. I'm not looking for anything from you.'

The crowds are thinning out. I wonder where Tony is.

'You're a beautiful woman,' I say suddenly.

'Where did that come from?' she says. She starts to sing out, 'I'm In Love With a Beautiful Woman.' She throws her arms all over the place.

'What else did Tony tell you about me?' I ask her.

'Not much. Just that your wife is a bitch.'

'He got it back to front. I'm the problem in the relationship.'

'Is that why you came here tonight?'

I don't want to go into it with her. How can I explain my life to someone I've just met who's about ten years younger than me?

'I don't know. Life is going a bit crazy for me at the moment. We're talking about moving house. We have a baby on the way. I'm under pressure at work.'

'It sounds like you're one seriously fucked-up dude.'

'There are a lot of new responsibilities. Pauline had to give up her job because so we're living on my salary. It's causing a bit of tension.'

'Pauline being your wife.'

'Yes.'

'So Tony helps the situation by getting you a bit on the side.'

'No, he just makes it worse.'

She laughs.

'Why is that?'

'Because he thinks I need an affair. He thinks I'm like him. His own marriage broke down.'

'I know. I caused it.'

I'm not sure if she's joking me or not.

'Do you think he wants to bring you down with him?'

'I didn't say that.'

'You implied it.'

We sit in the silence. The room is almost empty.

'Maybe we should go,' I say.

'Look,' she says, 'I took you for a different type of guy. I'm sorry. Maybe I'm mistaken but I thought we were enjoying ourselves. I'm not a marriage-wrecker but I'm not Snow White either. If you want to talk sometime you can tell Tony and we'll have a cup of coffee. Or hike ourselves off to Brazil and get married on a beach like Pammie Anderson.'

The night is ending as absurdly as it started. I don't know whether to be relieved or not. Am I being noble or just cowardly?

'I appreciate what you're saying. I'm sorry I'm not the kind of man Tony led you to expect.'

She kisses me on the cheek and picks up her bag. As she starts to leave I feel I shouldn't let her. It's always been like this with me, stuck in the middle of two alternatives. Tony has a joke about me: 'I used to think you were indecisive but now I'm not so sure.' His own split was more straightforward. He knows who he is.

She stops at the door to chat to some people. I watch her laughing with them. I envy her casualness. Was I this way once? No. I always had to make a three-act drama out of even the most minor event of my life.

I keep sipping the wine until there's just me and the bouncer left. He looks relaxed now that the crowds are gone, that any threat of disruption from the other drinkers has passed.

'What's the matter?' he says, 'Did she dump you?'

'What do you think?'

'I think you should probably try harder.' Maybe he's right. But with which woman?

179

I walk out into the night. The wind pierces me. A hobo puts his hand out to me as I pass him. At the end of the street a fight is breaking out. People watch it half-dazed, only mildly interested in it. I look for Tony among the couples locked in embraces along the wall but he's not there.

I hail the first taxi I see. A tinge of regret nudges at me as I sit inside. Have I let something slip away that might have been important or have I preserved something important by doing nothing? You're damned if you do and damned if you don't.

The taxi driver wants to talk but I'm not in the mood. He mentions some political scandal that's just broken out on the news.

'Zig and Zig should be running the country,' he says.

We pass Tony's car. Maybe he got lucky after all.

The heat in the taxi makes me sleepy. The streets slide by. Another night of my life has been wasted, Another night I've betrayed something in myself for no better reason than boredom. If I want I can blame the drink but it's a cop-out. I started drinking to make it easier for myself not to have to deal with my guilt.

Now there will be Pauline to confront, either with lies or excuses. It doesn't matter which. She doesn't care anymore.

I ask the taxi driver to let me out a few streets from where I live. I want to tidy myself up for her.

The light in the living-room is still on as I walk up the driveway. It's not like her to be up this late. It would have been easier for me not to have to deal with her until tomorrow.

She opens the door before I get to it.

'Well,' she says 'I thought you were out for the night.' It would have been the case more times than I care to remember. She keeps questioning me about these occasions and I keep blanking her. She usually backs off after a while. Maybe she's afraid of what I might tell her.

'Sorry I'm late,' I say, 'Tony brought me to meet some friends of his. It dragged on. How are things with you?'

'Not too bad.'

We go inside. She has the TV on but there's only static showing on it. The volume is up high. It makes a crackling sound.

'How is the bump?' I ask.

'I get cramps now and then but they pass.'

She's six months gone. I'm terrified of how I'll feel when she has the child. It will be like an unwanted visitor in the house.

'You were good to wait up for me.'

'I was worried. You hear horror stories about town at the weekends. There was something on the news about a stabbing in Garden Street.'

'I'm a big boy now. I know how to take care of myself.'

'I didn't mean it like that. How is Tony?'

'The same as ever.'

'You weren't out with a woman, were you?'

Sometimes she cuts to the chase like this.

'Why would you think that?'

'I don't know. Something in me makes me have to ask. It's when you have that look on your face.'

'What look?'

'I don't know. Forget I said anything.'

But how can I? It's always going to be the elephant in the room.

'Tony had a girl. I didn't.'

I can't keep blaming Tony forever. Maybe he's my cover for being me, the snake in the grass that's my own mind.

She sits looking at the static on the television.

'Why don't you turn it off?' I ask. She doesn't answer for a moment, confused at the question.

'How do you mean?'

'The television,' I say.

'Sorry. I hardly knew it was on. I'm in a daze these days.'

'Me too.'

She looks for the remote but she can't find it.

'I'll turn it off.'

Half way across the floor she stops. She clutches her stomach in pain. I move towards her to support her.

'Are you all right?' I say.

'I think so. He's just kicking.'

'It seems a worse one than usual.'

181

'The doctor said to expect it.'

'When are you having your check-up?'

'Next week.'

'Do you want me to go in with you?'

'That would be good.'

I lead her back to the sofa.

'Would you like a drink?' I ask. She shakes her head.

'The doctor said it wouldn't be right.'

'Okay. Don't then.'

'I wish - '

'What?'

'Nothing.''

'You wish I wouldn't drink so much. Isn't that what you were going to say? Well I wish you wouldn't smoke so much.'

She doesn't say anything. I go to the fridge. She's looking at the floor. I open a can of beer.

'Could we talk?' she says suddenly.

'We *are* talking,' I say. 'What do you mean?'

'I don't know. You're like a stranger these days.'

'What do you want to talk about?'

'Nothing in particular. I wish you'd stay in more.'

'When the baby is born I will.'

'Everyone says that.'

'So you don't believe me.'

She puts her face in her hands.

'I'm probably not attractive to you since I got pregnant.'

'What makes you think that?'

'Isn't that what they say? Don't a lot of husbands wander when their wives get pregnant?'

'If this is what you mean by talking I think I'll turn in.'

'Please don't.'

She starts to cry.

'I feel horrible.'

'Why?'

'Since I got pregnant I feel ugly. I think that's what's making you go out so much.'

'Stop it. You're beautiful. Pregnant or not pregnant.'

She takes out a handkerchief. She dries her eyes.

'Keep saying that and you'll believe it.'

'What did you want to talk about?'

'I'd like you to stop you going out with Tony.'

'Why?'

'I know how he thinks about women. How he thinks about me.'

'We don't talk about you. What are you saying?'

'It's the way he looks at me.'

'He likes you. He's always told me that.'

'I thought you said you don't talk about me.'

'That's not talking, it's a viewpoint. Do you have to pick me up on everything?'

'Every time you come back after a night out with him you're in bad form.'

'That's not his fault. It's mine.'

She takes out a cigarette but doesn't light it. It dangles from her lip for a moment. Then she puts it back into the packet.

'Sorry for annoying you. Let's not talk about Tony anymore. '

'Okay.'

She takes another cigarette out. This time she lights it.

'Did Reilly ring about the house?' I ask. Reilly is the auctioneer.

'He did. He said we have them worried. They've gone down a bit in the price. He says we're playing a good game.'

'We have time on our side.'

'He says they think we're losing interest.'

'Let them keep thinking that.'

'I hope it doesn't eat up what you got for your promotion.'

'Money was made to be spent. There's no point putting it under the mattress.'

'This is the first time we've had breathing space for years. Maybe the timing is wrong.'

'The timing is never right for anything in life. You have to move when you feel like it. I need to get out of this kip.'

'Don't say things like that. It's done us all right so far.'

'Has it? You can hardly turn around without bumping into something.'

'It's not as if there are dozens of us.'

'There might be yet,' I say, looking at her stomach.

She laughs.

'Let's get this one out first,' she says.

When we can talk like this it's like we've never had a problem.

'You won't know yourself in the new house,' I say, 'You'll have lots of wardrobe space for your clothes for the first time in your life.'

'And lots of places to hide from you if you come back from Tony in a bad mood.'

I put my arms round her. Sometimes I get tired fighting with her. We've battled so often there have to be better times ahead.

'Would you like a bite to eat?' she asks me.

'I had something in the pub.'

'I'll make you a sandwich if you like.'

'No thanks. I'll just sit here with my beer. I'm going to have an early night tonight. Go up now you if you want. You must be exhausted.'

'I fell asleep a few hours ago but I'm wide awake now.'

'Do you know what time it is? You need your strength for the baby.'

'All right I'll go up so.'

She stands in front of me with a cup of tea in her hands. She seems to be about to say something. Or expecting me to say something.

'I'm sorry,' I say.

'For what?'

'Nothing. Everything.'

She laughs.

'So am I.'

'You have nothing to apologise for.'

'We won't get into that. Anyway I'll go up now. The tiredness is hitting me suddenly. Do you think you'll be up long?'

'I'll just have this one,' I say, gesturing the beer, 'There's no need to stay awake for me. Do you want a hand getting up the stairs?'

'I'm okay thanks.'

She closes the door. I look at the blank television screen. In the street outside a car lurches into gear. I feel a million miles away from her and yet closer to her than any human being. Am I the problem or is it her? It's the situation, I tell myself, it's only a phase. She loves me at the back of it all and I love her. Tonight meant nothing. None of the nights with anybody else meant anything. It's Tony who's the problem. If I can get away from him everything will be good again. He's my bad luck charm.

When I finish my beer I'll go up to her. I'll try to re-kindle what we had, try to look forward to what we're going to have. I'll try and spend more time with her so we can build ourselves up as a unit again. The last few years have been all about me – my traumas, my midlife crisis, the Mount Vesuvius that is my head. I need to focus on the things that matter.

I tell myself life will change when we have an addition to the family. The discipline will be good for me. We won't be as conscious of one another. We'll be a family and I won't want to go out as much. I won't look back to the days when all her time was for me and we had no worries about money or other women or even getting old. I may not want the baby now but everyone says you change when it arrives. It will be important for me to have an extra reason to stay in. It will keep me away from the side of myself that's in love with illusions.

'You might bring me a cup of tea when you're coming up,' she says after what seems like a long time, her voice hoarse from the cigarettes.

I finish my beer and put the kettle on.

Neighbours

Oh yes, the Hanleys,
up with the lark for image
but we know the real story.
She drinks more than she should
and he's as mean as muck.
Pinched little face,
you can tell
he wouldn't spend Christmas.
As for her,
she tipples even with the kids around.
Thank God they'll be raised soon
and not have to face
the argie-bargies.

Don't want to give scandal
but you hear things, don't you?
I mean tongues wag
here in Gawk Street.
Nothing else to do but natter.
Blow your nose
and curtains flutter.
Full of curiosity boxes.
If Osama bin Laden was here
he'd have been found in a week.

He's seeing women too.
Know that for a fact.
My spies have informed me.
Not even lookers.
One like the back of a bus
and the wrong side of thirty.
But that's his business.
I mean the looks,
not the cheating.

Hypocrite.
Wears the knees out of his trousers
every Sunday at Mass.
Gets the pants off elsewhere
on the other days.

I'd say six months
before shit hits fan
and she gives him his P45.
Playing away from home,
can't go on forever.
God love her
she doesn't suspect a thing.
Or maybe she does.
Hence the bottle.
I wonder why she stays.
It's the children I feel for.

You never know people, do you?
Looked so nice when he moved in.
Butter wouldn't melt, like.
Wanted to cut my grass
with his new mower.
I was touched
but maybe he laid it on too much.
I'm not the suspicious type
but you get like that.
Life hardens you.
People become guilty
until proved innocent. Pity.

Beats her too, I think.
She wears some funny eyeliners.
Could be a coincidence,

or else she walks into doors
That's what he wants us to think.
Nudge nudge wink wink.

None of my business?
It is when they put stuff
in my bins.
No excuse for that.
Caught them at it twice:
food bin and general rubbish.
Who's fooling who?
I gave her a look afterwards
but she was too out of it
to notice.
In her PJs at the car. What next?
Self-respect costs nothing
but you can't tell them that.
You'd get more civility from the cat.

The last people were different.
We looked out for each other.
You can't put a price on that.
At Christmas they splurged out
on pressies for us and vice versa
to take the bad look off things.
.

Gone to Canada now.
The recession. Tough.
Oh well, must jolly on.
Deal with what's left.
Spike Milligan said
there are two things
you can't change in life:
neighbours and haemorrhoids.
Neighbours
 are a bigger pain in the arse.

Reunion

Time had deadened her sympathy.
They were people now, not progeny.
Southsiders with posh accents,
they discussed Sudan, the Lebanon,
in tones that seemed to say
she was irrelevant,
a creature of another day.
'You're pale,' they said,
'Have another gin,'
as if this would solve everything.
She indulged
and became a girl again.

There was a time, she thought,
a victim of her memory,
when their trivial little fears
were like nuclear holocausts
to her ears,
a time she would have sacrificed
the magic of her life
for the idiocy of theirs.
Such days are gone.
Detached now, or semi-detached,
she has become a witch to them
a killjoy standing in their light.

Well let it be on their heads,
she thinks,
indulging in her gin again,
solution to the decades of her pain,
laughing, almost,
at this new ability to switch,
in one fell swoop
from matriarch to bitch.

A widow with a bromide,
a complacent old whore
the iron of a thousand Mondays
harden the arteries of her soul.

Rite of Passage

It had never been a simple thing for him growing up. There was a kind of fighting with the universe inside him, almost a masochistic need for conflict.

'He suffers from sensitivity,' his mother used to say. It was as if it was some kind of disease

He was studious as a child, giving everything to the matter in hand, no matter how trivial. If his friends called to the house he hardly noticed them, lost as he was in his world

His mother was the dominant member of the family. She was a woman who quietly indoctrinated her children, a subdued technocrat. Sometimes he fell under her sway and sometimes resisted her. The pendulum swing of their relationship intrigued those who witnessed it.

'After all she does for you,' his father would say if he had a comeuppance with her. He'd be ashamed of himself even if it was of her own making. He might even apologise to her, retreating to her for comfort even though he realised the danger of her suffocating him.

The day he finished his Leaving Cert his father asked him what he planned to do with his life. 'I don't know,' he said.

There was nothing guiding him, nothing moving him in any particular direction. As a boy he'd had a fantasy of being a priest but that died. Afterwards he contemplated going on the missions as a social worker. He didn't know if he was trying to escape something in himself, something that would be blotted out by the helping of others.

In the end he decided to study Arts in the university. It was where most lost souls headed to buy time for themselves when nothing more obvious presented itself.

He watched the endless flow of students parading its corridors, united by an almost demonic sense of purpose. How was it that so many people seemed to know what they wanted so early in life?

In the cafes they talked of anarchy, of dropping out. It was the sixties, the decade of liberation. They spoke of sex as if they invented it.

He began to write poetry, carving words out of his head like a sculptor with stone. In his second year he produced a collection, nursing his words like a mother with a child. He wrote in the classical way but his poems were undercut by a modern sense, a sense of the disconnectedness of things.

The book gave him an exaggerated sense of his importance. He almost expected the world to stop spinning on its axis when it came out.

He spent a lot of his time hanging around town, his hands dug deeply into the pockets of an Air Force jacket he'd picked up in an army surplus store. He rarely talked to people. When he did it was in monosyllables.

He became involved with some drop-outs from the university. they were living in an abandoned house in the inner city. They told him about their fascination with the diseased imagination.

He started dating a girl from the History faculty. She'd already had an abortion, already a string of illicit affairs. Her body was punctured with dope, her mind a prey to every whim. This was fascinating to him. He rose to it like a bait.

'You were too cautious before you met me,' she said. She thought he was terrified of his feelings, of what giving in to them might do to him.

'Just because I don't wear my heart on my sleeve doesn't mean I don't have one,' he said.

'That's exactly what I'm trying to say to you. Put it on your sleeve and see what happens.'

He loved her openness but after a few months living with her it became like a new form of oppression. When you were doing something audacious every day it didn't become audacious any more.

One night when he found her with a needle in her arm. Her eyes were gone back in her head. He thought she was dying. She recovered but the experience changed him. He told her he couldn't live with the uncertainty of what she might do next. He went away from her, went back to his original love, the love of words.

He began to write a novel now, a predictable one maybe, something subconsciously autobiographical. It was the story of a man searching for a mother who deserted him in childhood, a man craving an anchor.

It had his secretiveness in it, the quirks of a style infatuated with its own excesses. He worked at it like a man possessed but it refused to let him finish it. As he read through it he became almost afraid of it. It was as if it had a life independent of him. Sometimes it seemed to have his soul in it. Sometimes it seemed to be sucking that soul out of him. When he got lucky the words flowed onto the pages but there were also times when they mocked him. They were as elusive as a woman.

After he got his degree the question of getting a job presented itself. He wanted to postpone anything smacking of real life. His parents worried about the sense of irresponsibility his studies seemed to have bred in him. He found himself becoming more distant from them. When he talked with them they seemed to kill his mind, kill all creativity. He spent most of his time outside the house. When he wasn't reading he walked the streets, nipping into restaurants for injections of caffeine.

There was a gloom over the city. It was like a physical thing, a black cloud of hesitancy that seemed to dominate everything. People walked with lethargy in the streets, uninterested in anything but the getting through of days.

There was a heatwave. Some days it got so warm he imagined the sun burning up the earth before his eyes. People stopped walking to catch their breath. They got winded even when they were strolling. He watched the sky turning into a kind of milky colour. Everything became foggy.

He looked for a job. Employers didn't want anything to do with him. They saw him as a misfit. When he filled in application forms he put the answers in the wrong boxes. He didn't know if he was doing it deliberately or not. It might have been subconscious.

He was every interviewer's nightmare. He gave the wrong answers there too. Rejection letters arrived in the post with such regularity it became a source of amusement.

It was the seventies. He thought back to the euphoria of the decade before, pining for it even if it was naïve. You could have too much reality.

He sought solace in those who failed to find roots in the same way as himself, drowning himself in the indulgence of it all. They affected a superiority over those who had jobs. Maybe part of it was jealousy. Doing nothing in the university had a kind of licence to it because he was suffused with dreams. Now he was just a malcontent in people's eyes, a loser.

One night at a party he took an overdose, heaping a pile of barbiturates into himself. He didn't take enough to do any damage. Most people saw it as the proverbial cry for help but in his own mind he'd meant it.

'What possessed you?' his mother said when she saw him in the hospital with tubes coming out of him. She was more hysterical than he'd ever seen her before.

'I don't know,' he said.

'You don't know why you wanted to die? What kind of an attitude is that?'

'I was out of my mind,' he said, 'It won't happen again.' She believed him but he wasn't sure if he believed himself. Sometimes he thought he didn't know his own mind.

'Nobody in the hospital seems to want to know what's wrong with me,' he said to the nurse who'd been taking care of him.

'You're low priority,' she said, 'They look on you as a university brat.'

'Which of course I am,' he said.

He was attracted to her, to the way her hair fell down on her shoulders. She had kind eyes.

They made smalltalk. She said her name was Maria.

'You wouldn't be interested in coming for a drink with me sometime, would you?' he said.

She was amused.

194

'Why do Irish people always put a negative into a question?' she said.

'I haven't a clue,' he said, 'Is that negative enough of an answer for you?'

They went out a few times. Most of their nights involved her telling him about her past. She said she was trying to fix a broken heart. He told her his was broken too.

'Maybe we can heal one other,' she said. He said she sounded like a character out of a soap opera.

He enjoyed her company. She put no demands on him.

She exuded serenity. Nothing could bother her. She sat like a bird as life became chaotic around her.

'What's your secret?' he said. She said she didn't have one. It was just the way she was made.

They spent most of their time in her flat. Often they didn't talk. They looked into the embers of a fire as records played in the background. He felt he was back in the sixties. On other nights they argued. Her serenity became too much for him sometimes. It came across as smugness. There were times when he started arguments merely for the sake of it. Maybe he was trying to uproot her from her stability. He'd be remorseful afterwards. He'd forget what the arguments were about.

He spent long spells away from her. He didn't think he was ready to commit himself to a relationship in the long term. He didn't see himself as the marrying kind. University friends warned him about clingy women.

His parents liked her because she stabilised him. They thought all nurses were beacons of sanity. She had a wild side too but she didn't show it to many people.

Sometimes he felt they were too close to one another. He thought of her like a drug he needed and then needed to get off. Her own attitude was more straightforward. She didn't put any pressure on him to commit himself to her.

He wandered around the streets like a war veteran, his mouth twisted into a kind of stunted articulation. There were times when Dublin had seemed like an ocean of possibilities to him, the only place where he could really be himself. Now it was no more than a place to live. He watched couples courting on the benches of Stephen's Green and longed for a return to the person he'd been when he first entered the university. Jadedness had crept in. He longed for the fantasies he'd nurtured when he was a child, somebody in love with great philanthropies.

'Why do you fight with yourself?' Maria asked him one night when he was unusually quiet with her.

'I'm not aware I'm doing it,' he said, 'I get bored with things are going too smoothly.'

'What kind of things?'

'What we do every day, day in day out.'

'You can't avoid routine. The most important people in the world have it. The President, the Pope. Why should you be different?'

He began to build his days around her. He told her things about himself that he'd been too inhibited to share with anyone before. The more time they spent together the more she drifted into a part of him he hadn't known existed.

One night she told him he was different to all the other men she knew. when he asked her why that was she said, 'Because you didn't try to get me into bed with you.'

He didn't know what to say to that.

'You're afraid of me that way, aren't you?' she said, 'If you got me pregnant it would probably make you think you'd have to marry me.'

'Would you think that?'

'No. It would change nothing.'

'What if I didn't get you pregnant?'

'I don't mind if we go on forever as we are.'

They did, but he felt it couldn't work that way indefinitely. All relationships had to move in one direction or another. go forward. If they didn't, something got in the way. Life. And so it happened.

Another man came into her life, a doctor she knew from her training days. She started seeing him. She said he was only a friend but he didn't believe it.

They broke up. The first few weeks away from her were almost like a liberation to him. It was as if his university friends were right, that she'd been a bind, a yoke around his neck.

Then the deprivation set in, the old feeling he'd had of her being a drug. He searched for alternatives to fill the void. Drink worked for a while but then it became a bigger problem than the void itself. Then he started living with other women. None of them matched her but he couldn't admit that to himself.

He went to Australia for a year. He worked for a television station that produced wild life programmes. Maria stopped seeing the doctor. They kept in phone contact.

After he left Australia he went to Europe. She told him he needed to settle somewhere. He said he would but once the thirst for travel got into him it was like a self-perpetuating need. It had to be filled over and over again.

He spent some time in London as a library assistant. Then he went to Greece. The people there were fascinated by him, by his Irishness. What did being Irish mean, he wondered. That he was screwed up?

He did farming in Tuscany. He became a lover of nature, of the way the sun went down in strange places. He travelled for the sake of it, not staying anywhere too long.

Women warmed to him. They sensed something to mother in his lostness, his reserve. Some of them wanted to possess him but he couldn't commit to them. The adventurer in him was never fully satisfied with them. He retreated to the sanctuary of other places when they got too close to him.

At the back of his mind there was always the pining for Maria. He resisted it, seeking instead the company of those who didn't know what it was to love, only to make love. In bed at night his body tossed endlessly between the sheets, his mind a mass of contradictions.

Occasionally he threw himself into his writing again, looking at his manuscripts sometimes the way a woman might look at an aborted child, as a part of himself he'd flushed out to nothingness, something that came from nowhere and went nowhere.

When he got to thirty he spent some time in the army. He thought its regimentation might cure him of his restlessness but it didn't work like that. He resented being told what to do. He got into trouble because of his insolence.

He felt he was running out of things to do. Would he stay away forever or come home? He thought of Ireland again, the old sow that ate her farrow as James Joyce had once put it. If he went back he wondered whether it would be from desire or need. He promised himself he'd only go back if he had to.

'We're lonely for you,' his mother said to him one night on the phone, 'We're not going to be around forever.'

In the end he thought it was guilt that brought him home. He resented the interruption in his life. He was stern with his parents for the first few weeks but then he mellowed. Both of them were in poor health. He became as much a carer to them as a son.

The country he returned to was different to the one he'd left. It seemed to be overladen with perversity, a will to death. People moved with brashness, irresponsibility. In the bars he saw a generation growing vindictive almost without being aware of it, a generation defined more by what it was aggressive to than by any other quality.

The aftermath of liberalism had left its mark. Marriages were abandoned like you'd abandon a household pet that turned on you, relationships were terminated like the end of a musical beat. It was as if two people had woken up simultaneously from a bad dream.

He postponed contacting Maria. It wasn't because he didn't care about her. It was because he cared too much.

One night he ran into an old acquaintance from the university. He told him she'd had a child some years before. He was shocked. Could it be his? If it was, why hadn't she told him about it? Maybe she felt it would place a burden on him, the burden of returning to her without wanting to.

He didn't visit her until he'd been home a few weeks. He wasn't sure how he'd be received. Would she be welcoming to him? Would there be some other man in her life?

She was living in an artisan dwelling in Ringsend. He was nervous approaching it. He had to steel himself before he rang her bell.

When she opened the door it was as if he'd never seen her before. It was a few seconds before he was aware of her beauty. He wanted to put his arms around her but something held him back.

'I can't believe it's you,' she said. Behind her a young child romped around a kitchen.

He asked her if he could come in. She said, 'I think I can extend you that courtesy.'

He went into her sitting-room. The child looked at him as if he was some kind of alien.

Four years, he thought, four years he fought the absence of her, four years that could have become a lifetime. Did she want him back? Would she tell him if she did?

They didn't know what to say to one another. Instead they just laughed at her son, laughed stupidly as he turned a toy upside down and then fell on top of it.

He saw himself in him. There was the same frenzied confusion about the eyes. It was as if the world had betrayed both of them.

In the dagger-cold of winter she married him. It sobered him into the acceptance of what was left over when you have no stamina left for excess.

He was quiet with her most nights. The city was quiet too. It seemed to go to sleep, content after all the decades of strife to become implacable again.

Their evenings sank into a cocoon of unambitiousness. The tumultuous tides of history were less important to him now than the small events of his days. The routine he once hated was now to be welcomed.

Maybe, he thought sometimes, his childhood dancing like a flame inside his head, maybe it was something to do with the passing of the years, with a death that felt like a regeneration.

He watched her son – their son - playing on the carpet. He thought of a boy who would be moulded by a world saner if not more ecstatic than the one he knew. He wondered if he'd forgive him for his absence as he grew up. And if she would forgive him.

They would cope somehow, he told her in the nakedness of the dawn, and one day if she was patient enough, as patient as she'd been during the years of his travelling, one day maybe he would return to the innocent he always was and, throwing his arms around her searchingly, invest her with his love.

Feministy Stuff

Two drinks and she's anyone's.
Three and she's everyone's.
That's about it really.
The ladette culture.
Always thought it a bit funny
calling depravity culture
but there you are.

It wasn't done in my day.
I can tell you that for nothing.
Women were women then, not slags.
They didn't wear dresses   .
up to their arses.
You have to leave something
to the imagination.

Of course live-ins
are all the rage nowadays.
No one bothers
with marriage any more
When they do
it's like a temporary arrangement.
'I'll stay with you
till you piss me off,'
that kind of thing.
Then 'I'm out of here'
and off to the solicitor with them
for the big pay-off.

My own good lady
comes from the old school.
We didn't do anything
till we jumped the broom.

That's the problem with people now,
They want everything yesterday.
Whatever happened to
deferred gratification?
If you get the honeymoon
before the wedding,
life is an anti-climax.
Girls have to set the example
for men who'd go to bed
with anything in a skirt.

My first girlfriend used to slap me
if I ever went above the knee
when I was courting her.
That was the deal.
I stuck to it - reluctantly.

Her mother used to say to her,
'Don't come home with anything
you didn't go out with.'
Today they're having babies
before you can say
'Brace yourself, Brigid.'

I know this lass
who's been on the mailboat
three times in as many years.
She goes to Liverpool.
There must be some quack over there
who does the dirty in a back street.

Have seven sprogs myself.
Nothing wrong with the old mojo, eh?
Herself says it's the only holiday
she ever gets from me.

My missus doesn't mind me
having a gargle
as she reproduces.
'You'll be seeing them long enough
after they come out,'
she tells me.

I haven't been to her deliveries.
I'd probably pass out.
Don't go for this New Man stuff.
Nuisances is a better word for them.
They're doing everything
but cutting the cord.
Jesus, one of the breed
will produce a nipper yet.

When that day comes
I'll happily perform a hara-kiri
on myself
without an anaesthetic.

Neophyte

As the lovers struggled onwards
to their distant purposes
I held you,
clutched at destinies.
As the schooners sailed sublimely
to their foreign shores
I watched you,
furled in fortitude,
a winsome kind of plaything now
a wife.
With seaspray in your hands
a stargaze in your eyes
you ran to me,
a sadder,
more amenable resort
a central heated nullity
though yet you were
too young,
too rich
to know.

What Lies Beneath

Winter came suddenly, snow tufting the edges of the rose-bushes, the wind with a sucking in it as it tore slates from the roofs. The football games have been cancelled. Old men on park benches blow smoke into the air. I watch teenagers straddling bicycles along the icy roads. The evening has a cleanliness in it, a wiping away of the sultriness of summer. The air is white.

I sit in my room and reminisce. It's like this every night. I enjoy being away from people. I'm my own protection, free from the scars of the past.

The trees look rigid. The branches reach outward for something indefinable. They're like the men frozen on the benches, frozen in time. The sun is like a football as it goes down. It's the last gesture of warmth on an insulated evening. On the pond I hear the ice crackle as children skate along on it. Their voices screech like out-of-tune violins, plangent and then dim.

The park attendant appears. He's a gruff-faced man with a whistle around his neck. He throws bread crumbs to the birds. They peck at them greedily. Two beggars argue about who owns a coin. When they start to fight it rolls into a gutter. Afterwards they fight even more heatedly.

A man who comes here every day starts to fall asleep. He has to be tipped on the shoulder to leave. A sheepdog snaps at his trousers. He wants him to play but there's no play left in him. Hunch-backed he slinks home, transported more by the force of the wind than his energy. I try to write his history in my mind. Sometimes I imagine he's my husband.

He sits tensely on his bench, his hands held tightly around a lunchbox. I see him as a man denied in love, a dreamer frustrated by the currents of time. Or maybe he's someone who's learned to regret his inability to love, a man who dies with every sun.

The streets are filling up now. The buildings stand out like sculpture in the clear night, encased inside their symmetry. Traffic hums quietly around me with its spider-like pace.

I watch drivers in their trucks. They sit behind steering wheels with a bored look on their faces, expecting nothing from a winter's night in the city. A newspaper boy is shrieking about a coup in Spain, a rise in the price of petrol. Nobody is listening. Exhaust fumes cough at me like human things.

Maybe he'll return to me tonight, tonight for no more reason than any other night. To ask him to come back would be like asking him why he went away. It would be a non-question. But I need to ask it. Women always need to ask.

I feel something special in the air tonight. It's a night in which anything could happen, a night in which a man could recognise a mistake and come back to something he deserted a long time ago. It's a night when you can be content with little things, with anything that might wash away your fear.

What would I say to him if he came back? That the flowers came into bloom? That I became old and unbeautiful? That I needed him, despite how pathetic that sounds for the modern woman?

No doubt I'd drive him away again with my need. Or else he'd be just coming back for an experiment. To see how I was. Out of that vague curiosity he might have when other women momentarily fail to satisfy him.

I tell myself I don't need him anymore, that I need nothing now, nothing except the adventure of my mind. But deep down I know I don't believe that.

The wind is getting stronger, grinding itself against the trees as if it's trying to uproot them. It moves eel-like through the room like a burglar.

I look at his photographs on the wall. His eyes used to follow me around the room once. Now they avoid me.

When I fall asleep I dream about him. My dreams are always of the early days of getting to know one another. That's the happy time for me, the time he was all over me, when everything I said or did seemed to enthrall him.

It's morning when I wake up. I listen to the sound of a factory opening up for the day, the whirring of a drill singing into wood. Machinery clanks like the siren of a police car.

Workers make their way in the doors in huddles, their voices wafting up to my room. I hear them discussing economic cutbacks, rises in tax. Sometimes they look up at me, they look up at this strange woman who gazes at them through her curtains as though she has nothing better to do. And she doesn't.

Cars groan to life. I watch them beginning their journeys towards obscure destinations, so many beasts of burden moving reluctantly along dark streets. I envy the people in them. Where are they going? To what jobs? What rendezvous? Sometimes I decide to go away with them but when I have my bags packed I change my mind. I tell myself it's more comfortable here, that beauty is around me. Even if it's the beauty of sadness.

The showers are beginning again. Rain falls like fingertips on galvanised roofs. It will continue all morning. Then it'll stop. It will seem emptied of purpose. It will be as if there's no good reason for it to go on. I listen to it falling inside the trees. Birds skulk on the branches. They seem to beckon me to fly away with them, to fly away and be with him wherever he is.

We're in Greece, in Spain. I hear the click of flamenco dancers on a ballroom floor. Colours are flashing before my eyes. When we get to France he puts on a trenchcoat. We giggle together over our ignorance of the language.

'I love you,' I say. He smiles.

I don't know how long after that it is when we marry. When we cross the threshold he orders me to swear slavery to him. It's a joke. I give out to him for it but secretly I want to be owned.

Our life together is one of contrast. He's the travelled one and I'm the homebody. He says that's about to change now that he's married but it doesn't.

One night I find out he's been with another woman. He doesn't confirm or deny it. I forgive him. Or maybe I just go into denial. I know there are others. He doesn't have a problem living a double life. He's out a lot of nights. I stop asking him what he does on these nights. It's boring listening to his lies.

Another night he carries a bottle of whiskey home in his pocket. When I spill it down the sink he hits me. Afterwards he begs forgiveness. It's no good. He's crossed a line. I didn't think he was capable of that. Now that I know he is, things can never be the same again.

That's how it ends between us. I don't kick him out. He just drifts away from me. I don't know which of us he hates most, me or himself. I hear he's with someone else now. I'd take him back but I can't say that to him.

What's my next move? Do I have one?

'You think too much,' my doctor says to me, 'You need to surrender yourself to the moment.' She says to watch the wonders of the dawn. 'The dew,' she says, 'looks like diamonds in the rain.' Isn't that beautiful?

She gives me pills. Every time I swallow one of them they bring him back to me. His footsteps are louder than the pounding of my heart.

Foreign Affair

From the hilltops of the Abruzzi
to the communes of Nepal
you carried a torch for me.
The sky blazed fiercely above us.
The sun shone on scenes
that were already half fading
even as they happened.

I fought a war inside myself.
You were like an accessory,
amused by mv awkwardness
as I checked deadlines
to my other life.
Together we immersed ourselves
in a madcap odyssey of pain,
my battered heart
carrying us through countries
we felt we owned
merely by visiting them.

On the journey home
I looked at a photograph of you
and found myself shivering
with a kind of dazed relief.
It had you sitting in a field
surrounded by sheep.

You seemed to be seeing through them.
You always had that clairvoyant sense.
It was what frightened me
about you.

That doesn't matter now.
The sun still breaks

over the harbor wall.
The sailors still stalk
the pier
with the kind of crassness
we once tried to emulate.
Meanwhile you've returned
to an old flame
with a winter face.

I was a man
who dated you
for two whole months
while each of us
etched in our future
without realizing
what lay ahead of us
on that forgettable Tuesday
in the museum
when you looked up at me
with shock
and we shared the ecstasy
of hope.

Cormac

Those early autumn nights were always tinged with promise, anticipation wafting through the air like a human thing as you made your way up the steps to the campus bar. Cormac would always be standing there with the inevitable Gauloise dangling from his lips, muttering 'What's your poison, man?' as he walked to the counter for as many neat whiskies as he could stomach.

He had a permanent array of witticisms on his lips in those days. Listening to him in full flight I was reminded of what Oscar Wilde must have been like in his prime. By the end of the night he'd standing on a table reciting Ginsberg. Or, if he was up to it, his own demented ravings. He was able to compose poems on the spot. Short stories took him a little longer. I envied him his talent but he disavowed it. We never respect what comes easily to us in life.

I was usually as drunk as he was at these parties. Sometimes he brought a guitar with him. He belted out every song he ever knew, his voice getting more raucous with each drink.

We were young then. We could cope with the hangovers. Often on the following mornings we'd have a hair of the dog, or many hairs. We stayed together in a flat in Swinford. He was usually up at the crack of dawn with a ready smile on his lips.

'Well, old buddy,' he'd say, 'We didn't need to go to Lourdes to get the cure.'

It helped that our excesses had an academic base. We'd have dog-eared paperbacks of people like Roland Barthes or Merleau-Ponti sticking out of the back pockets of our Levis, or some banned book we smuggled over from Holyhead on the boat after yet another drinking spree there with our equally dissolute friends. We'd discuss things like 'The Death of the Novel' for hours and then throw up over our Heineken. It didn't matter that most of our conversations were balderdash. You could get away with anything as long as you pronounced it properly.

When Sheila arrived in my life, Cormac's attitude to me changed. Two was company and three was a crowd. We'd been so close before that I was taken aback. Some people who knew us even thought we were gay. He was the first person I met on campus. Three years later he was still my best friend.

Sheila shattered the bond we had without realising it. She wasn't the first girl I was ever involved with but she was the first who posed a threat to my relationship with him. He'd had a lot of girlfriends but they slotted themselves into the life we had together rather than threatening to replace it.

I needed to be with Sheila seven days a week. 'I fell for her at second sight,' I told people. The first time I was out of my mind with cider. She was crushingly bored by me.

I thought I was being entertaining with her. She told me afterwards she was within an ace of slapping me in the face. When I sobered up enough to ask her out I realised what great beauty lay in those untouched features. Either because of these or her incredible nonchalance she became like a drug to me.

Cormac could only chortle when I talked about her. For him she was one of my well-known Ten Day Infatuations. Either he believed this or he pretended to himself that he did. But my infatuation with her didn't go away in ten days. Or ten weeks.

We were married within a year of meeting each other. I hadn't a cent in the bank or any prospect of a job. I'd rammed my final exams. She said if we cared enough about each other that didn't matter.

'What do you plan to live on?' Cormac asked me, 'Fresh air?'

I was shocked at his attitude. He'd always thought money grew on trees. If he wanted something it was never an object. But then he was always good at quoting scripture for his purpose. He wanted to hold on to me for his binges. Most of his other friends had drifted into jobs by now.

'You're turning into a choirboy,' he informed me.

He pretended to be glad for me when I started giving English grinds to earn a crust. He was a poor actor and I didn't fall for it. Sheila had a job minding children in a crèche. I wasn't sure how he survived financially. It was probably because of his parents. They were well off and indulged him. Maybe a bigger problem for him was me going off the drink. When I met him now our conversations were less felicitous. I knew he blamed Sheila, 'the ball and chain.'

She was as practical as I was reckless but I sensed that we'd last the pace together somehow. She had a contempt for the slings and arrows of life that seems to render them impotent. Nothing could dent her composure. She didn't care enough about anything to let it. She lived her life 'as grass grows on the weir.'

Her feelings for me were another matter. I didn't analyse them too much in case they disappeared. As long as she continued to hang around that was enough. I convinced myself she'd grow on me.

Cormac's resentment grew with time. He trotted out the old line about an Irish queer being someone who would walk over a bottle of Guinness for a woman. I used to say that kind of thing too when we were in college. We were supposed to be growing up now. Was he still locked in that bubble? Was he afraid of growing up?

To protect myself from his abuse I tried to turn him into me. I arranged dates for him with women I knew who might quieten him down. It was a forlorn hope. They usually failed miserably. On these nights he usually went out of his way to be as obnoxious as possible. It was a throwback to our irresponsible past. I wasn't amused.

Then Jo turned up. Sheila knew her from school. She was almost as intellectually aggressive as he was and that was saying something. He liked her for her spirit. She wasn't afraid of him and gave as good as she got. Was this the woman who could finally tame him? I watched them sussing each other out like boxers before a prize fight, each looking for weaknesses in the other that they could exploit. They traded insults merrily, the frequency of them rendering them harmless. Anyone who looked at them from a distance thought they'd probably gouge each other's eyes out one day but I saw a tenderness growing between them. It was more powerful for being subtle.

Jo also allowed Cormac into her bed. That was usually the quickest way to lose him but this time it didn't.

The longer they stayed together the more people's curiosity grew. What was her secret? Maybe the fact that she didn't have a plan to hook him. Previous girlfriends tried strategies with him but he always saw through them. Jo was just herself. He wasn't able to bully her because she saw him for the child he was. The fact that she seemed to love that child was the bonus.

They decided early on that they wouldn't marry. They existed in a limbo together, throwing wild parties that went on till the dawn and then sleeping through the following day as they got ready for the next one. People arrived at their flat unannounced. They stayed days or even weeks. Sometimes Cormac followed them back to where they lived, either in Ireland or out of it. Sometimes Jo went with him and sometimes she didn't.

I told Sheila they were the only hippies I ever knew. Other people played at it but they were the real deal. She thought they were going to spontaneously combust. 'Once the excitement dies down,' she predicted, 'they'll have nothing to fall back on.' Just this once I hoped her practical woman's logic was on the blink.

Money became a problem for them. Cormac's weekly drinking bill was like most people's annual budget. Then there were the months he was away from her getting up to God knows what as he busked his way around France with all sorts of deadbeats. The photographs he sent home from these escapades were enough to let both of us know this leopard hadn't changed his spots.

When his funds ran out he always seemed to have friends to rescue him. It was like the way you'd take in a stray dog. Nobody could ever say no to Cormac. The lower he fell, the more people queued up to mop his brow.

It was probably inevitable that he'd go back to his old ways of bedhopping. I'd been at parties in the flat they shared together where I'd see him pawing some student he was getting ready to seduce. Jo tried her best to look the other way. By now she was working as a secretary in one of the plusher insurance offices in town.

'It's not the Ritz,' she said, 'It's either that or starve.'

He was more interested in his liquid diet. I wondered how long he could go on before doing a Brendan Behan on himself. Every few months he 'd sign himself in somewhere to get dried out. Then he'd go on the wagon for a while. He inevitably fell off it when the temptation to imbibe got too much. On the odd occasions when he didn't succumb he became self-destructive in other ways. I saw him doing wheelies on corkscrew bends in his Volvo that would have been a challenge to Evel Knievel. His window had a sign on it that said, 'Don't Come Near This Vehicle If You Want to Live.'

We only saw one another by appointment now. If he deigned to talk to me on the street he'd usually make some sardonic jibe about Sheila and myself. It was often a kind of veiled reference to me having sold out with her. I'd catch the innuendo but pretend not to. He 'd try to cushion it by inviting us round to his next party.

Jo bore through it all like a martyr. Occasionally there were murmurs of discontent from her. He'd quash them almost before they were voiced. Either she was afraid of him or she still loved him or both. She might have been perversely fascinated by his excesses. Most of the other people he knew were.

Only tenuously was I a part of his world now. I tended to conk out at his bashes around midnight. That was when they were just warming up.

One night he threw what amounted to a wife-swapping party. It was one of those ones where everyone threw their key-ring into a basket and it was twirled around. People had to close their eyes and dip in. The idea was that you went home with the person whose keys you picked out. He embraced it with glee. Apparently he'd seen it in a film once. When I told him I wasn't going to join in he called me every kind of puritan under the sun. I doubted he really wanted to play either. It was the concept that appealed to him. He liked embarrassing us.

A crazy kind of bravado made him continue to cheat on Jo. I felt he wanted to be caught and one night he was. She found him with an au pair in their bedroom. He'd never had sex with a woman in the house before. For Jo it was a bridge too far. Her nerves weren't good at the time. She went bananas and threw him out. He got a shock at her reaction. So did I. Their relationship, I thought, was just about absurd enough to last. I imagined them in old age saying, 'Nobody could have had more problems than us. That's why we're so good at dealing with them.'

The next time I saw Jo she looked beaten. Out of some kind of mawkish loyalty I pleaded with her to take him back.

'Hell will freeze over first,' she said.

I'd heard stories about him being distraught without her.

'He'll kill himself if you don't go back to him,' I said.

'He'll kill himself anyway. What's the difference?'

'The difference is he loves you.'

She went quiet at that.

'Would you not give him another chance?' I said.

'I've given him a hundred. Each time it gets worse. Maybe he gets a charge out of it, this pathetic woman hanging off him, trying to stop him pulling the plug.'

He called in to me a few days later looking sheepish.

'She's finished with me,' he said.

'You asked for it.'

'That doesn't mean I wanted it.'

'What's next?'

'You tell me. You were always the ideas man.'

'Just now I'm out of them.'

I tried to contact him over the next few weeks but I got nowhere. He wouldn't answer his phone. Anytime I called to him he was either out or not interested in opening the door.

The last time I saw him he was working in an inner city car park pocketing the spare coins drivers threw at him for looking after their vehicles. It was a joke. There was a time I thought he could have run the country. Now he was just a step away from the drunk tank.

He threw his arms around me when he saw me.

'A blast from the past!' he beamed. I tried to return his hug but the stench of brandy from his breath nearly knocked me out.

'I can't believe you're doing this,' I said. He said he was fed up trying to live up to other people's expectations.

'For the first time in my life I feel truly content,' he said. He reached into the pocket of his coat and fished out a set of coins. Half of them went rolling around on the ground. He went down on all fours trying to retrieve them but they fell into a drain.

'How's Jo?' he asked with mock-casualness.

I didn't know what to say. She'd just got married to an architect from the midlands.

'The same as ever,' I said, 'Obviously concerned about you.'

'Oh but of course.'

'She never stops asking about you,' I said. It wasn't true. I wanted to say it because I felt she loved him more than she was admitting.

'She's kept all your writings from way back,' I added. That wasn't true either, though she used to read some of them to me now and then when she was feeling nostalgic.

'I'm writing The Great Irish Novel in my spare time,' he said. I didn't know if he was joking or not. Anything was possible with him now.

He saw a car coming in.

'Must go,' he said, breezing off, 'Adios amigo.'

He started hassling a motorist for a few coins. I didn't know whether to laugh or cry.

I found myself in the same car park a few weeks later in the middle of some forgotten task. I expected to see him. I wasn't looking forward to it but I needn't have worried. Someone else had taken his place.

'Where's the guy that used to be here?' I asked.

'He was arrested,' I was informed, 'for trying to pick someone's pocket. A fight broke out and he got stabbed. Did you know him? Apparently he was a bit of a character.'

'Was?'

'I'm not sure if he pulled through.'

That was how I heard the news. I wasn't sure how to take it. Had he brought it on himself? Had the real Cormac died years before?

I rang Jo. She was philosophical.

'I can't grieve properly,' she said, 'He hurt me too much.'

At the funeral we tried to be jolly for his sake but it didn't work. Most of us just felt sick, especially Jo. She thought she could have done more to save him. The rest of us knew that would have been impossible. He was the most stubborn man I ever met.

'You'd have walked on water for him if he treated you any way decently,' I said to her at the graveside.

'Maybe the problem was that he wanted to walk on water himself.'

'For a long time he seemed to.'

In the following nights I tried to get my mind off him. That was easier said than done. He owned us as much in death as life. One night I had a dream about him. I was trying to murder him in it. What Freudian message was I trying to give myself by that? Sheila held my hand to try and stop me shivering.

'You blame yourself for everything that happened, don't you?' she said.

Maybe I did. I'd been there since the beginning, I'd egged him on and when the heat got too much I backed off. Maybe it was true what he said about me being a choirboy. The bottom line was that I ran out of energy sooner than he did. That's probably why I'm still here.

Compromise

In the end we all surrender.
We substitute fire with ice
the scream for the whisper
life for the analysis of life
the scratch for the itch
the slug for the sip
the peck for the kiss
the moon for the sun
the bite for the taste
the cat for the dog.

I turned sideways
on the road to her,
tore a gearbox asunder
as I looked for her.
She was cool and hot.
That was when I didn't know
what was good for me.
Her memory outshone the enigma
of being with her.
Theorists explained this to me
as I nursed a broken heart
on a stony beach
somewhere near Barcelona.

This is a metaphor for all of life,
even the religious impulse
or artistic achievement -
sculpture, music, dance,
rounding the Cape of Good Hope
or being nice to children.

What we're left with
after families sunder
is dead wood,
the dull aftertaste of want
as your heart collapses
and you crumble
like a deck of cards
someone has shuffled
the wrong way.
And yet you have the surge
towards tomorrow…
if it comes.

Beckett told us to fail better
but failing worse
is more fun.

Done Deal

So it was ending this simply. Relief nudged out the pain he felt, the agony of anticipation dulled into this bland complacency.

'What will you do now, go back to Scunthorpe?'

'Does it matter? Don't worry, I won't be annoying you wherever I am.'

'That's not what I meant. You need a change of atmosphere.'

'Maybe I'll slit my wrists. That would make it tidier for you, wouldn't it? Then you wouldn't be walking away from anything.'

His face became sullen. It was like that of a censured boy. 'I didn't ask for this to happen. We always agreed that if it did we'd behave like adults.'

'That's right. There would be no malice on my part and no guilt on yours. What am I expected to do - handstands?'

Elaine had been right after all. There was no point coming here. She'd have her pound of flesh.

'I was trying to explain myself to you, that's all.'

'There's nothing to explain. I don't even know what you're doing here tonight.'

'I'm going back tomorrow. I didn't want to leave without seeing you.'

'Is this the part where we get out our handkerchiefs?'

He wondered if she'd always had this poison in her. Had he been blind to it before?

'Where would you be without your hatred?' he said, 'Sometimes I think you enjoy it. You'll have to find a new target for it when I'm gone.'

'Finding targets for hatred in this town is never very difficult, ducky.'

They sat in silence as the night stretched out around them. On the dance floor couples weaved in and out of one another. .

'Did she twist your arm or was it mutual?' she said after a while.

'What are you talking about?'

'I heard you're going back with her.' So it wasn't only in Dublin that gossip spread.

'Who told you that?'

'A little bird.' She was almost smiling now. She had a new power over him.

'The little bird was wrong,' he said, 'There's nothing definite. She came over for the trip, that's all. If you think she's anything to do with what's happening between us you're wrong.'

'How pathetic you are. Why do you always play the sheep? I might respect you more if you owned up to yourself.'

'What do you mean by that?'

'She's not that shameful. You don't have to apologise for her.'

'Now you're being ridiculous,' he said, but his face told a different story. He'd always felt guilty about her. She was an escape hatch for him, a way of avoiding confrontation with his other self.

'Did she bring the manacles with her?' she chided. He thought she must have been enjoying herself now.

'Your parents will be relieved too,' she went on. 'No doubt they'll see her as rescuing you from me.' His mother disapproved of her ever since she found them in bed together one weekend. After that she was just a 'hussy' in her eyes. That one weekend probably knocked a year off her life. Was there anything as obnoxious as the mind of a reactionary old woman?

'If you're going to go on like this I'm leaving.'

'I'm sorry. I can't help it. Of course you always knew I was a bitch, right?'

'Don't do this, please.'

'I mean you've behaved so honourably in the whole business, haven't you? You with your nobility. It's making me feel doubly worse.'

Her words droned on like a song out of key. His mind blanked out. He dragged on a cigarette as the tapestry of the summer crystallised itself before him. It seemed unreal to him now. It was like another life. He might have been here three years rather than three months. The time had crawled by like a film in slow motion. A few weeks ago he thought he wouldn't have been able to tear himself away from the place. Now he hardly cared one way or the other.

She sat across the table from him like a judge, her eyes burning a hole in his head. It would have been easier if she hit him, anything rather than this relentless wearing down. And yet what did it matter? There was only the night to be got through. Then he'd be free.

Tomorrow he'd return to the world of normality, a world that had in it a cushion against dreams, a cushion against the destruction of dreams.

'Would you like a drink?' he said, anything to deflect the derision of her sarcasm.

'If you think you can stand my presence for that long.'

He thought about the early days, the days when she was an obsession to him, how he used to follow her everywhere she went, intent on witnessing every movement, every thought. He'd watch her on stage and be fascinated and repulsed almost at the one time, a kind of animal grace in her as she slunk across it in her leopardskin suits to titillate the men in the front row. One night she promised to give it up for him but he talked her out of it, telling her it was what she did best.

Was this why he was leaving her now, because she shocked the puritan in him? He sampled her like an exotic dish and was returning to the bacon and cabbage of his existence. 'You'll marry a virgin,' she said to him one night, 'like all the emigrants who become promiscuous for a while when they're away from the womb of mother. Or who want to swap one womb for another.' The remark had stung him, probably because he couldn't deny it.

He looked at the couples on the dance floor again. The last dance was being called. It highlighted the difference between those accompanied and those alone. He knew the feeling. In a few moments the single ones would come to the bar. They'd drink until they were approached by one of the hostesses. It was the way it was each night in this house of dreams, a series of Master Cards procuring love on the instalment plan before the taxi ride home to domesticity.

'Will you stay here after I go?' he asked.

'Any better suggestions?'

'You're too good for this.'

'Try telling that to my bank manager.'

'So that's what it is all about – money?'

'That's right. Money that buys happiness. By the hour.'

He looked at the syringe marks on her arms, the lines under her eyes. 'You're not happy,' he said, 'Don't fool yourself.'

'I was talking about my clients.'

He thought he saw some frailty in her, some warmth. Could he leave her with a clear conscience after creating a need in her she didn't know she could ever have?

'So you don't matter.'

'All right, I'll rephrase that. Money that can make misery less miserable. That applies to those of us on both sides of the transaction.'

She looked pleased with herself at this conclusion; it seemed to take the harm out of how she spent her days. But then her expression changed again.

'Come to think of it, though, you're right,' she said, 'I'm probably really just a nymphomaniac at heart.'

He felt an anger burning inside him.

'Why are you destroying yourself? Is life that repulsive?'

'Don't judge me unless it makes you feel better about your own life. I thought you would have spared me that speech tonight. Tonight above all nights. Don't forget your halo as you leave.'

'Why are you being like this? I loved you. You know that.'

'I do but it's the past tense, isn't it?'

'Maybe it's the present too.'

'Sure,' she said, 'Don Juan reincarnated. So what do you do to the women you *don't* love – marry them? No, what you were in love with was the idea of converting me. Converting me to your own banality.'

She felt purged of something, the abuse acting as an antidote to his desertion of her. Maybe she even felt relieved. He might have saved her from a worse fate by leaving her. The more she thought about it, the more she felt there was something trivial about all the nights they'd spent together. There was nothing lost because there'd been nothing there to begin with except mutual convenience. He

224

tried to think of something to say to her, something that would make the night more than this limbo. But his mind was empty now.

The house lights came up. A man beckoned her from across the room. She went over to him. After a moment a few other men appeared, the ones who organised her contracts for her, dark-suited figures who were always in the background, men who seemed to arrive always in the dead of night, who seemed to watch her even when she was on her own time. He'd mentioned this to her from time to time but she was hardly aware of it.

She came back a few minutes later with Giuseppe. He was the man who organised most of her contacts for her, the only visible authority figure in the whole operation. Though his name was Italian he spoke almost with an Etonian accent, making people conclude he was born in England. She used to date him once. There was talk of marriage for a while. Was he still carrying a torch for her?

'I have to go,' she said nervously. 'Something came up.'

'Just like that?'

'You know how I operate. I have to escort someone somewhere.'

Now that she was the one going he started to want her.

'Will I ring you?' he asked.

She looked surprised.

'Why?'

'I don't know. I just thought – '

'If you want to,' she said. Giuseppe was looking at her crossly. She seemed nervous of him.

When he gestured to her she stood up. She disappeared a moment later through a jet bead curtain. It was the one that led to the other half of her life, the half he knew nothing about. He wanted to follow her but he knew it would be dangerous.

He watched her fading into the shadows in that suggestive walk she had, a movement that seemed to invite the world to be a part of it and yet at the same time say it was nobody's for keeps. In that tension was her main attraction.

Now that she was gone he felt a vacuum, the vacuum they all left when it was over, even though he'd been the one to end it. He thought of Elaine, his worldly-wise fiancée, the woman he was going to marry at Christmas, the one everyone said could save him from himself. Elaine who knew the price of everything and the value of nothing. Putting pennies together for their impending nuptials by working as a cleaner in one of the downmarket hotels in Castlebar for the past year, sitting back in the bedsit now wondering what would have happened to him.

He'd told her it would be a quick visit. It was a duty trip. There was nothing much to be said. He was an hour over the time now. It would be difficult to face her questions, her unassailable practicality. He imagined her thinking he'd got cold feet at the last minute, ensnared once again in the arms of this Jezebel. She'd be sitting in front of the television set if he walked in. Either that or poring over some train timetable.

She'd want a quick drink to round off the evening. Maybe she'd suggest an early night to make sure they woke to the alarm before the journey home in the morning. She was as trite to him as anything else in his life.

The music died down. He felt conspicuous sitting alone at his table. The other drinkers were looking at him. He could always sense it in the sudden silence of their conversations, the way they looked away when you became aware of their attention.

He didn't know whether to go or stay. The place was like a tomb to him now. Without her it didn't have any atmosphere.

He went to the counter and ordered a drink. He was like any other customer now that he was on his own, like any of the other men in the bar who looked like they'd left half a marriage behind them somewhere, their eyes filled with more passion than they cared to admit as they primed themselves for the moves that would bring a lethargic night to the boil.

A girl came over to him in a G-string. She gave him a come-on look. He wasn't surprised. Why else would she think he was here at this hour of the night, nursing his desire towards the communion that was her livelihood.

'Hi,' she said, 'I'm Naomi. Would you like a good time?' It was the familiar opener. It marked the terms clearly just in case there was confusion later on, or an argument about money.

He looked at her querulously, almost amused at the absurdity of it all. A good time was the last thing he wanted now; it would have been anything but good. But he found it difficult to say no. There was something almost waif-like about her. She couldn't have been more than half his age, he thought, another teenager sucked into the vortex that was Soho at night.

'Hello Naomi. Sit down if you want but I'm not staying.'

'That's all right,' she said, either not caring or not pretending to, 'I've had a busy day myself. I need to unwind.'

She started to tell him about a truck driver she'd just been with, somebody who'd asked to be beaten up. He smiled at this, relaxed by her openness.

'I saw Lisa with you,' she said.

'How do you know her?'

He was surprised at the lack of privacy in a place that prided itself on such a quality.

'I work with her.'

'You must be new here. I haven't seen you before.'

'There's a girl sick. I'm filling in for her. I normally work in Maida Vale.' She might have been a nurse talking about doing an overtime shift in a hospital.

'Would you like a drink, Naomi?' he said. She nodded.

He flicked his fingers. A barman came over with a tray. Half the glasses on it had water in them but they were all classed as wine. The water was given to the hostesses and the wine to the clients. They were then charged for two glasses of wine. That was how it worked, the small rip-off before the big one upstairs later in the night. It didn't bother him. He didn't care what was in the glass. Most of the money was going to supplement a salary that would have been low in the slack part of the season.

'You're Irish, aren't you?' she said, 'I believe you made a kill in the bar trade over the summer.' He wondered if it was Giuseppe that would have leaked this to her. In his pocket he was carrying the bulk of that kill, a sum he'd collected earlier from the bar. It was more money than he'd ever seen in his life but it meant nothing to him. He hadn't even bothered to count it.

227

'I earned a bit. Most of it is in the till over there.' He kept the bar going on the quiet days. They used to joke about giving him a share in the company.

'But some more is in your pocket, right?'

'How do you know that?'

'Lisa told me about you.'

'I hope she didn't tell you too much. Or too many bad things anyway.'

'She thinks very highly of you. You're not like the usual bastards who come in here.'

'Why did you not go upstairs with her?' she asked then. Was she programmed to come to the point this quickly? Maybe her frankness towards sexual talk extended itself to all communication.

'It's over between us,' he said, 'We've been finished for some time now.'

She drew herself closer to him, her leg brushing lightly against his.

'There are more fish in the ocean.'

'That's right. Or sharks.'

'I'll pretend I didn't hear that.'

She wasn't amused. Maybe she felt he was making her a part of the implication.

He felt the drink going to his head, the remorse of the early part of the night giving way to a pleasant anaesthesia.

'Why are you in this anyway?' he said out of the blue, matching her own familiarity, 'a pretty young girl like you with your whole life ahead of you.'

'It's tax-free!' she said, laughing.

Maybe it was the one haven left.

'Seriously.'

She looked at him thoughtfully.

'If you must know, I'm engaged to be married.'

He'd heard it all now.

'I don't understand.'

'I'm putting my boyfriend through college. If it wasn't for this, we'd be on the breadline.'

He wasn't as surprised at this as he would have been three months ago. He'd met many call girls since Lisa. A good half of them were well-to-do, using it as a stopgap. It was a long way from the women in fishnet stockings on the Holborn Road who looked the wrong side of thirty.

'You must be making quite a bit,' he said.

'Not after my lawyer gets through it.'

'Your lawyer?'

'I've been up in court three times in the past year. They keep raiding us. Instead of tackling the real criminals.'

'How much do you charge?' he said, more out of curiosity than anything else.

'For £50 I can give you a religious experience,' she said, laughing. 'Are you interested?'

'I'm afraid I wouldn't have the energy, but you can stay here and drink my vodka if you like.'

She blushed

'I suppose Lisa put you wise on that one.'

'I found out the first night. They mixed up the drinks by accident. I got hers by mistake. Would you like a real one now?'

'That would be nice.'

'Maybe I'll be like Jesus at the wedding feast of Cana.'

'I'm sorry?' She hadn't a clue what he meant.

He went up to the counter and ordered two glasses of wine. He was glad he had enough spare change in his pocket. He didn't want to take out the large billfold from his wallet.

When he brought the drinks back to her she gave him a kiss. The smell of her perfume nearly knocked him out.

'Here goes nothing,' she said.

She threw hers back in a swallow. He was starting to enjoy her, enjoy the fact that she was sitting with him even though he promised her nothing. The drink loosened her tongue. She started talking about her past, about a life of going from foster home to foster home, about a father who beat her. Her childhood put down the markers for this equally transient lifestyle.

They both got drunk on the wine. He forgot Elaine, forgot even Lisa. As the night went on he became more giddy. She reciprocated his idiocy. It was a night where he had nothing to prove and nobody to prove it to. They might have been brother and sister sitting in this thinly-disguised brothel even if she looked like Madame Cyn.

Eventually they were the last there. Their conversation died into the silence

He wondered what Elaine would be doing, what she would be thinking. He'd left her in a room full of packed cases, a practical exigency negotiated in the sensibleness of the morning. Tomorrow they'd accompany one another back to a world where questions would be asked, where you had an identity, where day was day and night was night and people sat in at the weekends instead of this mad abandonment to sudden ecstasies.

'Is there some other woman in your life?' she asked. She seemed to be reading his thoughts, to be seeing them in the concentrated distance of his eyes.

'Yes and no,' he said, the answer that's not an answer but maybe truer than one.

'You should have been a politician.'

Her eyes lit up. He found himself envying her student fiancé. How was it that desire shifted in him so often? How could an attraction gained this glibly last when beauty faded? Sometimes it took him less than thirty seconds to fall headlong for a woman. He thought of the words of the song: 'I'm going to keep on falling in love till I get it right.'

'What happened with Lisa anyway?' she asked. The confiding of the details of her own life gave her the right to be curious.

'It just petered out,' he said. Or had he ever got off the mark with her?

'You were probably too snobbish,' she said, a snap judgement he would once have laughed at. Was he ruthless enough to leave a woman for what she did rather than for what she was?

He wasn't interested in pursuing the point. He'd played it to the death too often in his head over the past few weeks. She was a tragic figure. That was a more relevant point. He was afraid she could one day infect him with that tragedy.

They sat without speaking. At times it felt like she wasn't even there. She rested her arm gently on his shoulder. He felt immune to any emotion. Nothing could hurt or excite him.

She stroked his hair. He thought how like an ordinary couple they would have appeared to an onlooker rather than a hostess and her client.

'Do you still want to go upstairs?' he said. She laughed derisively. Maybe she thought men were all the same at base, the same sex maniacs trying to act like they didn't want the package they paid for.

'Of course,' she said, 'unless you've got AIDS.'

He'd asked the question half in jest. Now he started to think he might follow up on it. What was to stop him? Maybe he needed to do something illogical, to bring this senseless summer to an even more senseless end.

'Let's get some more drink.'

He went over to the counter. This time he ordered a bottle of whiskey. It was like a spiral, this dance of death where sex and alcohol interwove, each being ratcheted up to another level at the same time.

The increased cost of the order meant he had to reach into his wallet for the extra money. When he opened it a wad of notes fell out. The barman's eyes widened.

'Wow,' he said.

He picked up the wad, replacing it quickly in his wallet.

'Keep the change,' he said. The bottle appeared on the counter. He brought it back to the table.

'A whole bottle?' she said, 'You must be planning a big night for yourself.'

'Let's go.'

They walked towards the stairs, his feet unsteady with the effect of what he'd had already. When they got to the top she led him along the corridor to her room. He felt like the text book emigrant having his last fling on the night before getting on the boat at Holyhead.

The room had nothing in it but a wardrobe and a bed.

'What do you want to do?' she said. He shrugged. She went to the wardrobe, taking out some chains and a whip.

'We could use these,' she said. He let out a whoop.

'I suppose that's all the rage now.'

'You're out of touch. We have new ways of entertaining people now. This stuff has been flogged to the death.' They both laughed at her unintentional pun.

She sat looking at him, waiting for him to call the shots.

'Are you ready?'

'Why don't we just talk?'

'You'd pay £50 for a conversation?'

'With you I'd pay £100.'

'Flattery will get you everywhere.'

He didn't know why he said it. Maybe he was trying to pretend to himself that he was seducing her.

He threw his wallet on the bed.

'Help yourself,' he said.

Her eyes grew wide as the bills spread out before her.

'I couldn't,' she said, 'We haven't done anything yet.'

'I thought you girls demanded your fees upfront.'

'Not if you have an honest face like you,' she said. She tweaked his nose.

'Whatever you want. Why not take it for your boyfriend? I've always had a secret ambition to contribute to the education of the youth.'

'Are all the Irish as generous as you?'

'Even more so. You should go over there sometime. You could retire young.'

He tried to kiss her. She pushed him away.

'That's not in the deal. It smudges my make-up.'

It was ironic, he thought, how she would offer the ultimate favour but not this incidental one.

'Let's just drink,' she said.

He wasn't sure if she was joking. Maybe she wanted him to fall asleep so she could make off with the wad. Did he care now? Hardly. Even if it meant blowing in an hour what it took three months to earn.

They took their clothes off. He got into bed with her. She ran her hands over him. He smelt her perfume. It was like an intoxicant. He started getting woozy. Then everything went black.

When he woke up he didn't know how much later it was. His head ached.

He jumped up in the bed. The room looked different. He was disoriented. He tried to remember the night. It came back to him only in snatches.

She was still beside him. She looked at him amusedly.

'You nearly finished the bottle,' she said.

'I went out like a light.'

'You sure did. It was boring for me here waiting for you to make love to me.'

'What time is it?'

'The middle of the night. What does it matter?'

He sat up in the bed.

'I need to go to the toilet,' he said.

'Be my guest.'

As he walked to it he banged his head off the wall. He hardly felt it.

He didn't really need the toilet. He just wanted to wash his face, to get into the day.

He came out. She kissed his head.

'If I did that I'd be unconscious,' she said, 'You must be made of steel.'

'I'm probably still drunk. It's an anaesthetic.'

He lay back on the pillow.

'Hey, you're no fun,' she said, 'Do you not want your money's worth?'

She went over to the window. He looked at her standing there, a vision of beauty in a nightie. What was she thinking about, what lost chapter of her youth?

When she came back to the bed he started to talk about Elaine. He told her too much about himself. He always did that with women when he had drink taken. He wasn't sure how much she was taking in.

He didn't remember what happened afterwards. It was a night that was part dream and part fantasy. At one point of it he appeared to be on the brink of a solution to every dilemma he ever had. At the next all solutions became inane. She cradled him like a mother. He found himself crying into her arms. It was as if a new innocence was being born in him, an old identity expunged.

He wondered what would have happened if he'd met her three months ago. She was like a *tabula rasa*. He spoke to her with the freedom that comes from the knowledge that you're leaving somewhere for a long time. She talked about her past too but when he asked her about her boyfriend she clammed up. Maybe this was part of the deal too.

Morning came. He reached across the bed for her but this time she wasn't there. He sat up. The sun stung his eyes. He wondered if she'd taken his money. His wallet was open on the locker. He looked through it. He didn't think it was as full as it should have been but he couldn't tell for sure.

His head was exploding with pain. He dragged himself over to the window and looked out. There was nobody on the streets. It seemed a long time since he'd talked to Lisa. She probably spent the night with Giuseppe. She was his again now after her aberration with 'the Irish import.'

He looked around him. On the mirror she'd scrawled in lipstick, 'It's been a business doing pleasure with you.' Underneath the message was a heart. It had an arrow running through it.

He started thinking about the money again. He was annoyed with himself for not counting it when he got it. Such things didn't matter to him then but now, in the cruel light of the morning, they were suddenly important. As far as Elaine was concerned it was the only reason for the trip.

He thought of the way he'd face her, how he'd justify it. She'd set her hopes on him making a king's ransom during these months. It was supposed to set them up for their future. What future could they have now? It lay in the bottom of his whiskey glass. It was in the garters of a whore.

He tried to piece the night together. All he could remember were moments.

Sounds started to come from other rooms. The cleaner women were about. He heard a vacuum cleaner going next door. It bored through his head.

He dressed himself. Every movement was still causing him pain. He felt like an old man. When was he going to start listening to the messages his body gave him?

He went down to the lounge. It was empty. He looked around him at the rows of chairs upturned over tables. Was there anything in life as depressing as a bar before opening time? The smell of drinks that had been discarded from the night before made him retch.

The barman came out. He smiled knowingly at him.

'Did she live up to expectations?' he said.

'I'm looking for something for a hangover.'

He laughed.

'You know what they say. If you stay drunk you don't have to worry about hangovers.'

He took a capsule from a drawer.

'They say this works,' he said.

He swallowed it without looking at it.

'I'll have a drink too.' Disease and cure in the one order.

'Of what, sir?'

'Anything.'

He poured him a glass of brandy.

'That's on the house,' he said.

He went over to a table with it. The capsule seemed to be working. He felt relaxed.

He searched in his pockets for the phone number of the bedsit Elaine was staying in. She was going to give him hell for not coming back last night. He didn't mind that. In fact he expected it. He'd grovel to her. There would be a row. She'd suspect him of having slept with Lisa rather than anyone else. She wasn't a patient woman and she wouldn't be patient today. With a bit of luck he might be able to win her round. It was a question of damage limitation. He had the rest of his life to make up to her.

The first thing she'd query him about would be the money, how much he'd spent in this stupid, reckless night. He'd lie about the amount but she'd know, she always knew. She'd castigate him about this, castigate him about the fact that she'd spent three months scrubbing floors to save up for the deposit on a house while he'd been contemplating his navel in a bordello. He'd let her rattle on because it was more peaceful that way. He needed her to be an opposite to him, needed someone to regard as important what he would have cast to the four winds. It might have been the formula for most successful marriages.

He left the bar, emerging into the coldness of the day. He decided the first thing he'd do would be to buy the tickets for the boat. That would be better than ringing her. It would pacify her better than an apology. The apology would come later. It would be accompanied by fawning and a promise to behave himself. It had been the pattern of much of their relationship, this sudden transition from an intensely indulgent phase to an intensely pragmatic one. She was like the brakes on his feelings. She prepared him for the world of ordinary people, the one most people lived in.

He stood at the corner wondering if there was someone he could ask for directions to the ticket office. He hoped it was nearby. He was too hungover to walk any distance looking for it.

After a few seconds he saw Giuseppe. He seemed to come out of nowhere. What was he doing up at this hour of the morning? His was a night world.

Had Lisa spent the night with him? He felt a vague choke of envy. Maybe that was the direction her life would take now. But what did it matter to him one way or the other? He'd be better off pretending she never existed.

He came over to him.

'How is the last of the red hot lovers?' he said, a grin playing round his lips. 'I believe you're leaving us.'

'Who told you that?'

236

'Lisa. She said you dumped her.' He could imagine the tone of voice she would have used to say the words. He could almost taste the sarcasm behind them.

'That wasn't what happened. We're just friends.'

'That's not what she said.'

'What did she say?'

'She said you led her up the garden path.'

He felt threatened. He wanted to go away from him but he felt something pinning him to the ground, something intangible. It was a kind of spell Giuseppe could weave without doing anything.

'You must have made quite an amount of money over here,' he said.

'Have you a problem with that?'

'I don't think it's very mannerly coming over here using our women and then running back home with your stash.'

'I earned it honestly.'

He tried to walk past him but he stood in his way.

'Excuse me,' he said.

Giuseppe didn't move. He just kept grinning.

When he tried to walk past him a second time, Giuseppe grabbed him. When he looked down he saw a dagger in his hand.

'The least you could do is make a donation to her,' he said, 'after all she's done for you.'

Another man appeared from behind a wall. He recognised him as someone who always hovered behind Giuseppe whenever business was being done, one of the many parasites in his world. He had a scar that ran down his cheek.

'Get out of my way or I'll call the police,' he said.

The two men laughed. It was only when the words were out that he realised how ridiculous they sounded.

'Call them' Giuseppe said, 'Call the Irish ones as well if you wish.' He laughed again. He was enjoying the game now.

They waited for him to make his move. As he looked at the other man more closely he realised he had a dagger too.

'Is it my money you want?' he said.

'We wouldn't say no to a few pounds, would we?' Giuseppe said, 'Are you offering it?'

He took the wallet out of his pocket, throwing what money was in it onto the ground. He was glad Naomi got some of it. Would Lisa? According to her it was blood money. She told him once that the bar he worked in was run by the same organisation that employed her.

Giuseppe picked it up. As he spread the bills through his fingers he whistled. 'There's more here than I thought,' he said, 'You're either the best barman in London or the cleverest thief.'

Some fury that was buried inside him erupted in him at this. He lashed out at Giuseppe, hitting him a glancing blow on the face. He reeled for a second, then caught his balance. As he fingered his jaw he had a smile on his face, a smile almost of gratitude.

'The good old Celtic temper,' he said.

He ran his finger along the edge of the blade as the blood trickled down his cheek. He seemed to be debating within himself whether to use it or not.

'What do you think of that?' he said to the man beside him. 'Not very polite for a foreigner, is he? After our great welcome and all. Not three months off the boat and already he's beating up the natives. I think he needs to be taught a lesson. Would you agree?'

'You've got my money,' he said, 'Let me go now.' But he seemed to know he wasn't going anywhere. His show of temper would cost him.

He tried to run. A foot went out in front of him. He fell. He felt himself being grabbed from behind. A blade went into him. It went in cleanly, like a key slipping into a lock. There was no rage in Giuseppe as he did it, no passion. It was almost a self-righteous act.

'Why did you make me hurt you?' Giuseppe said, 'I hate it when people make me hurt them. It's so unnecessary.'

He fell down. Blood gurgled out of him. When he put his hand over his stomach it came away red. There wasn't much pain but he started to feel fear for the first time now. He tried to look down at his stomach but his vision was blurred. Above him the two men were quiet. Giuseppe seemed surprised by what he'd done. He looked at the dagger as if it belonged to someone else, as if he hadn't been in charge of it.

'You shouldn't have hit me,' he said.

He tried to stand up but there was no strength in his legs. He put his hand on his stomach to gauge the flow of blood. He felt it trickling between his fingers and onto the pavement. There was a red circle under his shirt. His trousers were wet. He felt as if he'd spilled something on himself. He wondered if he was dying.

The two men were still watching him closely. Their faces were blank. He wondered why they weren't running away. A man passed by.

'Help me,' he said to him, stretching his arm out. Giuseppe and his friend started to run away. The knife fell.

He felt everything getting suddenly far away, everything inside him and outside him. As he looked around him he saw the dagger beside him, silver in the sunlight. Why had Giuseppe dropped it? Was it by accident or had he meant to? Beside it lay his wallet, a few stray bills floating through the air in the wind. One of the notes had blood on it.

He heard the footsteps of the two men growing fainter. For a moment he thought he saw Lisa. He tried to open his eyes but he couldn't. The sun was too strong.

The blood was coming out in gushes now and the pain getting worse. The lightness in his head was almost pleasant.

He didn't know how long he was there before he heard an ambulance screaming down the road in his direction, the siren whirring above him like an omen, or maybe a reprieve.

Flight

The light looked different
that day.
A beige filament
crept through the sky.
At the airport
 a woman's hat blew off.
The plane was delayed.
I sat on the platform
watching students lugging backpacks.
Filipino salesgirls offered gifts
of customized products.

A university professor cried
into the arms of his daughter.
I tried to act cool
as we embarked
but my heart
was jumping inside me.
When we rose into the sky
the land spread out beneath us.
The handkerchief fields
were like a chessboard,
the rivers like veins.
Smoke billowed from factory furnaces.

We zoned in on Dublin.
We were above the clouds
for a while
and then we started to fall.
My stomach fluttered.
It was like
when you were
on the ferris wheel
at a carnival.

In the distance my woman waved
from a balcony.
She was crying with relief
that I survived
the long months away –
the robbery in St. Tropez,
the suicide roads of Milan,
the diabolically cruel sun.

I felt embarrassed
talking about these things
as we got the taxi to Artane.
It began to rain,
inevitably, at Santry.
We laughed about that
and about my wanderings.

I tried to ask
what she'd been up to
but she wouldn't say.
It was as if it didn't matter.
I watched strange houses
streaming by,
the dull throb
of what was once familiar.
The night came down
and before I knew it
we were home.
She opened the door
with a sense of pride,
showing off the new check carpet.
We went inside.
Both of us felt drunk
though we hadn't been drinking.
We fell over the threshold
onto my luggage.

She put the kettle on.
She said,
'Is it still two lumps of sugar?'
I said,
'I don't take it at all now.'

There were photographs of me
on the wall.
I looked triumphal
in the Vatican, in Turkey,
among the ruins of Greece.
All these places
seemed irrelevant now.

'Hail the conquering hero,' she said.
I was home for good.
I scanned the room
for things I thought
I'd forgotten –
the wedding vase,
the curtains with the leaf motif,
her CD collection of Mozart,
the cat that walked in
walked out
walked in
walked out
and continued to look
at us, as if we were the tenants
and she the landlady.

'It's good to be back,' I said.
We fell asleep on the floor
with all our clothes on,
having emptied two bottles of duty free.

In the morning it was still raining.
Dublin still looked miserable
but I knew I'd never leave
the city again
no matter what exotic promises
Europe held.
There was a security in the rain,
the broken furniture,
the peeling paint.
I knew that,
being old,
I was suddenly
terrified of happiness.

Christmas

On a quiet street
the cars crawl by
and shoppers loll
and men of Mammon
shine their wares.

Reilly bows beaten
to recessionary prices,
forks out overtime cash
for Donal's Action Man
Imelda's precious Panda bear.
His wife thanks God
her heart is strong.
They've survived
another year.

On Stephen's Day
Imelda weeps,
realising Panda bears
don't come from Santa
after all.
On an apple box a priest
is telling everyone
to think of love.
Reilly lurches back
to the lounges
that are open again
after the soul-destroying limbo
of yesterday.

In the distance fires burn.
Crimes begin.
Knives are pulled
after the Yuletide lull.

Guns go off
and people die
but no one really hears them
on this quiet street
where cars crawl by
and shoppers loll
and men of Mammon
shine their wares.

Homecoming

Stranded with the nothingness
of their return,
anglicised,
to a dark Bohola home,
she lights a candle
in the local parish church,
drops widow's mites
unthinkingly
in boxes emptied
once too much
to feed a curate's dreams.

She pines for early loves,
has Guinness in O'Donoghue's
to dull her thoughts.

At teatime
she chats with neighbours
who barter their talk for food.

The knocker thuds.
She musters up a face
for her famous girls,
makes promises to herself
not to attack.
But as she listens
to their tales of city life
she's already looking forward
to their going back.

'You've lived too long,'
their faces say
when they're not thanking her
for being there.

They've all done well
she thinks
as shadows fall
on ghosts of the past.

What's next?
she asks herself,
What's last?

King Bob, Approximately

It was one of those ideas that looked good on paper. Everyone was going to Larry's place dressed up as a character from a Bob Dylan song. I chose 'Napoleon in rags.'

I arrived with one hand inside my coat to look like the man himself. The other one held a six-pack. Everyone was there. All the old potheads I thought I'd outgrown. They were people I usually only ran into when I was making a late-night trip to the off-licence and wanted to make a fast getaway.

There would be no fast getaway tonight. Tonight we were looking for a rub of the relic. We were on BobWatch.

I was high-fived by a few of the potheads. It took me an eternity to get to the fridge to deposit the six-pack. Now all I had to worry about was whether it would be lifted before I got around to drinking it.

Norma made a beeline for me. She was an old flame of mine, or rather an old ember. We never quite ignited.

She now had 'Brownsville Girl' emblazoned on her chest. I took it as a progression.

'Napoleon in rags,' she said, 'How original.' .

'It was all I could think of,' I explained.

I placed one of my hands strategically inside my coat. It was important to get in character early.

The room looked like the set of a medieval melodrama. Ken McCarthy was Jack of Hearts. Dessie Sheedy was Mr Tambourine Man. John Murtagh was Dylan with the fuzzy hair and the Cuban heels. Gary Cullen was Jokerman. He took the lazy route to him, putting on nothing more than a clown's outfit and a red nose. Blind Willie McTell was Paudie Ryan with a pair of shades. A man in a black suit called himself the Guilty Undertaker. Alongside him was a Lonesome Organ Grinder.

A man I didn't know had a flowerpot on his head. As he walked by me I thought: What song was that from? Maybe you didn't need to be anyone to wear a flowerpot on your head at a fancy dress party devoted to Bob Dylan. Or maybe Bob had a new song out called 'Flowerpot On Head.' Stranger things had happened.

'I Want You' blasted out of the hi-fi. Clean Cut Kid had sellotaped the dial at max volume. Surely this wasn't Billy Kennelly from First Arts? Larry started dancing to it, if you could call it dancing. He looked more like an octopus trying on a tuxedo.

'If you don't stop that,' I warned, 'It could become permanent.'

'Shut up,' he said, 'It's my party. I'll fly if I want to.'

The song ended. He came off the floor dripping with sweat.

'What did you think?' he said.

'Don't give up the day job,' I told him. It wasn't good advice. He didn't *have* a day job.

'What's new?' he asked me.

'Nothing. What have I missed?'

'Not much.'

He gazed derisively at my Carlsberg.

'Would you not like something more interesting?' he said.

'I'm staying off the hard stuff tonight.'

'Not even a nip?' He waved an airport-style bottle of whiskey at me.

'Maybe later.'

'We have some other alternatives if your taste inclines that way.'

'How do you mean?'

He gestured somebody putting cocaine up their nose.

'Becky's been in the bathroom since she got here. She brought her own supply. If you're nice to her she might share.'

Becky was my favourite person in the whole universe next to Bob. She's an anorexic. (That isn't the reason.)

The door opened at that moment and she emerged. She looked high. But then Becky always looked high.

She was dressed as Queen Mary. She'd brought the tiara to complete the effect.

'Holy Christ,' she said, throwing her arms around me, 'You.'

'What made you think I wouldn't come?'

'You've been ignoring my phone calls for the past month.'

'I don't always get them. The answering machine is in the hall of the flat. People who pass by tend to delete them.'

'Can you not come up with a better excuse than that?'

'Sometimes the ones that sound the phoniest are the true ones.'

'Phoniest. That's a good pun. Okay you bastard, I forgive you. Anyway I need to talk to you. Can we go somewhere?'

She led me out to the conservatory. Jokerman was behind us. He was laughing himself silly. Blind Willie McTell was in a heap on the floor. He'd fallen over a footstool. Jack of Hearts was busily attaching himself to The Queen of Spades. Her voice started to get shaky as soon as we sat down.

'Dad fell in love with another woman,' she said. 'Or should I say another child. She looks about fifteen.' Her parents had been married for 23 years.

I looked into her eyes. As I did so it struck me that they had ten million millennia of longing in them. Why hadn't she come as Sad-Eyed Lady of the Lowlands?

'I'm sorry to hear that,' I said. I vaguely remembered meeting him once. He didn't look like the type of man to walk out on a 23-year marriage. Which begged the question, what did a man who would walk out on a 23 year old marriage look like?

'Where are things at now?'

'He's been dumped. He wants to come back but Mam won't have him. She wants to make him suffer.'

'What do you want?'

'I just want us to be a family again.'

I tried to think of some advice for her. Kim came over. I used to go out with Kim once as well. All my previous girlfriends were big into Dylan. It was a precondition of my going out with them.

'Hi, Kim,' I said.

'Hello, loser.'

For the first year of being with her I used to pray she wouldn't leave me. For the second I prayed that she would. After we broke up she became a lesbian. I hadn't seen any signs of this when she was with me. On the night we met we met when she tried to take my trousers off as the same time as she was unzipping her dress. This is quite a complicated manoeuvre at the best of times.

'Nice costume,' I said.

250

It looked like she'd taken down the curtains to make it. Was she trying to be one of the characters from 'Visions of Johanna'? She had something taped around her mouth that looked like mercury.

'Hi,' she said, 'This is my friend Cordelia. She gestured a sullen-looking girl with a leopardskin pillbox hat on her head. I presumed Cordelia was her latest lover. Kim changed lovers like the rest of us changed our socks.

'Hello Cordelia,' I said, 'That's a lovely name. Were you named after the character in *King Lear*?'

'Everyone asks me that,' she said, 'Can you not think of anything more interesting to say?'

'Okay, you have lovely hair.'

She had. It was done up in curls. I wondered if she was trying to be the girl from 'Just Like a Woman.' I decided not to ask this in case she went for me again.

Becky was still in a state about her father.

'He has to come home,' she said, 'I don't care what it takes.'

'Maybe you could talk your mother round.'

'It's no good. She has her mind made up. She wants to rub his nose in it.'

I could see her going on about her problem all night. When you've put a drug into your body, as I knew myself, you fixated on certain subjects. I didn't feel we'd be able to get her father back to her mother at a Bob Dylan fancy dress party. I thought it might be better to try and get her mind off him.

I asked Becky if she'd like a beer.

'No,' she said, 'It puffs up my stomach too much.'

'Would you mind if I got one?'

'Be my guest.'

I walked to the fridge. The music continued to pound. We were now on to 'Don't Think Twice, It's All Right.' Everyone seemed to know the words. Dessie was lending accompaniment with his tambourine. Jack of Hearts was kissing The Queen of Spades under the coffee table.

When I got to the fridge I discovered that my six-pack had been pilfered. There was just one miserable can left. Fuck it. Not that I was surprised.

I told my tale of woe to Larry. I thought he'd feel responsible seeing as it was his fridge.

'Well at least they left you one,' he said.

'I can't get through the night on one beer.'

'We'll get something for you. Relax.'

'If you don't I'll have to leave.'

'There must be some way outa here,' he sang, 'said the joker to the thief.'

'Shut up, Larry,' I said, 'You have a voice like a crow.'

'I know, but at least I'm better than Bob.'

'No heresy please.'

'Go back to the party and chill out. That's an order.'

I returned to Becky.

'You're my reason for travellin' on,' Johanna said to me as I passed her.

'Be nice, Kim,' said Blind Willie McTell.

'Fuck off, Willie,' Kim snapped.

I held up my single beer to Becky.

'Some bastard decimated my supply,' I told her.

'It's your own fault for not keeping an eye on it. Maybe you should have taped the cans to your stomach like one of those suicide bombers. You know what Larry's parties are like. Everyone's a parasite. Anyway you're better off without that stuff.'

'What's your alternative?' I said, 'Smack?'

As soon as I said it I was sorry.

'What kind of crack is that?'

'Crack. Now *you're* starting to make puns.'

'If you get any funnier I might throw up on you.'

I looked at her pale face. It made me feel sad. I found myself becoming nostalgic for an age when people just got drunk instead of retiring to bathrooms to put stuff up their nose.

Paul Finn tapped me on the shoulder. I used to work in a record company with Paul before he went off to London to pursue a career as a hip-hop singer. Now he was living with his mother in Morrison Terrace. He had his face painted all the colours of the rainbow.

'What gives, stranger?' he said.

'Same old same old,' I said, 'How about you?'

'I'm thinking of taking off across the pond again.'

'I thought you were just back.'

'After a week in this hellhole I find myself becoming terminally depressed. Do you not find Ballina toxic? As soon as the old lady can stump up the plane fare I'm off.'

'To London?'

'To anywhere, man. Just give me that ticket and I'm out of here.'

He took a can of Carlsberg out of his pocket.

'Fancy one?' he said. In the same movement he got one for himself from another pocket. As I looked at him a certain penny dropped. I was speaking to the thief.

'Everybody must get stoned,' he sang. I fantasised about stoning him in a different way. I was going to say, 'Why did you take my beers from the fridge?' but I didn't. It would have created a bad atmosphere. He'd been a leech all his life. Why should he change now?

Instead I said, 'Why have you painted your face all these colours?'

'Do you not get it? Bob's a chameleon, right? Why would he just have one colour on his face?'

'How slow of me.'

'I was going for the *Renaldo and Clara* look.'

'You certainly got that.'

Becky wet her finger. She touched his face.

'Why did you do that?' he asked her.

'I wanted to see if the paint was dry.'

'Okay.'

'Was *Renaldo and Clara* when he broke up with Joanie?' she enquired. 'Joanie' was of course Joan Baez.

'I think it was earlier. Probably when he went electric.'

I listened to them warbling on. Were we all mad to be talking about something that happened thirty years ago? What if Dylan was to suddenly appear. Would he think we were mad too?

'I'm bored,' said Becky, 'I've lost my father and I'm depressed and bored. Let's dance.'

She dragged me onto the floor. 'Song to Woody' came on the hi-fi. Jokerman swayed to it. Cordelia's leopardskin pillbox hat fell off. I was able to see her lovely curls. Jack of Hearts had his hand up The Queen of Spade's skirt. The Guilty Undertaker and the Lonesome Organ Grinder were doing their thing out the back.

As soon as Becky started to dance she got weak.

'Let's sit down,' I said. As I went to grab her she collapsed like a rag doll onto the floor.

Larry ran over to her. He slapped her face.

'You need some air,' he told her.

'I don't want air,' she said, 'I just want to go to bed.'

'Naughty girl,' said Dessie.

'Why don't you bring her upstairs?' Larry said to me, 'Napoleon would have, you know.'

'Not tonight, Josephine,' I told him.

I walked Becky towards the kitchen.

'Where are we going?' she asked me.

'Somewhere that we can bring dead girls back to life,' I told her.

'That's sweet,' she said.

I took her up in my arms. I don't normally take girls up in my arms but she was so light with the anorexia it was like carrying a child.

We went into the kitchen. Vinnie Keaveny was sitting at the table gazing intensely at nothing in particular. He was decked out as Mr Jones in a three-piece suit. We'd all thought of becoming Mr Jones for the night. He was Dylan's most famous character and all that. But Vinnie *was* Mr Jones, even in 'real' life. He had three square meals a day, a dog called Rover and fitted carpets in his house. In fact I sometimes thought Dylan must have met Vinnie to write the song. (The fact that he wasn't even a glint in his father's eye when it was penned puts a slight dent in this theory.)

'Somebody sick?' he asked.

'The situation is under control,' I assured him.

I splashed some water on Becky's face.

'What's wrong with her?' said Vinnie.

'Nothing,' I said, 'She just got a bit weak with the heat. Right, Becky?'

'Right.'

'Put her head under it,' Vinnie advised.

'I don't want to give her a heart attack.'

'You won't,' said Vinnie, 'Trust Mr Jones.'

I splashed more water on her. Her droopy eyes widened. I started to relax.

'Welcome back,' I said, 'You had us worried there for a few minutes.'

'I feel like I've been in another world.'

'Maybe you have.'

'Sorry about that, motherfuckers.'

'It would probably be best if you went home now.'

'I don't *have* a home,' she snapped.

'What's she talking about?' Vinnie asked.

'Nothing,' I told Mr Jones.

'I'm going upstairs,' said Becky.

'You can't. It wouldn't be good for you. You might conk out again.'

I wondered if she was intending to have a refill of the white stuff in there.

'Don't worry,' she said, as if reading my mind, 'I'll be a good girl. It's only for a pee.'

'Okay but if you're not down in a few minutes I'm coming in after you.'

'That sounds kinky,' she said, giving me a kiss.

'Don't be too long or you'll miss the party,' Vinnie said to her.

'The best parties are in your head,' Becky declared.

She tottered off. Vinnie shook his head. He was bewildered by this very un-Jones-like girl. He waved his pencil at me. Mr Jones had to have a pencil, didn't he?

'Nice uniform, Napoleon,' he said to me.

'Thanks,' I said, 'It could do with having the sleeves mended. Maybe I'll bring it to Elba next week. I heard they have some good tailors there.'

'So I believe. Elban tailors are the best.'

I told him I liked his outfit but the truth of it was that he hadn't really made much of an effort. Was there not more to Mr Jones than a three-piece suit and a pencil?

We got talking about the songs. There was so much happening it was easy to forget why we were there.

'It was his best composition, though, wasn't it?' he said.

'You mean 'Ballad of a Thin Man'?'

'Yes. Beckettian almost. Wouldn't you agree?'

I've always felt that people who use words like 'Beckettian' should be put away somewhere for a long time without any possibility of parole. They're like people who use words like 'societal.' Or 'infrastructure.'

'Maybe a bit obtuse, though,' I challenged.

'Wasn't that the whole point?'

'He's done better songs that have got less attention,' I continued. I was intent on bursting his Mr Jones' bubble.

'I think Zimmy is still on a journey,' he said.

'You mean the Never Ending Tour?'

'No, I mean an *inner* journey.'

'Ah.'

'Let's put it like this. It's a long way from 'Blowing in the Wind' to 'Idiot Wind'.'

I wondered how long it took him to make up that line.

'That sounds like a great insight, Vinnie,' I offered.

'Maybe I'll do a piece on it sometime.'

Vinnie wrote articles on music for *Hot Press*. They were always well written but every time I read one of them it always spoiled the music for me afterwards.

'You should,' I suggested, 'or even a book.'

'No. That would be stretching it too far.' He was getting worked up. Antime Vinnie got worked up you were looking at an hour of a discussion at least. I wasn't up for that.

'Listen Vinnie,' I said, 'I have to go. I'm bursting for a pee.'

'Peeing seems to be very popular tonight,' he said.

He went back to doodling with his pencil. Most likely you go your way, I thought, and I'll go mine.

On the way up to the toilet I ran into Con Connolly.

'Good evening, Bonaparte,' he said. A bit stiffly, I thought. Con was another old acquaintance of mine from the music business. He had his face blackened. I was trying to figure out who he was trying to be.

'Good evening Mr...Evers?' I said. I was thinking of Medger Evers.

'Nice try. It's Rubin Carter actually.'

Shit. I should have guessed.

'Let me congratulate you on a very imaginative choice.'

'Thank you. Listen, I need your advice on something.'

'Shoot.'

'I don't know how to put this. You know Norma, don't you?'

'Yes.'

I knew what was coming because I also knew Con had the hots for her.

'Is she, how shall I put it, available?'

'That depends who you are, Con.'

'What's that supposed to mean?'

Everyone knew Norma fancied Larry. She'd been out with Con a few times but only to make Larry jealous.

Con always believed Larry was a closet homosexual. If he was it would have suited him down to the ground. If Norma believed it, he thought, it would clear the way for him with her. Except for one minor detail. She'd have preferred to date a terrorist than Con. The reason I knew this was because she told me one night in Costa over a latte.

'Maybe you should let Norma burn Larry out of her system before you move in on her.'

He put on a horrified expression.

'Larry? He's as gay as Christmas.'

'That's a matter of opinion.'

I knew Larry dated both men and women in the past. I wouldn't have put it past him to date sheep.

'Can Norma not see the light?'

'Maybe she will in time. Or maybe Larry will have a fling with her and then go off with another man. The point is, don't say anything to her about his sexual predilections. You'll only make her want him more.'

'That's a funny kind of logic.'

'You asked for my advice. I'm giving it to you.'

'Thanks, he said, 'for nothing.'

He walked off in a sulk. From the other side of the room Norma gave me a thumbs-up sign.

I went to the toilet. It took me an age to empty my bladder. What kind of nutballs had I landed myself with?

When I came out I had to step over Blind Willie McTell. He was lying in a heap on the stairs. Jokerman was trying to move him. The Guilty Undertaker stood beside him looking... guilty.

'Willie,' said the Jokerman, 'You need to get up. You can't sit on the steps all night. Someone will mash you.'

'Disappear, Jokerman,' said Willie, 'I'm happy here. It's relaxing.'

'Can you do anything?' Jokerman asked me.

'I'd leave him alone,' I told him. 'Maybe tell him a few jokes. Isn't that what you're good at?

'Fuck you,' he said.

I went downstairs. Becky was waiting for me on the bottom step. She was looking sleepy again. I thought she might have been up to her old tricks again in the little girl's room.

'I have a feeling I'm not going to live long, Napoleon,' she said. I was going to say 'Please don't fall apart on me tonight,' but I didn't. In her condition even a chance comment like that could have pushed her over the edge.

'You're going to live to be ninety,' I said, 'and your father is going to come home. You're going to be a big happy family once again.'

She gave me a kiss.

'Maybe I'd have that beer now,' she said.

'I thought beer puffed you up.'

'Maybe I need puffing up.'

You could never understand women. As Oscar Wilde said, you could only love them.

'Girl From the North Country' came on the hi-fi.

'I know the words of this,' she said.

She started to sing. I joined in wherever I could. She had a beautiful voice. When she sang she forgot all her problems and so did I.

When we were finished the man with the flowerpot on his head started clapping frantically. The Lonesome Organ Grinder mimed grinding an organ. It seemed appropriate.

'Thank you,' said Becky, 'Both of you. Whoever you are.'

Bob Dylan had also been listening to it.

'You were in the wrong key,' he said.

Becky gave him the fingers.

'What would you know?' she said.

'*Touché*,' said the Lonesome Organ Grinder.

'Maybe you could organise the beers now,' Becky suggested, 'Getting those few notes out recharged my batteries.'

I didn't need to be asked twice. At this stage of the night I'd have drunk my own urine if someone told me there was alcohol in it. I found myself eyeing people's half-drunk glasses on the table and thinking about helping myself to them. I cursed Dessie for his thievery again.

Norma was eating a cherry.

'Thanks for rescuing me from Con,' she said, 'He's a lovely guy but I'm not ready for a lovely guy yet. You have to date Mr Wrong before marrying Mr Right, don't you?'

'Where do I fit into that sequence?' I asked.

'You're Mr Wrong but I feel like going wrong tonight.'

My Napoleonic pride was shattered.

'I could have you executed for that,' I said.

'Ooh,' she said, 'Very sexy. Power is an aphrodisiac, you know.'

'So they tell me.'

'Any good battles coming up?' she asked.

'One at Waterloo but I've got a bad feeling about it. I may pass on it.'

I heard a voice behind me.

'If we don't learn from the lessons of history,' it said, 'we're condemned to repeat them.'

Mr Jones had entered the room.

'I met him once, you know,' he said.

'Who?'

'The Main Man.'

'Did you speak to him?'

'I wanted to but I froze.'

'You never told me that. Did you get his autograph?'

'I was only a kid. It was in a café beside where he was appearing once in London. I went up to him with my programme. He had a "Get lost" look on his face.'

'I wouldn't worry about that. He's like that all the time. What happened?'

'He put a scrawl on it and went off.'

'What a way to treat your fans.'

'Agreed.'

Blind Willie McTell approached me.

'What's it like out there?' he said.

'What's what like?'

'Everything. The room. The people.'

'The room is hot. The people are cool. How are you?'

'Lonely.'

I didn't know if this was part of the performance or if he meant it. We'd been playing these roles so long they'd actually started to become us.

'How long have you been like this?' I asked.

'For as long as I can remember. It's not much fun. But at least I can hear the music.'

Jokerman walked in. He tried to cheer Willie up. He was pulling faces at him.

'It's no good,' I said, 'he can't see you.'

'I know that, dummy,' he said, 'but he'll sense it.' He gave him a shake. 'Can't you sense me spreading the love, Blind Willie?'

'You betcha,' said Willie.

The Tambourine Man appeared at the door.

'Where's Bob?' he asked.

'I think he was in the garden with Joan earlier on.'

'I'll check it out.'

He marched off. I went over to Becky.

'I couldn't find any beers,' I confessed.

'Don't worry about it. It's you I want.'

She had the untouched look of a neophyte, a changeling.

'You're beautiful,' I said.

She put her arms round me.

'When are we going to be a united family again?' she said.

'I don't have a crystal ball,' I said, 'Why don't you ask Bob? He knows everything.'

'You really believe this crap, don't you?' she said.

'What crap?'

'The crap that's all around us. Are we clever dicks or are we just afraid of facing reality? Is that why we do it?'

'Sometimes you have to,' I said, 'to get you through.'

'It doesn't work that way for me. Most of these people haven't lived yet.'

'Probably not. Maybe they never will. Maybe they'll be better off.'

Kim and Cordelia walked in. They were holding hands.

'We're in love,' said Kim.

'Good for you,' I said.

Dessie traipsed in behind them. He was high as a kite on something. He started shaking his tambourine.

'What gives?' he said.

'Kim and Cordelia are in love.'

'I'm glad someone is. Would you like to hear a song?'

It wasn't a question, it was a statement. The Clean Cut Kid turned the hi-fi off. Dessie fetched a guitar from behind the sofa. He started to sing 'Stuck Inside of Mobile with the Memphis Blues Again.' I always admired people who could memorise songs that had more than 500 verses in them.

Bob Dylan arrived in during the last one. He seemed to be impressed. He nodded at Dessie.

'You're even better than me,' he told him.

Larry popped his head out from behind the sofa. He started giving out yards to Dessie for using his guitar.

'Who gave you permission?' Larry said, 'You'll make a pig's ear of it.'

'Sorry,' said Dessie.

Everything seemed to go quiet suddenly. Now that the hi-fi was off we were all thrown back on our own resources. On our miserable Bobless lives.

'He betrayed us all,' said Larry, draining the last of his airport whiskey.

'What do you mean?'

'He betrayed us by pretending to bring us to nirvana and then hooking off to his luxury pads with his fortune.'

Jokerman looked crestfallen. Queen Mary adjusted her tiara.

'He never said he was a communist,' I suggested.

'He was a rebel,' said Larry, 'Now he's cosying up to the Pope. How consistent is that?'

'He's probably looking for fire insurance,' said Dessie, 'now that he's tipping the eighty mark. Knock knock knockin' at heaven's door? Zimmerman, zimmer frame?'

'Take a chill pill, Larry,' said Kim, 'He's just a song and dance man. Give him a break.'

'He can't even sing anymore,' said Larry.

'Could he ever?' said Cordelia.

Jokerman looked at Larry.

'I don't know why you threw this shindig if you have these views,' he said.

Larry looked downhearted.

'Maybe I'm addicted to bad karma,' he said.

My head was lifting. I stood at the French doors. The party was ending. I felt sad. Would we ever meet like this again, all of us freaks and weirdos? People told us to get a life, to get our own thing going, but sometimes you could have more fun jumping on someone else's bandwagon.

I went back in. Jokerman tweaked his nose. Queen Mary bowed. Blind Willie McTell pulled off his shades. He showed us his babyblue eyes.

Napoleon in rags, meanwhile, surveyed his empire. He felt proud of Mr Jones and sorry for Con. He was ashamed of Becky's dad.

Larry still looked downhearted.

'Do you want to know what my attitude to Bob Dylan is? Fuck him.'

'I wish I could,' said Norma, 'but I don't think he'd let me.'

What's It All About?

When we're young
everything is dreaded.
We go on about the meaning of life,
where we came from,
where we're headed,
all that boring eschatological strife.
Then we enter a different league.
We get bouts of bad health,
metal fatigue,
maybe a problem with drink.
We visit a shrink
to unload our petty woes
and hopefully earn a dose
of Prozac,
bleating about depression
to create
a pseudo-intellectual impression.

After paying him a king's ransom
we look for a handsome partner.
We hunker down to a relationship,
the woosome twosome trip
that will define us,
not realizing security minus
love equals desperation.
There follows the house,
 children,
hollows in the soul
as the years roll by.
We don't bother to salvage
what little hope was there,
content to cry bitter tears
in carpeted rooms
as divorce looms.

It's not our fault.
Some short-circuit
in our DNA
brought things to this.
God's to blame
for the whole dastardly game,
filling us up
with an infatuational fit
and turning ecstasy to shit.

Life is about emotional health.
We play the hand we're dealt.
There's no point aping Hamlet.
looking for ants
 in the picnic basket
but ever since Adam ditched
the Eden deal
mankind's been pitched
into this unholy mess
where we sin and then confess
what we don't understand
just because it's ready to hand.

The French call sex 'the little death'
The big one doesn't cause them
quite as much distress.
They think about religion
when they're in deep pain
fire insurance a worthwhile gain
for agnostics searching for catharses
as they slump on their collective arses.

Call From Afar

I am trapped
inside the exactitude
of the moment.
You speak to me
of an unknown body,
an unknown mind.
My senses are extinct
my identity unknown to itself.

Call me
when you find yourself
tell me you were the one
who knew me when.

Days disguise themelves
as battalions
that deceive me,
claming my voice,
my mind,
the other things
you toyed with
when it was important.

A building claims you.
You drown inside it.
Meanwhile I float outside
on a dangerous street
hearing the way
you used to be
waving at the things
we shared
in a rainy month
when everything was promised
in that street
under that sky
covering the yellow walls
of my mother
and us.

Norfolk
sabotaged you.
It held you for a moment
before letting you go
into the wider world
beyond my laments
and my imprecations.
It enclosed you
in other cocoons,
the worlds you hid from me –
people, plastic,
a block of ice
you looked at
like a mirror
and then became.

See-Saw

What did I drink last night? Who did I insult? No longer are these outings matters of enjoying oneself. They're damage limitation.

The clock says 1.21. Three hours ago I pressed the Snooze button. It's been alarming me every seven minutes since. I press the button now by rote. There's nothing to get up for. But we must preserve the illusion. Forward the great password. Onward Christian soldiers. Arise, arise and do your worst. You get out of life what you put into it. Lately I've been putting in zippo.

I crawl downstairs. Turn television on low so as not to upset my hangover. Look at smiley early morning faces telling me about earthquakes and murders. Buttonhop to the 40th repeat of *Friends* for escapism, or the 80th one of *ER*. What's George Clooney's secret that he can look almost the same in the last episode as the first? Refrain from checking self in mirror as realise am not George Clooney.

Ring Greg. He was the one who told me not to have that last whiskey last night. A good friend even though I almost socked him one for his solicitude.

He isn't in. The answering machine says call back later. It's one of those Happy Voice messages that reminds me of the happy TV faces. Would prefer one that goes, 'Fuck off. I'm not here.' I'd always respond to that

Hitler, my glorious ex, rings It's as if she times it to the moment when I'll be near a phone. She's always had this ability to read my mind. Is this what they mean by women's intuition?

She wants me to bring Sam, our joint creation, to the park. I've forgotten it's her day to have him.

'You're always like this after a night on the town,' she tells me.

'I'm always like this, period,' I reply.

There's some chitter-chatter about how to dress him and what to bring with me. It flies over my head, like all of her ruminations have flown over my head during the last two years.

268

I go into Sam's bedroom to wake him. Everything is all over the place. That makes it look like my own room. Monkey see, monkey do. As Darwin said. Or was it Spock?

He wipes the sleep from his eyes. We're both slow to wake up in the mornings but for slightly different reasons.

'We have to meet your mother,' I say. Summit conference of the EU.

'You were supposed to bring me to the swimming pool,' he complains. Children have better memories than elephants.

'That's next week.'

He grunts as he slides out of his bed onto the floor. Then he somersaults over to the wardrobe. It's all done in the one motion. Oh to be young again. If I tried that I'd probably end up in the A&E department of Beaumont Hospital.

'What would you like for breakfast?' I ask him. He shrugs his shoulders. I look in the fridge but there's nothing there. This simplifies matters.

'You can have toast or toast,' I inform him.

'I think I'll have toast,' he says. He's already shaping up to be a stand-up comedian.

SpongeBob Squarepants has come on the TV. He guffaws loudly at it, almost knocking himself off the sofa in the process. He laughs so much I think he's going to throw up. I yawn so much I think I'm going to throw up. Hey, the day is on the road.

The toast pops up. He munches it. Meanwhile I drink coffee.

'Are you not having breakfast?' he says.

'This *is* breakfast,' I say.

Coffee makes me sick but it puts my brain into first gear. If I still have a brain.

The programme finishes. He's left three-quarters of his meal behind him. He wants me to play football with him. I tell him there's no time, that Hitler is waiting on us. Except I don't call her that. It would get back to her. Anyway, he'd want to know who he is. He's too young to hear tales about Der Fuehrer not being A Nice Man.

'Are you ready to hit the road?' I ask. He nods. Of course he's ready. He would be ready to fly to the moon if I asked him. Which might be a good idea.

I search inside my anorak for my car keys. They're not there. What was I wearing last night? Did Greg take them? I remember him telling me to walk home. Maybe he drove me.

'What are you looking for?' he says.

'Nothing,' I tell him. He's at the age where he thinks I have all the answers. It wouldn't do to let him know I was footless last night when I sent the child-minder home. If Hitler heard about that it would be the end of my visitation rights.

I find them under the seat. Eureka. First victory of the day. From now on everything is possible.

I drive towards the park. There's ice everywhere. Our breath fogs the air.

'It's freezing in here,' he says, 'Can you not put on the heater?' I turn it on but the engine hasn't been engaged long enough for it to take effect. It only blows out cold air.

'You must have the dial wrong,' he tells me.

'Just keep jumping up and down and you'll get warm,' I say. So he does. Until his head is banging off the roof of the car.

'That's enough,' I say.

'You told me to do it.'

He starts asking me questions about every building we pass. Who lives there? Do I know them? Who owns that shop? Do I go to it? Maybe I was this curious once. Oh to be seven again. Oh to be even thirty-seven again.

'Look!' he screams, 'There's Jimmy Barrett.'

Jimmy is hobbling along a footpath in his football gear. He waves at us. The day has hardly begun and he's already played a match. I'm envious.

'Why can't we go to the pool?' he asks me as we reach the park. 'Why do I have to go with her?'

'Because she's your mother.'

'But it's boring. We do nothing.' I'm flattered that he prefers life with the person she calls The Bad Parent. And a bit surprised that life in a Georgian house in Castleknock with a tennis court in the back garden doesn't float his boat as much as a crap flat in Whitehall with a leaky roof.

'She'll feed you up with healthy food,' I say 'so you'll grow up big and strong.'

'I don't want to grow up big and strong,' he says, 'and I don't want healthy food. I want toast and coffee.'

'Good choice,' I admit.

We arrive. Hitler approaches us as we get out of the car. As usual she's got here first.

'Your front tyre is bald.' she informs me. It could be worse. It could be me. Won't be long for that either.

'I know,' I say, 'It may have escaped your notice that I lost my job. Good tyres are luxuries these days.'

She beckons Sam to her. 'Come to Mammy, Puddles,' she says. I don't know why she calls him Puddles. He doesn't either. He's probably too young to tell her he despises the name but I know he does. His face says it. It'll probably come out in therapy when he's about 55.

She swings him around. In her car I spot a gigantic teddy bear, probably her latest present to him. Is she trying to buy his love?

'You owe me money,' she says. The expression 'cut to the chase' should have been invented for her.

'I know. I'll give it to you when I get my dole.'

'You really need to start looking for a job.'

'Do you know any that pay more than the dole?'

'Slacker,' she hisses, 'How you love your layabout lifestyle.'

We've reached one of our familiar impasses. No matter how much a couple love or hate one another, how is it that every situation always ends up with a discussion about money?

'You're first on my list,' I say, 'If it's any consolation to you I scan the Situations Vacant column every night in the paper.'

'For leisure reading maybe. Now that you're too drunk to read Dostoevsky anymore.' Ouch.

I look around me at the other sets of parents. Some of them are playing with their children on the climbing frames. Some are on the see-saws, some on the swings. In an ideal world we'd be there too with Sam. We'd be a nuclear family. But this isn't an ideal world. It's a world where I fantasise daily about her driving a Nissan Almera off Howth pier.

'I have to go now,' I say, 'See you next weekend.'

'Don't forget the chicken's neck.'

She drives off. In an hour they'll be sitting down to dinner in Castleknock with her new lover. He's a landscape artist with a goatee, a man who's 'going somewhere' in life as she puts it. Meanwhile I continue my backwards march towards depravity.

The park is quiet. I wonder what to do with the rest of the day, with the rest of my life. 'Get a job,' is her familiar refrain. Would that be a possibility? Maybe I could emigrate to somewhere like Canada. I believe they still have work there for people who want to pick fruit or stack supermarket shelves on crap wages. If I worked for thirty years maybe I'd make enough for a down payment on another crap flat in Whitehall with a leaky roof.

Another alternative would be to audition for *X Factor*. Or get rich from a record deal. Or study acting and win an Oscar. Or first prize at the Cannes Film Festival. Or the Lottery. Or find the cure for cancer or Aids or even multiple sclerosis. In the meantime I need a packet of fags.

Greg tells me I need to think about Part Two of my life. 'Hitler is history,' he says, 'You need to get her out of your mind. The hate will eat you up.'

He's right, of course. Last night he introduced me to another woman, a workmate of his who seems to like me. We had a nice conversation but it didn't really go anywhere. Maybe I'm blocking myself. He told me I needed to 'move on.' Unfortunately I don't want to move on. I've always preferred standing still. It seems easier.

I try to remember the girl's name. I think it was Gillian. Greg told me half Dublin was looking for her phone number. But then that's the way he always talks. 'A year's pension for just fifteen minutes,' he said to me when he looked across the bar at her. Greg is also separated. Surprise?

I wrote Gillian's number on a bus ticket that I stuffed into my anorak. I may or may not ring her. The last thing I want is to appear too eager. That always scares them off. But at my age it's probably not a good idea to play games. I believe she's a Second Time Arounder too. Is there anyone who isn't these days?

A cold sun bleeds into me as I walk down the street. It's 3 p.m., the time of day when it's too early and too late to do anything. I think it was Jean-Paul Sartre who said that.

I wander into a cinema. They're showing an Arnold Schwarzenegger film. I give myself up to it. Arnie is blowing away half the population of South America for no better reason than they look sideways at him.

After it ends I start thinking about Gillian again. Will I ring her? I feel as nervous as I did the first time I asked a girl out at the age of sixteen. What should I say? 'How's the going, love, would you like to go out tonight? And then spend the rest of your life with me?' You can't afford to dilly-dally with Second Time Arounders. It might work or she might tell me to take a flying jump for myself. I don't mind either way.

Gillian. Nice eyes, nice smile. Much nicer than Hitler anyway, especially when she gets into one of her rages. That's a whole other story. Remind me to tell it to you sometime. But be warned: It's X-rated. And she comes out like the devil in it. She'd probably say the same about me.

That's the thing about life. We all try to make ourselves out to be God and the other person in the marriage the devil. After a few pints it evens out. After a few pints we think we're all God and the devil mixed. That's closer to the truth.

Waking

Milk going sour on the sideboard
a half drunk bottle of wine
her blouse on the sofa
as I wonder
what happened last night.

The phone rings.
When I pick it up
she says she's fine.
She asks how I am.
I say I'm fine too.

I turn the radio on,
look out at the day
as the sun spears the blinds.

I'm in a stained vest
my head bursting
with dim memories
of last night.

I sip the stale wine,
draw on a cigarette butt
as the day takes shape.

Do all parties end like this,
I ask myself,
with broken furniture
and broken relationships?

A radio blasts my ears.
I fall on the ground,
half-remembering insults hurled
and received.

Drink is the great leveler.
It's a pleasant amnesia.

Spilt whiskey
looks up at me
from the carpet.
Her blouse is torn,
meshed into the sofa
as if it grew from it.
I can taste her presence,
her European aura.

The morning is an eternity
until my dog walks in.
He licks my face.
At least he forgives me.

It's the beginning of a new day
press
pause
delete
oblivion
rewind.

Responsibility

I wrecked my car
walked out of my job
got angry at the sun
for shining.

Smoke rings fill the air.
Calypso music surrounds me.
I'm drinking Southern Comfort
as if I invented it.

It's like a day off school,
a night off from your parents
or your wife.
There's mud in the sky,
the lizard is in our hearts,
the scorpion spits at the fire.
We go down
to the dungeon of ourselves,
light matches at harvest moons,
suck dust from powdered roads,
hitchhike to nowhere
under a moon that's bursting
like a potato.

There's no fool like an old fool,
my advisors tell me,
but they're young fools.
They know less about life
than an amoeba.

The soft air calls to me
like a magical old friend
coming home.

My father would turn in his grave
if he saw me
surrounded by people
whose lives have deserted them.
And yet they give me
something to identify with.
I could have been that soldier.

I'll ride my horse
into the horizon
dismount at the gulch of death
as the buzzards of hope
wait patiently for a premature release.
My soul falls out of my body
onto the scorched earth
as I salute
something,
nothing,
everything.

Strategic

You settled for the first shot,
cast yourself in dull regimes,
deserved,
in a perverted way,
the dirt of your divorce.
He cased you at the discotheque,
a predator with charm,
you fell into his arms
with glee.

In time you saw the subterfuge
that made you swoon,
you repossessed
your purity too late.
In moments you forgave him,
soldl your love to chimeras,
made promises in stupors
that tomorrow would be clean.

The doctor gives you pills
to stall your thoughts.
You function well for days.
He writes about the children
and you prime them for society,
erase somehow the detritus
of women on the streets,
a man across the water
chasing women on the streets.

Your days drive on,
and futures,
like the waxworks of your dreams,
pass by.

Perhaps you'll reach relief,
you think,
in dream or fantasy
but night brings thoughts
of youth again,
the pornographic men.

The Ex

I was always a tomboy. More interested in sport than men when I was a teenager. Afterwards work became my thing. People started to speculate. Would I wind up an old maid? Marriage was like a holy grail.

Then one day the job stopped doing it for me. I started to look at men, at children. What was happening? Was my maternal instinct starting to kick in? My mother breathed a sigh of relief.

What she didn't know was that I wanted a child more than a husband. A lot of my girlfriends felt like that as well but they wouldn't admit it. They waited until after they'd gone up the aisle to tell the man in their lives they were dispensable. Baby made three. That was one too many.

My friends told me you had to travel half way around the world to adopt nowadays. I didn't feel like going to Russia or Vietnam so I decided to have one myself. I knew a few men who were willing to be sperm donors. Men never mind you asking them things like that. I chose Liam, a bank manager I knew from Tubercurry. We did the deed and, lo and behold, a month later I got the good news from my doctor.

The problems started when I began to fall in love with him. Liam might have been after sex but I wasn't. Tomboy or not, at least I had one female characteristic: clinginess. So when he tried to drop me, as men do when they've got what they want out of you, I threw a fit.

I made him feel so guilty we ended up getting married. It was that crazy. He thought he was rescuing me and I thought that too. I can't think of any other reason why I would have tied the knot with him. Me, a woman who campaigned almost singlehandedly for the abolition of marriage as an institution… because it turned perfectly normal people into barbarians.

Maybe I just wanted to try it as an experiment. I was always into experiments. Have baby, live with man, get married. I was hardly a poster girl for originality.

We had two good years together but the marriage lasted three. Therein lay the problem. In the final one we were attending an inquest of the emotions. Presuming any were ever there at all.

'We suited each other,' was one of his milder descriptions of our time together. 'We were insane to hook up,' seemed to hit the target better.

Everyone else was breaking up all around us at the time. I didn't think too much if it. We weren't much more than statistics. It was only when he was gone that I knew he'd been there. As someone used to being surrounded by people I took him for granted. I expected him to be there forever, like a bad smell.

We're apart now. In a way that seems more normal. When we were together we spent most of our time arguing. He comes over to see Jerome, to tell me all the reasons it went wrong between us. I prefer it when he just sees Jerome.

He met someone else, a girl half my age. He's dressing younger to fit in with her. He's also talking about young things, like what's in the music charts these days. Do young people still say things like 'music charts'?

One night he told me I should find a toyboy for myself. 'If I did,' I said to him, 'maybe your toy girl would go off with him.' He didn't like that.

I drink to make the time pass. That's what you do when your man leaves and you have no job to occupy yourself.

I love Jerome but I never saw myself as being the type of woman to spend all day with a child. Sometimes he gets on my nerves. Like when he wakes me up in the middle of the night. And sometimes I'm sure I get on his. Like when I give out to him for waking me up in the middle of the night.

My mother cries about me. She thinks I threw away my future. Maybe I did. I tell her to find something more interesting to worry about than me. Like crosswords, for instance. Or origami.

People ask me where my life is at the moment. 'Nowhere,' I say. I watch the soaps and mooch around the kitchen. I meet my friends occasionally to bitch about the male of the species. That's my favourite hobby these days. We all have stories to tell, most of them ending up with the conclusion that when men are circumcised, the doctors throw the wrong bit away. Ho ho.

Lately the talk is about property rather than love or love's end. We discuss bridging loans, inheritance tax, VAT. That doesn't hurt. What hurts most of all is the fact that I don't care. As one who was slow to give love I'm even slower to give it up. As he would say himself, 'Women, can't live with them, can't live without them.' When he's drunk he says, 'Can't live with them, can't live with them.'

He wants the house. Does he forget the fact that I raised his son here, that I rescued him from his demons here, that I picked him up when he had his breakdowns here?

'That's history,' he says.

We meet lawyers. They know nothing about us. They're thrown into positions of great power because they have more money than we have. We tell them what divides us and they tell us what can join us. But it always boils down to money. Who has it, who controls it, Who can get it out of those magic holes in the wall that they have outside banks.

I try to tell a story of the night Jerome was born, a night he was meant to be with me but wasn't, a night he was with another woman, a night I forgave him for. It was the beginning of a pattern of other nights when sons weren't being born but his wife was pining for him. Foolishly.

But they don't want stories. They want documents, lists of expenses, plans for what I'll do with my future. We joke about meeting in McDonalds in a few years to exchange Jerome, the engine running outside the restaurant as one or other of us picks him up or drops him to soccer practice. The new Irish family. Son with Man United, Mother with Man Disunited.

He's clever with the lawyers. I'm not. He knows their language, what they charge by the hour. He might even go drinking with them. That could help with the bill.

'Where to now?' my mother asks. It hardly matters. My life has been lived already.

282

From now on it will just be explanations, memories, people trying to tell me what I should have done differently. Woulda, coulda, shoulda, didn't. My main mistake was falling into the trap women have fallen into for two thousand years: Getting Involved With A Member Of The Opposite Sex.

He told me once that I was the right woman at the wrong time. And then, inevitably, that he still loved me even if he wasn't 'in' love with me. I wonder if he gets these kinds of things from books. Does he read them in fortune cookies? In a way it feels nice to be the right woman at the wrong time. It's certainly better than being the wrong woman at the right time.

'Irish women make better mothers than wives,' he said to me one night. I was breastfeeding Jerome at the time. Was this a defence mechanism? Would he have preferred me to have him at my bosom? Was Jerome the straw that broke the camel's back?

I have no bitterness about anything. How could I have? Most of my friends are divorced. It's the new elitism. Happiness is only for dullards. What we should plan for is that all-important second relationship where one piece of damaged goods meets another piece of damaged goods and they click in their makeshift flat on two post-marital salaries.

In the old days people fixed what needed mending. My mother would know. She was married to an alcoholic and she offered it up. I didn't want to be that soldier. He probably sussed that. It made him run, boy, run. He wanted the shrinking violet but instead he got Maggie Thatcher. Thatcher dressed up as Mother Teresa in his eyes, forever looking for pity from 'the girls.'

He thinks all women are hypocrites. Maybe we are. I don't analyse things like that anymore. All I know is that tonight I'm staring at a television screen with a remote control in one hand and a child in the other wondering where it all went wrong.

Time

I think of you
behind a desk,
no longer beautiful
no longer young,
filling in forms
as dusty
as the shelves you stack,
too far away to care.

Where did we lose it,
little one,
so close to the finish line?
Childhood lovers,
destined to be paired,
I remember the dress
you always wore,
I remember a night
on a beach in Sligo
when we were immersed
in our dream.
So arrogant,
as if we had the right
to happiness.

Tonight as I write these lines,
imagining you behind your desk
I wonder if that night
comes back to you
like it's always done to me.
We embraced our future then,
running against the wind,
the sand in your hair
as I said to you,
'What now?'

not really knowing
what I meant.

In the long months afterwards
we forgot
my careless words.
Our lives went on like before
but there was a question now
unvoiced
and worse because of that.

You changed your dress,
you talked less,
embarking on a trip
that brought you here,
to the habitat you claim to love
2000 miles away
as you sit vacantly
filling in forms
with the kind of energy
you once devoted to me
before either of us were born.

Teeling Street

I sit in the dark
watching leaves cluster.
There are lives
I don't know about,
will never know about.
There are only windows
that occasionally emit light.

Voices become raised.
The suggestion of drama
permits me to conceive
the vague promise
of a random event
that might transform my life
or someone else's
from this deadening
frightfulness
of repetition.

A song rings out
in the cool of the evening
reminding me
of other nights
when different promises
were available.
Cars huddle past,
their movement the only diversion
on this street
where nothing happens.

Meanwhile the dawn awaits.
Milkmen prepare our daily diets.
We try to court sleep

postponing the scars of intent
the things that keep us ticking -
meetings, meals,
polite chit-chat
while inside we know
that the banter
hides secrets
that can only be revealed
at weekends
when defences are down
and a truckload of tension
spills out
to the person who just happens
to be sitting beside us
in the pub.

This is the new confessional.
We commune under the influence
of liquor, Sky TV,
remonstrating over the price of a pint
and thinking of the girl at the counter
the one with the lovely face
who speaks to PJ
at the fruit machine.

Forget the mortgage
and collecting the kids.
Such inconveniences can wait.
It's a war we've won
without weapons or even words.
Time permits us this quiet reward
even while it's killing us.

Repossessed

Every class had one. Ours was called Rod Traynor. I remember him at the back of the class doing dissections on spiders. 'For posterity,' he explained. Sometimes he put mice into people's satchels to see their reactions.

He fell in love for the first time at 12 years old. The following year he began a life-long love affair with drink. 'If you took more interest in your work there'd be less time for that sort of thing,' the English teacher said to him. 'But I don't,' Rod replied.

Various methods were used to deal with him. Sometimes letters were sent home to his parents. For Rod it was his first taste of being a celebrity. 'He'll grow out of it in time,' his father told the principal, 'he's going through that difficult phase.'

'So are we all,' said the principal.

'He'll never stand in a dole queue,' his mother liked to boast. Rod begged to disagree. It was his life's ambition to stand in one.

I don't know why I befriended him. We were opposites. He either came first or last in exams. I seemed destined to inhabit the anonymous middle. I was a plodder. He was a lazy genius.

He opened up a world to me, albeit not the one my parents planned for me. He introduced me to people who were on the fringes of society - petty criminals, speed freaks. My father tried to stop me seeing him. He had me earmarked for a future in the bank. To help me on my way he introduced me to 'the best people.' He once said to me, 'All you need to get through this life is a word that's written on every·door.' In my innocence I thought he meant 'Push.'

He threw me across the room one night when he heard I'd been out with Rod. 'That boy will bring you to the bottom of the barrel,' he said. It was where most 15-year old boys dream of being.

Rod was a writer as well. As editor of the school magazine he monitored what the rest of us did. I couldn't match him in this either. My own pathetic attempts at writing stories usually ended up in bathos. Maybe I was too awed by him to find my own voice. His pet topic was the loner, the freak, the misunderstood hobo. The last verse of one of his poems had a junkie in a Parisian bordello having his last fix before he slit his wrists.

'Hardly Muredach's material,' I observed. One day soon afterwards he urinated on 'The Prelude', our official text, in the middle of the English class. The teachers couldn't wait to see the end of him. In the exam hall for the Leaving Cert he turned on a laughing machine. It caused panic but it wasn't traced to him. If it was he'd probably have been expelled.

Out in the world he turned smooth. He tidied himself up and got a job in a hardware shop. He also gave up the gargle. Everyone wondered what was going on. Had he found God? Gone bonkers? Met a girl? The latter proved to· be the case.

Elizabeth Keegan was a Social Worker from Galway. When Rod met her he said he'd keep her in business for life. She'd heard about his exploits but thet didn't seem to bother her. She liked the little boy lost in him. They began a whirlwind romance.

The first time I saw them together it struck me that she was the first quiet girl he'd ever dated. I had to do a double take when I saw him taking a non-alcoholic drink with her. If she married him, I thought, his mother would die a happy woman.

'When are we going to see the tux?' I taunted as I was leaving. He waved his fist at me. A couple of days later I met him on the street. He was shaking.

'What's wrong with you?' I said. He said Elizabeth was doing his head in.

'She's too sensible for me.'

'That never bothered you with the other ones.'

'I can't stay on the dry anymore. I have the DTs. She's destroying me.' Only Rod could use the word 'destroying' to refer to someone trying to make him healthy.

'There's something else. She's pregnant.'

Two weeks later they were married. Rod's father believed he was reformed. He gave him a loan for a mortgage. It acted as a deposit for a house they'd been looking at in Geesala. They moved into it shortly afterwards. There was a lot of land at the back of it. Rod started building a cabin on it. He said it would be like a den for the pair of them. He was more interested in that than the house.

He didn't have any job at the time. Elizabeth's pay packet supported the two of them. He seemed infused with a new vigour. They bought a dog to complete the family set-up.

Everything seemed to be running smoothly but then one night Rod was taunted by someone he used to go drinking with.

'I hear you're being pussywhipped,' he said to him.

There was no way he was going to take that. He knocked him out. The man sued him for damages.

Rod went back on the bottle with the stress of it all. He stopped building the cabin as well. The house was re-possessed when Elizabeth couldn't meet the mortgage payments. The two of them split up. She rented a flat in Ballina as the birth of the child approached. Rod moved between her flat and the cabin, not sure where he wanted to be in the long run. The bank was trying to repossess the cabin as well. Rod dug his heels in.

'That wasn't part of the mortgage,' he said.

He was right there. It was a messy legal situation.

'He left me last week,' she told me one day soon afterwards when I met her in Garden Street.

'Is there another woman involved?' I asked.

'I don't know. Somebody said they saw him with one.'

She started to get emotional. I suggested a drink. A few minutes later her head was in her hands as she went on about the mad life they had together.

She thought he still loved her but didn't want to admit it. I asked her if she wanted me to visit him. She said she wasn't sure. He was staying in the cabin all the time now. It had no heat or electricity. She feared for his health.

I went up to the cabin a few days later. I could hear the sound of music from inside as I approached it. I knocked. When he came out I couldn't believe the decline in him. He looked like a man of fifty. He had nothing on him but the bottoms of a pair of pyjamas Tomato ketchup was dripping from his mouth.

He threw his arms around me.

'Come in amigo,' he hailed, 'A royal welcome awaits you.'

As I walked in I got the stench of stale liquor. Records were strewn around the floor. Cobwebs hung from the ceiling.

His dog charged at me as I took in the surroundings. After he calmed it down he motioned me to a corner. I sat down.

'Excuse the mess, old fellow,' he guffawed, 'It's the cleaning lady's day off.'

It was only then I spotted a woman in his bed. She looked like a gypsy. Her hair was streeling wildly over her face.

'Oh yes,' he said when he saw me looking at her, 'You must meet Maria. What do you think - hot stuff, eh? Can't beat the bit of home help, can you? Service with a smile.'

I said nothing.

'Give us a few minutes, will you, sunshine?' he said to her. When she got out of the bed I saw she was naked. He watched her dressing. She made her way out the door.

'Amazing creature really,' he said after she was gone, 'Can't get a word out of her to save her life but she makes love like one to the manor born.'

'What's happening between you and Elizabeth?' I said.

'You know the answer to that. She wanted me to go straight. I told her I couldn't. It was as simple as that.'

'You fool,' I said, 'Do you realise what you're giving up?'

'I'm doing her a favour. Are you too thick to see that?'

'She loves you.'

'It's too late. Where were you when there was a chance for us? She wouldn't have me back now anyway.'

'That's debatable.'

He gazed into the fire.

'Do you know I almost stabbed her one night?'

'That's the past. She's willing to give you another chance. She told me so.'

'What's it to you anyway? Are we in Good Samaritan week?'

I resisted saying 'I'm worried about you.' It would probably have brought on another onslaught.

'You're about to have a child in a few months' time,' I said, 'Do you not care about that?'

'I'll throw her a few quid when the nipper arrives. Beyond that I can't go.'

He dragged on a cigarette butt.

'The marriage to Liz was a mistake. It should never have happened. I don't know why it did. She caught me at a moment in my life when settling down seemed like a good idea. I'm like that. I don't make sensible decisions like the other 99% of the human race.'

'You made one sensible one.'

'Don't try to be clever.'

'Would you not go back to her for her sake if not your own?'

He laughed.

'It's an interesting suggestion but no. Look, she'll make out fine without me. She'll fit nicely into the deserted wife category. There'll be lots of visits from people who'll let her cry on their shoulders. They'll tell her what a lucky escape she had from me.'

There seemed nothing else to say. I told him I respected his decision.

When I went to leave he tried to hold on to me at the door. He started to open a bottle of whiskey.

'No, Rod,' I said, pushing him away from me, 'I have to go. Really.'

His face fell.

'You used to be great craic once,' he said, closing the door.

I told Elizabeth what happened. She wasn't surprised, even about the other woman. She cried again. I held her tight.

I asked her if she'd meet me some night for a drink. She said she would. I'd always been attracted to her. I never mentioned anything to her when she was with Rod. Now it was different. I knew she liked me too.

I went out with her a few times in the next few weeks. One night I took her to a show. As we sat sipping coffee afterwards in the foyer I saw a strange look in her eyes. I asked her what was wrong.

'I dream about him every night.'

'Maybe your subconscious is trying to tell you something.'

'I don't believe in going into things like that. I have enough on my plate trying to figure my mind out during its waking hours.'

'Do you think he'll try and get back with you?'

'If he does, the door will be closed.'

'I don't understand. I thought you wanted him.'

'I do. It's him that doesn't want me. He never loved me.'

'Why did he marry you so?'

'Maybe out of a sense of guilt. He wanted to create a fictional image of himself. It was like something out of one of those novels he used to write at school.'

'Were you happy with him in the beginning?' I asked her.

'Sometimes I thought I was going out of my mind. We'd take off on weekends together in his uncle's car. He'd speed down the road at 70 or 80 miles an hour with a bottle of whiskey in his hand.'

'Did you ever crash?'

'Only once. It was a miracle we walked away from it. After that I never sat in a car with him again.'

Over the next few weeks l visited her most nights. I still saw us just as friends but people began to talk about us. Then one night I slept with her. Rod heard about it and blew a fuse. He came up to my house reeking of beer.

'Why don't you find your own woman?' he roared at me.

'You told me it was over between you two.'

'That's not the point. You don't move in on another man's wife. Especially someone who used to be a friend.'

A few nights later I heard he threatened to kill me. He'd been getting worse with the drink. He was also in trouble with the law. He went back to a pub he'd been barred from and the manager rang the guards. They arrested him but the man didn't press charges. He slept it off in a cell.

It wasn't until the birth of Elizabeth's baby that I met him again. He came in to see her in the hospital but didn't show much interest either in her or the child. He was sitting on the bed playing with him when I went in. When I saw the pallor of his face my heart ran cold. He seemed to have aged a decade even in those few weeks. His coat had so many tears it was like a patchwork quilt. There was a bottle of whiskey sticking out of one of the pockets.

In his hand he held a hurley stick. He wielded it at me as though he was going to use it on me.

'Go ahead,' I said, 'Hit me if it makes you feel good.'

He stared at me like a madman. I could see he didn't know what he wanted to do. Then he broke out into one of his guffaws. Elizabeth looked from one of us to the other. She asked me to leave them alone together. Rod took the bottle out of his pocket and had a swig of it. As I went down the corridor I heard him singing to the baby. For a moment I envisaged him running away to his cabin with it, locking it away from the universe.

I walked around the grounds for a while. Then I sat on the grass. After a while he came through the door, staggering on his feet. He didn't see me and I didn't approach him. I was relieved to see him go off. When I got back into the ward Elizabeth looked distraught. .

'He's out for blood,' she said.

'Did he bother you?'

'Not really. He just talked nonsense. He said he was thinking of going to South America to dig for gold.'

'Did he say he wanted to go back to you?'

'I can't remember what he said. He doesn't know what he wants anymore. He's eaten up with hatred. I'm afraid of what he might do to you.'

'Why don't you move in with me?' I said suddenly, 'That way we'd have a kind of protection against him.'

'It could make things worse.'

I knew there was that danger. Maybe I wanted to bring things to a head.

'Will he always be the thing that comes between us?' I said.

'I have no feelings for him now at all except fear.'

In the next few weeks I heard stories of him threatening me in the bars again. Nothing ever happened except for a stone thrown in my window one night. He stayed in his cabin most of the time now, emerging only to chase away the children that ran around it. He was almost permanently drunk. Sometimes I saw him outside the main house. The bank was trying to let it to tenants. They hadn't been able to re-sell it. Elizabeth said Rod wouldn't let them, that he frightened away a prospective buyer one day. It was as if he still had hopes they could be there together again - or maybe he was just there to wallow in the memory of what it represented.

One night I saw him curled up outside it in the rain, the inevitable flask of whiskey in his hand. I was tempted to go up to him for old time's sake but I didn't. Two nights later he was taken in to hospital with double pneumonia.

He spent a few weeks hovering between life and death. Elizabeth spent most of her time by his bed. Sometimes I went in with her. If he saw me he went ballistic. He was on so many pills he was only half-conscious most of the time. The only thing he enjoyed was playing with his child. It seemed to represent a side of his old life that he still wanted even if he wouldn't admit it to himself.

The doctors didn't give us much hope for him. Rod said he didn't care if he lived or died. Whenever food was brought to him he threw it back in the nurses' faces. He was so thin he hardly made a crease in the bed.

Elizabeth stayed with me some nights. More usually she spent the night by his bed or in a room the hospital allowed her to sleep in that was near his ward. I spent most of my time hanging around the canteen. She joined me there every few hours to give me an update on his condition. I thought she was more faithful to him than many women who'd spent twenty or thirty years with their husbands. It made me love her even more. But it also made me worry about whether he'd always been in her mind.

He died within the month. By now we were just waiting for the call. My one came in the middle of the night. As soon as the phone rang I knew what it was. I couldn't feel too much sadness for him but Elizabeth was in bits.

'I'm shocked but not surprised,' she said when I asked her how she took the news. It was the way I felt too. How could Rod Traynor be dead? He was my hero, my role model, my soulmate. He was the worst of me and the best of me, the person who created all the things I loved and hated about myself.

I was more upset for her than for myself. She told me he was already dead for her the first night she saw him with the pneumonia. After that it was just like a playing out of an inevitable story. She didn't allow herself to grieve. She wasn't sure she'd be able to cope with it if she gave in to it.

She told me she wanted me to be with her all the time now. I felt that wouldn't be the right thing to do. I stayed away from her for the next few days out of respect for what they had.

Old friends from the school appeared at his funeral. People who hadn't seen him for a long time were in shock when they heard what happened.

Those of us who lived in the town were more philosophical. I was asked to give a eulogy but I refused. The priest spoke of a highly intelligent man who took the 'short path' to his destiny.

A vigil was held around his cabin after the burial. I didn't answer any questions about him that were put to me, playing down our friendship for reasons I wasn't quite sure of. Maybe I was nervous about how my relationship with Elizabeth might be perceived. For a part of the night it was as if we were mourning some kind of rock God, a man who pointed us all the way to some dark ideal.

A lot of drink was consumed. At a certain point of the night someone started a bonfire. They lit a piece of wood and threw it in one of his windows. We watched it sending the cabin up in flames without doing anything to prevent it. I felt it was fitting. What we were watching was a kind of Viking ritual. When it fell to the ground it was as if an exorcism had been performed.

Afterwards I walked with Elizabeth up to the house where they'd lived together for that short time. It was still uninhabited. As we looked at it in the night light it seemed to resemble a Greek ruin. She cried as we dallied briefly outside its doors, remembering the days when he went off the drink at the start of their marriage, busying himself wheeling wood from trucks to his cabin.

When I asked her if she thought our relationship contributed in any way to his death she said no.

'What killed him,' she said, 'was that he wanted to want me but he couldn't. That was the most insufferable thing of all for him.

When he made great claims of passion for me it was like a scene from one of his novels. I was a· symbol for him rather than a real person.'

I knew she was trying to forget him but I wasn't sure she could ever do that, or ever fully replace him with me in her affections. The more she talked, the more she seemed to be trying to convince herself he was gone from her life. I wondered how true that was. I felt she was protesting too much.

I told her that when I moved into the flat with her. I said I'd have preferred if she said she still loved him. That would have been less likely to pose problems between us down the road. As we sat talking I saw a tear in her eye. I wiped it away.

I couldn't get the image of Rod out of my mind. I was haunted by the thought of the life they had together all the time I was on the sidelines.

She kept telling me she loved me and that the baby had really taken to me too. The more she said it the angrier I became. Eventually I found myself begging her to stop. She didn't seem to know what my problem was for a while but then she did. She put her arms around me and told me not to worry, that she was mine now. But I still felt hollow inside.

Later on in the night I went for a walk in the grounds behind the flat. When I got back she was just sitting there. We didn't talk. We just stayed in the darkness thinking about everything that happened. I sat for hours in the silence looking out at the leaves shaking in the trees. She stayed sitting at the far side of the room from me, both of us trying to understand the glue that bound us together and the ice that kept us apart.

Getting it Together

She watches infomercials
on the plasma screen
then rollerblades to the park
to tone her muscles up.

Mornings she despises,
especially with a head
like World War Three,
which is most of the time.

She's about to give the bullet
to her beau
who's so 'yesterday,'
and unhygienic to boot.

A chicklit confection
crowns the coffee table.
The fridge has yoghurt
and yalacta cheese.

She texts Cindy
to say 8.30 will be fine
at the hip-hop club
for two Red Bulls
and a skinny latte chaser.

At the club she'll meet Damien
who swings both ways
but not hers unfortunately.
Damien is into bowling
and *nouvelle cuisine*.

She's not up for a relationship
at the minute

because she needs her space.
Commitment will come
in its own sweet time
like everything else
in her life.

She wants two kids
before she hits thirty.
Till then it's partytime.
Work is to make ends meet.
Keep the head down
until you punch that clock.
Ducks in a row
so no one suspects
the mad binges.

It's not a bad life really.
A few bob for doing nothing,
two weeks in Lanzarote
in August, fake tan
and the latest Marian Keyes
and maybe a bit of nookie
after a dance.
Holiday romance, no strings.

Weekends are for chilling out,
slumping round the apartment
like a tramp,
catching up on the gossip
with her mates
before visiting the old lady
with the weekly wash.

Tonight she'll put on
her cleanest dirty negligee
and snuggle up to the box set

of *Sex and the City*
with a double vodka
and diet coke chaser.
Nothing like a night in
with her facepack
to mark time
before meeting Mr Right
or even Mr Wrong.
'Love is blind,'
she tells the last sad sack
who failed to float her boat,
'and marriage a tin-opener'.

But enough of that.
Who's got the remote?

Alternative Lives

'The Kennedys are inked in for eight.'
'What are we going to do about the sitter?'
'Can you not organise these things in advance?'
'I don't have a crystal ball.'

Groceries in the Lexus,
appointment at the squash court
and Dave, always Dave to the rescue,
to cancel the *hors d'oeuvres*.
'Love you,' she says,
pecking him on the cheek.
'Have a good trip'.
He revs up, waves, tells her
they'll do it next week instead.

At St. Patrick's Well he removes the ring,
takes his new suit from the boot.
Sharon is on the mobile
as he squats in a traffic jam.
'How long have you got this time?'
'Just the night. She's starting to ask questions.'
'Is she on to us?'
'No, but you can't be too careful.'

They totter to the run-down hotel
that serves tine usual stale tea
with the usual good grace
Afterwards they slink upstairs.
He takes her clothes off clumsily.
She enquires about access, custody,
the possibility of a future.

They take beer from the f ridge with a key,
one of those funny ones you pay for.
He lies awake listening to the traffic,
his mind gone, not part of anything.
She asks him what's wrong.
but he doesn't know.
He misses something,
maybe a part of his old self.

He drifts into a half-sleep.
When he wakes it's still dark.
She's lying beside him
without her make up.
She looks like his wife.
Was this what he fell in love with?
What he still loves?

A waiter wakens her.
She senses something wrong
but she's afraid to ask.
'When you look for commitment
men leave skid marks.'
She read that
in one of the glossy monthlies.
'Coffee?' she suggests.
He paints on a smile.
Water bubbles out of the kettle
as he sits on the duvet
wondering.

The Six Year Itch

The last words she said to me were, 'We didn't fail. We just didn't bother trying.'

Nobody told us it wouldn't work. My grandparents stayed together and so did my parents. Everyone we knew, even the miserable ones, even the ones who were eating each other for breakfast. 'You have to give problems time. They'll sort themselves out.' And if they didn't, tough.

If you divorced, what would the neighbours say? We were engaged in emotional investment here. Building blocks for the future. It was the way life worked. Tip one domino over and they all fall down. It wasn't like changing your fridge or your TV set. We were people, godammit.

The last balloon popped. We sang 'Auld Lang Syne' to everyone around us. Not because we liked them but because they were there. We were drinking Prosecco, the make-believe champagne. And making make-believe love.

'Champagne for my real friends,' she said, 'and real pain for my sham friends.' I'd heard all her jokes before. That didn't stop her repeating them. What else was there to do now but go through the motions. We spoke our lines like two bad actors in a play most people had stopped caring about.

I was the last one at the party, a familiar situation for me. Too drunk to stay up and too drunk to go to bed. I emptied other people's drinks into me as I sat in the half-dark waiting for the sun to come up. She sat across from me checking her watch, her hemline, her future.

'Well,' she said.

'Well what?'

'It's time to go.'

It might have been a metaphor for the night, for all our nights together. Marshalling the practical details to relax herself. Discipline was important to her, as were deadlines. And we were dead.

What were we going back to? I looked at her through bloodshot eyes. I wondered who she was, who I was, where the day would bring us. We were in Act Two of our marriage, the scene where the outraged wife throws the alcoholic husband out.

'What drink would you like, dear?' she asks. He replies, 'Gin and tonic, dear, without the tonic.' But unfortunately this drama wouldn't play out quite as efficiently as one on Broadway or the West End.

When I was drunk I saw everything crystal clear. When we were dating she accepted my weakness, indulged it. Now she'd sooner have me drink hemlock.

Everyone was gone. We were alone with our mutual hatred. I smelt the oncoming dark. Could we make one last stab at tolerance, pretend the last six years hadn't happened? No, no, a thousand times no. We were like Adam and Eve in some poisoned garden - without our fig leaves. Like any other couple bereft of a place to hide we mortgaged our lives.

She accused me of drinking away our fortune, a fortune that was never there in the first place. It didn't suit her to admit that.

'It's the economy, stupid,' I said to her, 'the economy and your spending.'

'So your booze expenditure had nothing to do with it?'

How could it, I thought. Like most alkies I didn't see alcohol spending as reckless. You never do. Why waste money on cabbage that could be spent on Cuvée Speciale?

She rang the taxi, poured black coffee into me, apologised to the host. He sighed as she dug out my coat from under the fifty others in the utility room.

'Now, buster,' she said, 'one arm at a time.' She spoke to me as if I was some stranger she was rescuing from a dead-end dive in the sticks.

'Why do you drink so much?' she asked me after she got it on.

'Why do you nag so much?'

'Is that an answer?'

'If it keeps you off my back, yes.'

'Every alcoholic has to give himself reasons to guzzle.'

'Maybe, but you're a better one than most.'

Did I drink because she fell out of love with me or did she fall out of love with me because I drank? It was the old chestnut.

The taxi arrived as the sun came up. We drove to the home that wasn't a home. Here every room was a utility room. Or rather a futility room.

When I got inside the door I started crying. Was it for myself or for her? Or for what we'd become?

Six years. Six summers of separate holidays. Six long winters of hunkering down in dead rooms with the aftershock of our plan to live happily ever after.

In sickness and in hell.

We were thrown into the nakedness of the morning. The silence mocked us. I looked out at the billiard table lawn, the rolling fields. Space and more space. That was what the six years had been about. Expanding our house and reducing our emotions.

The insanity of the night turned into the insanity of the dawn. Could we ever forgive one another for the sin of meeting, or the later sin of falling in love?

The taxi driver drove her to her mother after dropping me off. No doubt they'd bitch about me as they worked out the details of the divorce. Mother-in-laws were good at that kind of thing.

She married me for money and divorced me for more money. That was the mathematics of marriage. Afterwards she took up with a man from Wolverhampton. He was more humble than the usual Brit.

'He's an antidote to you,' she said.

I was grateful to him for taking her off my hands. If she was happy, I thought, she wouldn't needle me. Was it possible for her to be happy? I feared I'd ruined her for other men. She enjoyed hating me too much.

How was it that two lives that seemed to be going swimmingly for so long could take off so suddenly in another direction and cut out all the things that made them work? It was like a fugue missing a beat, a blot at the end of the rainbow, a lock without the combination. I racked my brains for the reason.

I remembered the first date we went on, sitting with her in the tense darkness of a cinema, holding her hand during a Gary Cooper movie and trying to reprise Cooper's profound silences. Other dates followed, each more perfect than the last. Then we got married, settling into the routine of just being together. She made plans for the house and I pretended to be interested. Then she became bored with that. She got into yoga and TM. There was even something called Kabbalah. The very word itself scared me. What had I married? Was I so boring that she'd go into the realms of the occult to get away from me?

She organised coffee mornings, tried to get in touch with her inner feminist. All the beautiful people attended them, the ones who were infatuated with finding how many angels could dance on the head of a pin.

I started going out with some of my old friends, people she referred to as lowlifes.

'Why would you see *him*?' she'd snort, regardless of who it was. .'He de-stresses me,' I'd say back, regardless of who it was.

The problems didn't start with us going in different directions. That was just a symptom of the disease. The disease itself I put down to wedlock, emphasis on the 'lock.' My father used to say that a cat and a dog could happily sit by a fire without fighting but if someone tied their tails together they'd go mad. We were like a feral cat and a rabid dog.

'I despise you,' she said to me one night.

'I bet you say that to all the guys,' I replied.

The death of our love became a kind of protection to us. It would have been worse if one of us still loved the other. This way the fight was fair. It was to the death.

Where did we go wrong? One day a friend of mine said to me, 'Sometimes there doesn't have to be a reason, sometimes it's just the way things are.' He consoled me when I lost my job over her, when the solicitor told me I'd probably lose the house as well. You never knew a woman until you met her in court.

The worse she got, the more philosophical I became. I told myself it was as simple as the law of diminishing returns, even the law of gravity. What went up had to come down. The moon in June became the bitter harvest in September. What I didn't bank on was just how bitter that harvest could be.

As the divorce papers were being put together I ran into her with the new man in her life. She was wearing a leopardskin blouse I once bought her. It made her look predatory. I didn't know what to say to her so I just jabbered. She looked at me as if to say, 'Have you finished yet?' I felt like someone who'd just rung a doorbell in an empty house.

It was unlike her not to respond. I almost missed her abusing me. She obviously wanted to get away. Why? When I looked down at her stomach I discovered the reason: she was pregnant.

'When is it due?' I asked.

'When is what due?'

'Don't play games. This makes everything straightforward.'

'We're not sleeping together if that's what you're thinking.'

'The last time that happened there was a star in the East.'

I couldn't understand why she was being so demure. Did she think she'd get more money from me in the settlement if she didn't have a man? She walked off in a huff.

Her lover turned on me.

'Why do you always go out of your way to upset her?' he said. She obviously had him brainwashed. I could see her seducing him as she'd once seduced me. She was his property and he was her property. I was to be let out with the cat. Anything I said could be used in evidence against me. So I said nothing. I wanted to keep my billiard table lawn.

Tonight it's cold. Smoke billows from a chimney outside. The branches of my yew tree snake their way to the sky. In the distance two lights flash. I listen to the voice of Tom Waits droning like a rhinoceros with a sore throat. Time stands still. I have no regrets about anything that happened. We were who we were. I can forgive her if she can forgive me.

Tomorrow I'll be moving out of here. 'Exit at noon or the bailiff will fine you.' That was the way she put it. In the kind of voice that makes you listen. Tonight I'm an owner. Tomorrow I'll be a trespasser if I try to infiltrate these walls even for five minutes after that time.

Maybe I'll feel a sense of adventurousness in being homeless. Or maybe I'll just feel miserable.

The clock ticks like a metronome. The more I listen to it the louder it seems. Each second is precious to me. I gaze out at the empty streets, the changing contours of the sky. I've never liked goodbyes but tonight is different. Tonight there's nobody to say goodbye to.

I look around me at the walls, the furniture. Everything I'm bringing with me is in a case that's sitting in front of me, the heritage of six years. It's amazing how you can downsize when you put your mind to it. How much clutter do we gather around ourselves in a life? Maybe we need junk possessions just like we need junk food.

My life in a suitcase. Who would have thought it would end like this? She can have the antique furniture, the Dresden dolls. Where I'm going I'll hardly have room for such delicacies. You can't fit a cocktail cabinet in a phone box.

I won't be bringing our wedding photo. As I look at it now I smile. I'm standing there in my tweed suit with an expectant look on my face. It's as if I believe I have some divine right to happiness. She's more guarded. Maybe she knew something I didn't.

Earlier today I got drunk again. I thought about emigrating to get away from it all. But where would I emigrate to? No matter where I went she'd find me. She has the zeal of any number of FBI agents. So I got off that tack.

I'm too old to start Part Two of my life and too old to end Part One. I can't meet anyone new because I'm broke. If she takes any more money off me I'll be her slave. That may be what she wants. Maybe it would assuage some of her pain. The Germans call it schadenfreude. I call it sadism.

I think I know how it's going to pan out. She'll accuse me of hiding my money and I'll accuse her of hiding her fancyman. We'll both put our best foot forward for the solicitor as we once did for each other. In the end she'll probably win because she's better at lying than I am. For ever and ever, ah men. Pass Go. Collect half a million.

I can already see her in the dock. She'll be wearing her Burberry coat, standing at the front of the courtroom with a smile of victory playing about her lips. She'll trot out my spending habits, my emotional emptiness, my abject unsuitability for marriage. I'll see my life laid out before me like a cadaver.

She'll enjoy bleeding me dry. As for myself, maybe there'll be a kind of purity in having nothing rather than little. With nothing you can start your new life better. With a little you're more inclined to hark back to your old one.

The bottom line is that we brought out the worst in each other. We made each other realise just how cruel one human being can be to another when they're suffering. How wonderful an institution marriage is to facilitate this.

Today I fell off the wagon again. When you're drunk you don't feel the pain as much. My psychologist tells me I need something in my life to stop me drinking. 'It's like your second wife,' he says. He's probably right, except you can trust alcohol. A drink won't walk out on you in the middle of the night. It won't bankrupt you or go off with another man. When I find a wife I can trust I'll probably give it up.

I have a beer and then another. The second one is nicer. By then the guilt is gone.

There was a time I used to be an idealist. These days everything is more basic. You do what you have to do to get from A to B. Life is easy when it's mechanical. I don't think, therefore I am.

If she came back to me tomorrow I'd probably take her in. Why? Because she's the only thing I know. Something is better than nothing.

Life is simple these days. I watch people working their forty hours, licking up to their bosses, filling their petrol tanks, doing their shopping, not walking on the grass, getting their golf handicaps down, washing their teeth every night, eating their greens, stopping at yellow lights, buying houses near schools as they plan families and only using bad language after the kids are gone to bed. Oh, and never looking at women with sin in their hearts. Or going the way of all flesh. Until one day on the road to Damascus the divine light shines on them and cause these massive big haloes to break out around their heads.

Maybe I'll make one last burst for grandeur. Maybe I'll sell myself to the highest bidder. Here's the ad: 'One ageing bachelor, cured of passion, capable of great things now, shopsoiled but optimistic, Contact Box 3C.' Maybe someone could buy me on eBay. 'Best before 2014.'

I keep asking myself how the dream died. Maybe I was too encased in cotton wool growing up. Maybe my parents loved me too much to make adulthood possible.

My world was a Hollywood one, a yellow brick road. Like all Irish mothers, my one thought I was God. Other women followed, those who promised the earth but delivered only that – earth.

Then she came along. She was the big one despite the fact that she promised less than all the others put together. Maybe that was why I thought we'd last.

Dawn is here. Pools of sun invade the room. It's coming up to the time of day I like best, the half-light that promises something intangible. The birds are fluttering in the trees, the moon sinking into a bed of its own creation.

I listen to Bob Dylan asking one of his paramours to please crawl out a window. That's how I feel too.

Like all men I preferred the chase to the conquest. I was Jason seeking the golden fleece. Once I got it I didn't know what to do with it. Or maybe it wasn't a good enough fleece.

What do I have left? My health. Or at least what remains of it. The memory of her when she loved me. Or pretended to. Those first dizzy nights when life spread in front of us like a canopy, the wind at our back. Love beckoned us along like the words of a mindless teenage song.

Rain creeps over the roofs. I feel my heart beating against my chest as I look out at the sky. I want to sleep so I can forget.

People give me advice on how to live but there's no advice you can give. There's only living. Advisors are just people who are in love with their voices.

Once upon a time the world was my oyster. Now an oyster is my world. But then things always look worse at night, don't they? In the morning I'll be calm again. The condemned man will eat a hearty breakfast. After I've finished it I'll put the last relics of the past into a kitbag, turn on the engine of my car and drive to the next good thing.

Pub Talk

The theory of evolution, of course,
is an insult to the monkeys.
All you have to do
is look around you.
The first man in the Bible
killed his brother.
Since then
we've been going downhill.
Genocide, rape, pillage,
and that's just the idealists.

You can't leave your house today
without protection.
A fellow down the road
got his arm broken
for jumping the queue
in a chipper.
Another chap got headbutted
in Fumbally Lane
in broad daylight
by a total stranger.
Evolution how are ye.
He got a suspended sentence.
I know the suspended sentence
I'd give him.
From the neck.

This country is going down the toilet,
mark my words.
No one opens the door for you now
or stands up in the bus.
I'm in my fifties.
I remember manners, decency,
people who'd buy you a pint.

I'm on the dole too.
Lost my job
to a bloody computer.
Yer man who wrote *1984*
had it right.

I got a package.
Attractive at the time
but it was gone in a year,
most of it spent in this kip.
Gave the best years of my life
to the gobshites
and they threw me out on my ear.
Probably lose the gaff next.

When my ship comes in
it'll probably be the Titanic.
What doesn't kill you
makes you stronger.
Name of the game is survival.
Do it to him
before he does it to you.

The wife is good to me though.
From the same generation as me.
We know what's important.
Christianity.
You don't have to be in a church to pray.
God is everywhere,
even in my pint.

Pity about the priest scandals.
Sure they're the same
as the rest of us.
Let him who is without fault
cast the first stone.

Who said that - Jesus?
If he didn't he should have.
Live and let live
and let the dead bury the dead.

Nippy tonight, isn't it?
What's your poison, head the ball?
You wouldn't get me a half one,
would ye?
I'd kill for one, that's the truth.
We're not here for a long time,
we're here for a good time.

I'll have a slash first if that's all right.
Thanks be to Christ I can still piss.
You don't buy beer, you rent it.
Next time it's my twist.

What did you say your name was again?
The old head is goin'
along with everything else.
Ah sure we'll be dead long enough.
Where's the bleedin' jacks?

Phone Watch

Velour would be good for the curtains.
Put them with the new carpet
and you're laughing.
It's maroon.
We had mauve last
but the dog destroyed it.
That's the thing about dogs.
Next up is the conservatory.
We were thinking glass
but then Sonny came up
with a brainwave.
'Half and half,'
he said, like the beer.
There's no end to DIY, is there?
Don't even talk to me
about the bedroom.
Have to get the garage sorted first.
Maybe when the kids grow up.
Jack is seven already,
seven going on twenty-one.
Eats enough for an army.
Probably be running his own business
before he gets out of his teens.
Dearbhla is slower but I like that.
They say you have a daughter forever
They're in the bunk beds now.
Fighting like cats and dogs.
All part of growing up.
Deep down they're thick as thieves.
Funny way of showing it, kids.
Fred will be home for dinner soon.
He's from the last generation.
Wants it all served up to him.
But he's good to me in other ways.

I don't complain.
You could, but who'd listen?
The kitchen is like a pigsty.
I close my eyes
when I go in there now.
You'd need a hard hat.
But at our age who cares?
It's just bricks and mortar.
Next week
I'll do a commando raid on it,
a lick and a promise.
Couldn't be bothered at the minute.
So exhausted I could drop.
But duty calls.
Himself and his bloody fry.
By the way
did you hear Eric died?